THE INFECTED

Michael McBride

FIRST EDITION PAPERBACK
ISBN 978-1-934546-15-4

DELIRIUM BOOKS
P.O. Box 338
North Webster, IN 46555
srstaley@deliriumbooks.com
www.deliriumbooks.com

Copy Editors: David Marty & Jamie La Chance

For my wife,
who waited a decade for a honeymoon spent chasing
iguanas through the ruins

Special Thanks to: Shane Staley, for believing; Paul Miller, for the pathology validation; The Delirium Faithful; Dennis Duncan; Greg Gifune; Leigh Haig; Brian Keene; Dave Kendall; Troy Knutson; Don Koish; Jamie La Chance; David Marty; Matt Schwartz and Shockliners everywhere; the unwittingly helpful docs at BCH; my mom; Kyler, Madison, Trent, and Blakey; and to you, dear reader, for supporting the specialty press and my insanity.

1050 A.D.

PROLOGUE

Chichén Itzá
Yucatán Peninsula, Mexico

The visions consumed him. They were now all he could think about, even with the sacrificial ritual transpiring right in front of him. *Kukulcán*, the feathered serpent god, would have to be favored with the blood of his enemies if they were to survive the coming assault at the hands of the *conquistadores*, an onslaught he had been dreaming of for more than seventy years. As *Ah Kin Mai*, he had been blessed with the ability to communicate directly with the gods in his dreams, as only the chief priest of the Mayans could. He had communed with *Chac*, god of the rain, and appeased him with sacrifices down the sacred wells, into the *cenotes*, where he guarded the gates to *Xibalba* and the afterlife. *Hurakan*, god of the storms, had negotiated with him for the drowning of children to keep the hurricanes at bay. They came to him often, when the crops were dying or when the winds arose to scream through the jungle, but Kukulcán had only asked of him one service, one he had spent the majority of his life upon. Kukulcán demanded that his impending death and the forthcoming slaughter of his people be avenged.

And he had shown Ah Kin Mai precisely how to exact his revenge.

On the day when the great serpent of light, the eternal Kukulcán himself, descended from the sun to consume the blood of his final enemy, the countdown would begin. Today was that day, the longest day of the year with the conquistadores carving their way through the jungle toward their temple to abolish it in the name of their God. All had been prepared according to the mighty Kukulcán's specifications, though only the lesser priests, the *Chilan* and *Nacon*, and the great chief knew of the divine design. And their descendents, those who survived to feign their allegiance to the Spanish God, would see Kukulcán's prophesy to fruition by the secret sacrifices of blood to his creations, now crawling through the caverns beneath their very feet.

The crowd gathered around the massive temple roared, summoning Ah Kin Mai to his natural state of consciousness. A naked man, the entirety of his body painted blue, reached the foot of the altar where he had been led by their greatest warriors, hands bound behind his back. Only the pointed metal helmet he had been wearing when they captured him remained upon his head, tears streaming from beneath eating through the paint on his cheeks. He screamed something in his evil tongue and fell to his knees before the chief to beg for his life, which only angered the great man, as to give one's life for the gods was an honor the foreigner should have embraced. The chief could only turn away, the gathering on the lawn below the monolithic temple falling silent.

The warriors watched the chief, awaiting instructions. With a single nod, the chief offered his blessing, the gesture sending the spectators into a frenzy.

His screams swallowed by the roar of bloodlust, the blue man struggled against the warriors to no avail, his best efforts only assisting them as they lifted him and dropped him onto his back on the stone altar. The Nacon descended upon him from the corners of the room, swaddled in the ceremonial robes of skinned jaguar, pinning his arms and legs to either side until his torso was firmly held.

Ah Kin Mai approached the altar from the eastern doorway of the sacrificial chamber, circling around the stone slab until he faced the west with the screaming Spaniard at his back. He drew the knife from the iguana-skin sheath in time for the sunlight to focus upon its chiseled facets, eliciting a throng of applause, allowing the energy to charge him until finally he turned and in one swift motion slammed the blade all the way through the blue man's chest just to the left of the sternum. Withdrawing the knife, he reached both hands through the man's ribcage, the fractured edges tearing at the backs of his hands until he cradled the heart in his palms, squeezing it though it beat spastically against him. With practiced ease, Ah Kin Mai forced his wrists apart to create a wedge to draw out the heart, blood spilling in freshets over the chest of the conquistador, until he was able to turn and raise the heart high above his head. As the blood rolled down his arms and dripped down upon his head, the solstice converging the sun god's rays onto him to announce the coming of Kukulcán, he was overcome with waking visions. Great Spanish galleons with sails as wide as the sunset against the turquoise blue of the ocean, conquistadores pouring off like ants from so many mounds of dirt, the sun glinting from their metallic helmets and crosses. A seething mat of flies in the darkness, scavenging the last of the meat from the bones

The Infected

on the floor, crawling all over walls glowing with phos-phorescence. The flash of slashing swords. The very temple he stood atop now crumbling, victimized by the ravages of time, slowly returning to the earth. Ages passed in the span of the fading heartbeat of the muscle in his hands until he could see white men standing atop Kukulcán's pyramid at the summer solstice, a cloud of darkness funneling from the glow of the channeled rays of the sun like a tornado from a birthing star. Screams. A tide of humanity washing over the jungle as the darkness descended upon them. Great fires and columns of smoke rising from buildings the likes of which he'd never even imagined. People tearing each other apart with teeth and claws. Flesh melting from disease. Eyes made of blood. A man in a purple chamber, his face riddled with fluores-cent pink sores, the gums in his smiling mouth lined with them. A woman in blue sobbing, cradling a child to her breast as insects swarmed out of a vent. And in that woman's face he saw a terror like the world had never known, the tears glistening on her eyes reflecting an image exclusively for him. The true face of Kukulcán.

Then blackness from which the chanting crowd drew him back from the abyss. He lowered the enemy's heart and squeezed the last of the life from it, the blood dripping down to the ground and slithering between the cracks in the stones, draining into the very heart of Kukulcán. Taking a single bite from that tough morsel, he passed it to the chief and turned to head back to the eastern door to the chamber. Voices rose into a tumult as their ruler stole a piece of the captured enemy, chewing it only long enough to remove his own knife, which he used to begin sawing through the prisoner's lifeless neck. In a matter of moments he secured the trophy that would hang by a chain from his neck for the finite remainder of his days, but Ah Kin Mai no longer watched, instead

10

raising his attention to the pinnacle of the pyramid where the serpent of the sun began his descent down the side of the stone creation.

The countdown had begun.

JUNE 19TH
PRESENT DAY

CHAPTER 1

Yucatán Peninsula, Mexico

Karl Walters stood atop the Kukulcán pyramid El Castillo in the middle of the Mayan ruins at Chichén Itzá, surveying the crowds already beginning to form on the grass surrounding the enormous temple and wondered if this must have been what it looked like from this vantage before they sacrificed the virgins on the alter behind him nearly a thousand years prior. He imagined the gathering chanting for blood in a long dead tongue and felt an almost electric tingle shoot up his spine as though he were walking over his own grave.

By morning they anticipated that more than forty thousand people would be packed shoulder to shoulder at the base of the monolithic stone construct, waiting for the true moment of the vernal equinox when the serpent of the sun would descend from the sky to the earth. The pyramid had been built in such a way, with precisely aligned corners and steps, that only on this one day each and every year would the sun light the stone borders of the infamous stairs leading up to the sacrificial platform,

The Infected

so as to create the appearance of an enormous snake slithering down to the base where it would meet with the enormous sculpture of a serpentine head. It was astounding to imagine such exact knowledge of the sun's cycle and the ability to craft a structure on such a grand scale with one of the four sides seven degrees off from the others, as to allow the snake of light to descend from the blue sky. The Mayans had a mastery of architecture and science that defied all primitive logic. That's why Karl was here now. To a professor of archeology, this was one of the most amazing sites on the planet. He was not only involved with the excavation, but the renovation as well, working with a skilled team of architects, sociologists, and anthropologists to rebuild one of the mightiest empirical seats the planet had ever known, while simultaneously trying to crack the code of their disappearance.

And on this one day, tomorrow, June 20th, he would be transported back to 1050 AD to see the world through the eyes of the dead.

"We have all of the cameras set up, Professor Walters," Kevin said. He was a graduate student in anthropology from the University of Texas. "We have three inside the El Coracol Observatory for when the sunlight converges in the center of the planetarium, one on each side of the main pyramid to watch from the outside, and four more up here in the altar chamber."

"Good work," Karl said, donning his faded tan baseball cap to keep the sun from his eyes as he came back to the moment and the work at hand. He took one long last look down the ninety-one stone stairs to the stretches of trimmed lawn expanding to the edge of the jungle that crowded in from all sides. The spectators were pushing forward to be right against the ropes keeping them from scaling the pyramid. A smile brightened his sun-leathered face and he turned his child-like brown

16

eyes back to his work, tucking a stray strand of graying bangs back under his cap.

Stepping over a bundle of power cords taped together into one enormous braid as thick as his forearm, he made his way to the closest of the cameras, mounted atop a tripod, and pressed his eye to the lens. It was focused squarely on the ornately carved stone altar in the center of the lone room crowning the apex. Adjusting the horizontal lock, he pivoted the camera from one side to the other, looking first to the open doorway to the left, past the one directly ahead beyond the altar, and then to the one to the right. The lens fought for focus each time it passed from the blinding light of the outside world back into the darkness of the corners, making it appear as though corridors of light reached from each threshold to converge in the center on the altar, where so much blood had been spilled in the name of gods no longer remembered in the land of their creation.

He raised the camera to the roof and back down to the floor, checking to make sure it would move freely when the time finally came. None of their past efforts had been able to successfully capture the event, which was how he imagined it must first look when one wakes after death at heaven's gates.

Something scurried across the ground in front of him, but by the time he drew a bead on the movement, all he could see was the spiny tail of one of the black iguanas that inhabited the ruins wiggling back and forth as it squirmed into a small fissure between the base of the altar and the rock floor.

Karl zoomed in on the spot where the tail had just disappeared. It looked like any of the cracks between the large square boulders used to build all of the structures on the site, but there couldn't have been anywhere for that iguana to go, even a smaller juvenile like this one.

17

The Infected

"Hey Kevin," he said, pulling his eye from the camera. "Could you grab me that pole over there?"

He dropped to all fours and crawled to the crack, sticking his index finger in all the way past the second knuckle without encountering the slightest resistance.

"Here you go, chief. Find something interesting?"

"I don't know," Karl said, raising his hand from the fissure to take the metal pole. It was one of the long rods they used to hold a microphone over someone's head while they were on camera without being seen. What did they call it, a boom stick?

He poked the end through the hole. It was barely thin enough to pass and stopped about a foot and a half down. Raising the pole, he slammed it down once, twice. There was a cracking sound and he heard what sounded like gravel falling into a dry well. Again, he raised the staff and drove it down.

The pole broke through the rock and slipped right through his hands and straight down into the floor.

It clanked against a stone floor somewhere beneath.

Karl looked at Kevin.

"Go get the others," he said, lowering himself to his belly to try to get his right eye as close to the hole as possible.

*   *   *

It had taken five of them with crowbars and a winch nearly four hours to remove the stone set into the floor at the foot of the altar. They'd chiseled the edges round, but the boulder now sat in the corner of the room away from the large hole leading down into the heart of the pyramid. Industrial spotlights ringed the hole, positioned so that the bulbs shone down through the swirling motes of dust to part the darkness just enough for them

18

to descend within.

The floor of the sublevel was only five feet down, making it so that none of them could stand fully erect, but that didn't matter in the slightest as they were all crawling with flashlights, brushing aside more than nine hundred years of dust to reveal an intricately carved design on the floor.

"I think it's a snake," Dr. Mallory Jenkins, one of the world's foremost experts on Mayan hieroglyphics said, grinding away the crust of dust from around her nostrils. She visibly struggled to breathe the stale air.

"But it's a square," Karl said. He couldn't bring himself to open his clenched right fist. Within was the multifaceted red gemstone that he had cracked with the pole while trying to jam it down from above. The hole had led from the floor above down through the mouth of a snake sculpted as though striking down into the cavern from underneath the altar, holding the gemstone between long upper and lower fangs. The iguana had apparently been able to squeeze out of the snake's mouth around the stone, but the boom stick had knocked it right out.

"All of the construction is square. Even this pyramid is built from enormous blocks. But feel along the edges," she said, taking his hand and guiding it around the outside of the design. "Can you feel how it isn't straight?"

"Yeah," Karl said, sliding his fingertips through the dust.

"Would you two quit screwing around and holding hands," Ray Thompson said. He had a trust fund that could bankroll the entire third world, which afforded him the luxury of pro bono work as it suited his whims, but he was also one of the most brilliant architects on the planet. Not to mention a full-time goof off. "Why don't you guys just get a room?"

"Knock it off, Ray," Dr. Gilbert Reid said. Professional to a fault, he was the senior anthropologist who managed all of the grants and finances. "Tell me how so many tons of rock are supported above our heads. How has it not collapsed and buried this chamber in a thousand years?"

"Look around," Ray said. "There are twelve wide columns ringing the room and some sort of grid running between them. I don't know if it's iron or what, but the tensile strength is amazing. It reminds me of the rebar frames we use to build bridges and overpasses under the concrete."

"And what about this 'snake?'" Reid asked.

Mallory directed her flashlight at the outermost edge of the carving and brushed off the seams until they were clearly visible like cracks in the sidewalk.

"This is really one big matrix, but not like a checker board, more of a giant spiral. See…each of these segments isn't exactly square, but more trapezoidal to allow it to taper inward. They're each like vertebrae in a spinal column, but following the pattern inward like a conch shell. And each one has a small carving within it." She brushed the square with her palm. "This one looks like a crown of sorts." She cleared another square farther toward the center. "This one's a crab."

"What function could they possibly serve?" Ray asked. "Everything else on this entire site has an alternate function to simply serving as structure."

Karl held up the gem toward the hole above, the overhead lights casting red squares on the walls as though from a disco ball. He turned it over and all of the facets directed the light into a fine red beam that put a dot the size of a nickel on the floor.

"My guess is that when the sun aligns just right in the chamber above, a beam is focused down through that hole by the altar into the snake's mouth and through this ruby to highlight one of the squares."

"So this is some kind of calendar then," Reid said.

"Too many squares," Mallory said. She was brushing the dust from all four sides of each segment in sequence. "I'm guessing there have to be nearly a thousand of these segments like links in a chain. Their calendars were precisely three hundred sixty-five days."

"What else could it be then?"

"Maybe a star chart," Ray offered.

"Please," Reid said. "The planetarium is domed to mirror the shape of the sky. A flat map would have been beneath their intellect."

"This entire temple is designed for use only one day each year," Karl said. "The summer equinox. Wouldn't it then stand to reason that this hole in the ceiling would also be designed to project the sunlight through the gem on just that one day as well?"

"So it is a calendar," Mallory said, her long dark bangs tangling into clumpy strands with the dust to hang across her face. "But rather than marking days of the year, it's marking the same day each year."

"Then each of the individual carvings within would somehow represent that specific year."

"What if it's like the Chinese Zodiac?" Kevin piped up from against the wall at the back of the room in the heavy shadows.

"What are they teaching you in school nowadays?" Reid asked.

"Maybe," Mallory said. She stopped freeing the edges and took a broad swipe across the floor. "I could be wrong, but no two designs appear to be the same."

"So if it's a spiral, what's at the center?" Karl asked.

Mallory looked at him for a moment, her brow furrowing, then crawled toward the center of the design, directly beneath the open mouth of the serpent as though it were trying to sink it's fangs into the top of her head. She brushed away the dust to reveal a small square, maybe an inch wide. Rubbing it, she could immediately tell that it wasn't made of granite like the rest of the floor, but rather something softer.

"It's wax," she finally said, pressing her fingernail into it and leaving a crescent.

"Wax?" Karl said. "Let me see. That makes no sense whatsoever."

He crawled over beside her and rubbed the square. It certainly felt like wax, but...he brought his finger to his tongue.

"Amber," he said.

"What's that?" Kevin asked.

"Tree sap," Karl said, coughing the dust from his lungs. "But why in the name of God would this small patch in the middle of the floor be made of tree sap?"

* * *

Karl had just closed his eyes when there was a knock on his trailer door.

"I've got it," Mallory gasped the moment he swung out the door. She looked like she'd run all the way there.

"Got what?" Karl asked, stifling a yawn. He was exhausted, but there wasn't a prayer of getting any sleep tonight in all of the excitement. Besides, Mallory often proved to be an excellent diversion.

"The design," she said, grabbing him by the hand and pulling him down onto the lone stair. "I know what it means."

Karl barely had time to grab his shoes before being hurried off into the night.

*   *   *

"We were right that each of these sections represents a year," she said. Her enthusiasm made her positively radiant beneath the overhead halide lights, the dust shimmering around her like glitter. "But they aren't representations so much as they're predictions."

"Did you stay out here after we all went back to our trailers?"

"I came back," she said. "Tell me you were going to get any sleep tonight."

"You're right. Another hour and I'd have undoubtedly been back out here myself." He smiled and ran his fingers through her hair to remove a cobweb. "So...predictions you say."

She placed her hand atop his momentarily before turning her attention back to the design on the floor.

"It starts from the center and moves outward. The carving in each square of the snake's body represents the defining moment of that year. Look here." She directed her flashlight at the fifth square spiraling outward from the amber plug, revealing what looked like a tidal wave. "Remember the hurricanes that flooded New Orleans?" She traced around the expanding circle until she reached another four blocks farther out. There was a bird covered in flames. "This is 2001 when terrorists crashed those planes into the World Trade Towers."

"I think you're stretching this," Karl said, trying to carefully phrase his words to avoid hurting her feelings.

"Oh yeah? How about this?" She traced her finger across the squares as the spiral widened, counting silently with moving lips. "Here. 1989. A carving of a block wall crumbling in the center. Berlin. And here..." Her spiral expanded quickly as she scooted backwards. "Twenty-one years prior, a snake in bamboo. Vietnam.

The Infected

Tell me any Mayan could have possibly traveled far enough to see bamboo."

Karl shrugged, but leaned in more closely.

"1945. A panther. Panzer. World War II, get it? And here...1917, two dragonflies. Biplanes dueling. Double check my count if you want to, but I'm convinced. These all line up perfectly."

"So the Mayans could not only chart the sun and stars, and create an accurate calendar a thousand years ago, but they could precisely predict the future as well?"

"You don't believe me," she said, looking wounded.

"I didn't say that."

"You didn't have to."

She turned away, but he took her by the hand, coaxing her eyes to meet his.

"It just sounds so fantastic..."

"This is what I do, Karl. This is the kind of thing I've devoted my life to trying to figure out."

"I didn't mean to question your expertise, Mallory. It just sounds almost...spiritual, you know?"

She nodded and leaned in to give him a gentle kiss on the lips.

He smiled as she withdrew.

"You present a compelling argument, Professor Jenkins."

"Does that mean you believe me now?"

"I'll believe anything you say now." He looked up at the stone snake poised to strike above the center of the design. "So you're saying this year is the very center?"

"Yes."

"So a gob of sap represents this year? Why are there no other years after?"

"I don't know the answer to either question, but if I'm right, we'll know for sure tomorrow."

JUNE 20TH

CHAPTER 2

Chichén Itzá Ruins, Yucatan Peninsula

Rather than watching the serpent of light descend down the side of the pyramid from the top as he had each of the prior five years, Karl awaited the vernal equinox on his rear end in that dusty chamber beneath the sacrificial altar with a video camera in his lap, anxiously awaiting the moment when the sun finally arrived in position. Mallory sat to his right with a camera of her own and a gallon of water to share between them. The others waited above their heads, having sealed a sheet of plywood over the hole where they had descended once they were all the way down. The only illumination came from their flashlights, and a pinprick of red light directed off-angle through the ruby in the snake's mouth, which glowed a warm crimson.

"What's your prediction?" Karl asked.

"Honestly...I don't know. You?"

"I'm worried that by cracking the ruby I could have skewed the results and ruined ten centuries of planning for whatever may be supposed to happen."

"Don't beat yourself up about—"

The Infected

A cheer arose outside, as loud as any stadium Karl had ever been in, regardless of the fact that they were down in the middle of that manmade mountain. The ground beneath them positively shook.

"Here we go," Karl said, bringing the camera to his eye and pressing the button to record. Through the lens he saw Mallory do the same.

Slowly, the room began to brighten by degree, the sunlight reaching through the ruby and bleeding the walls red.

Still, one thought plagued him...Why would such brilliant architectural minds consciously decide to place the hole leading down there so inconspicuously at the foot of the altar? Everything else was so elaborate...but his concerns were chased away as he focused on the gem and watched it intensify in brightness until it was like looking into the sun itself. The corridors of light must have merged directly above them now.

"It's beautiful," Mallory whispered over the awed hush that had befallen the world around them.

Karl lowered the lens, following that solitary red beam from the point of the precision-honed stone to where it formed a circle of light directly on the plug of tree sap in the center of the design. He zoomed in until he could see the reaction of the focused light on the amber. It began to bubble, just slightly at first, but soon the entire surface began to ripple and the level began to lower.

"It's melting the sap," he whispered. There was a brief moment of utter respect where he found himself staggered by the brilliance of these people who abandoned their temples so long ago. How advanced had they truly been to anticipate where a single beam of light would focus nearly a thousand years in the future? That notion led to a far more frightening question.

Why?

Michael McBride

The sap drained down through the hole, leaving only a small dark square.

Karl fought with the camcorder for focus, trying to peer through the blazing red into the now empty space.

A thunderous roar shook the structure. The light snake must have finally slithered all the way down the side of the pyramid to reach its monstrous stone head.

A red dot appeared at the edge of the hole in the floor. Karl fought to steady the camera enough to see it clearly: long spindly legs and a bulbous, hairy abdomen, like a cross between a mosquito and a fly, minus the most prominent features of each, a sort of fuzzy flying ant. There was no long sticker, only a lowered head with a pincer-like mouth.

Its clear wings vibrated with a hum as it took to the air.

"How could there possibly be anything living down under—?" Karl started, but had to snap his mouth closed as more and more sand flies flooded through that hole like a dam springing a leak.

The camera clattered to the ground as he lunged toward Mallory, throwing his weight atop her and pinning her to the stone floor. He could feel her trying to scream under him, but all he could think to do was to bury his face in her hair, slapping his hands over his ears and trying to shield hers with his elbows.

The dust whirled in the room like a miniature tornado at the behest of the myriad insect wings.

Karl felt hundreds of little legs on the back of his neck, but he feared uncovering his ears more as he could feel many tiny bodies trying to squeeze between his fingers to find their way inside.

He flinched as one greedy mouth began gnawing through the skin on his neck, and screamed as hundreds more followed suit.

29

The Infected

*   *   *

Ray stood just inside the northern entrance to the sacrificial chamber atop El Castillo, watching where the four channels of light came together just his side of the altar. Where they met it was like a birthing star, staggering white energy growing more intense by the second until it appeared to become a physical entity, hovering in the middle of the room. It was the most amazing thing he'd ever seen. He'd marveled at the glory of European castles and hunting lodges, stood at the thresholds of churches so elaborately crafted that it stole his breath away, studied at the feet of modern masters like Frank Lloyd Wright, but this was something else altogether. This was organic; a living monument to the gods of architecture, an animate thing. He imagined he could feel it breathing around him as though drawing its first breaths of life.

He tried to picture what the world would have become had the Mayans survived and the Romans perished, their great cities melding man with nature and fostering a celestial spirituality. An understanding of the physical intertwining of structure and functionality in a way—

At first it looked like the being of light before him became television static, but as it expanded outward, funneling straight out of that hole in the ground between the plank of plywood and the base of the altar, its signature was unmistakable.

Ray threw his arms in front of his face as clouds of sand flies fired past him, hitting him like so many grains in a sandstorm. Hooked feet lanced into the backs of his hands and forearms, driving him back into the wall and down to his knees where the minions began eating through his skin.

Michael McBride

*   *   *

Professor Reid had the best possible seat for the coming light show. After ten years at Chichén Itzá, he'd have been more than disappointed with himself if he hadn't found the spot where he was certain the Mayan chieftains had stood to watch this very same experience so long ago. Kevin was right beside him as he always was, and like a good dog, he stayed a half a pace behind his right shoulder.

It never failed to amaze him how many people made the pilgrimage to this spot every year to watch what he imagined they could only peripherally understand. It was like rolling out the red carpet for God and watching Him arrive every single time. This was a society that should have thrived, were it not for the primitive weapons of the Europeans that were beyond anything the Mayans had ever pondered. While this race of highly enlightened Mexicans built feats that still astound modern science, the white man—in all his professed wisdom—invested his mental prowess into making tools of destruction.

The world should have never evolved as it had. The societies built upon science and discovery should have ushered in a truly golden age, rather than those that conquered them hurtling humanity along the shortest path to extinction.

He could see that same sentiment of wonder in all of the eyes far below, trained up on the side of the staircase as the celestial serpent began his annual trek toward its missing head. It was truly a blessing in this day and age to be part of something greater than oneself; to bear witness to the humbling fact that mankind was but so many ants scurrying aimlessly around in the face of

31

something they would never truly be able to understand.

When the crowd cheered, Reid allowed it to feed him, reveling in the moment. Celebrating along with the masses. Watching a marvel of the ancient world more incredible than any modern skyscraper that reached for the sun, but could never come close to touching it. This temple was an invitation to that celestial orb, welcoming it to the world without trying to snatch it from the sky like a golden coin.

"That's incredible!" Kevin shouted to be heard over the thrum.

And on cue, the thousands gathered on the lawn fell to revered silence, all eyes trained upon a snake composed of triangles of light, slowly working its way down the rail toward the earth as a society centuries ago had envisioned it long before laying the first stone.

A shadow passed across the snake a heartbeat before the first of what would be a choir of screams filled the air. Reid turned to see a buzzing black cloud explode out of all four entryways to the upper chamber at once like so much smoke, but rather than rising into the sky, the cloud furled only momentarily before expanding outward.

He turned back around to see Kevin already leaping down to the next stone ledge and preparing to lunge off of that one as well. By the time his legs started to move, his ears were filled with frenetic humming. Sand flies flew past him to all sides so fast it made him feel like he was moving in reverse. As he threw himself down and swatted uselessly at the insects all around him, he saw the massive wave of people a hundred feet down rolling away from the pyramid like a crashing tide.

* * *

"Get up!" Mallory screamed into his face, trying to hold him upright by his shirt while his head insisted upon lolling backward.

Consciousness faded in and out, and, with it, his vision. It felt as though someone had butterflied the back of his neck like a shrimp. Karl could see her panicked face, and then nothing but blackness. His legs from the knees down were cold, though he could feel them bunched up beneath his rear end. There was a hissing sound like the room had filled with snakes, hiding beneath the piddling of enormous raindrops.

"Come on, Karl!" she screamed, jerking him back and forth until he fought enough to hold his head erect of his own volition. "I can't keep your head above the water and push the ceiling open above us at the same time!"

It was the sheer terror in her eyes that ushered reality back in. The entire room was filling with water from a geyser shooting straight up into the face of the snake statue on the ceiling from the hole in the floor. He remembered the sand flies that had looked like fat flying ants, but couldn't hear their buzzing over the rush of incoming water, even if they were still down there in the darkness with them. It felt as though someone had stabbed him in the back of the neck and then peeled the skin from his triceps and calves. There was pressure beneath the skin like the knife was still buried in his spinal column, but he swiped at it repeatedly only to find a knotted mass of swelling instead of a hilt.

"Are you okay?" he whispered. Whatever was lodged in the back of his neck was putting pressure on his trachea, causing each word to feel as though it ripped a strap of his windpipe off on its way out.

"Yeah," she said, leaning her forehead against his chin. "Thanks to you…"

He kissed her hairline and wrapped his left arm

around her shoulders, reaching straight up with his right to slide back the flat sheet of wood.

It was like opening the gates of hell. Screams of terror and agony followed the rush of fresh air into the darkness.

"Go on," Karl said, grabbing Mallory around the waist and hoisting her upward until she was able to reach the floor above and haul herself out onto the flat stones in the blinding light.

Karl wavered, the frigid water now nearly to the middle of his thighs, and jumped up to grab the stone lip. Mallory's hands were around his wrists immediately, giving him just enough leverage to pull himself up; enough to get his elbows braced on the floor to either side.

She moaned as she rolled back onto her haunches and pulled.

"Thanks," he gasped, pushing himself to all fours and crawling forward. Through the open doorway he could see the crowd below through the swarming reddish-brown flies, stampeding in every direction at once before fading into a haze.

"Stay with me, Karl," she said, but his eyes were already rolling back into his head, accompanied by visions of men and women trampling children in their rush to escape.

*　　*　　*

"The blood," he groaned. Someone was wiping a damp rag across his forehead. "The blood of the sacrifices..."

"He's delusional," Reid said from somewhere ahead.

Karl opened his eyes long enough to catch a glimpse of the back of the older man's head silhouetted against a windshield.

"Shh," Mallory whispered, again mopping his sweating brow. "Don't try to talk."

His body felt like it was on fire.

"...spilled from the altar and down the hole..."

"Just try to rest, Professor Walters," Kevin said from the passenger seat, loading ice from a cooler into a plastic bag and passing it to Mallory in the back seat.

"...fed them for...all these years...how?"

"Can't you drive any faster?" Mallory shrieked.

"I'm doing eighty kilometers now," Reid snapped. "These roads weren't made to travel this fast."

"I don't care what they were made for. He's burning up!"

"...the Cenote," Karl mumbled. "The water...must have come...from the sacred pool."

"Please rest, Karl," she whispered, kissing him on the forehead. He didn't have to try to see her to know that it was her tears that had fallen onto his face. It was in her voice. "Save your strength."

His head was in her lap, his legs crumpled in by the rear door of the Cherokee. He tried to stretch them, but they were unresponsive. With a trembling hand, he reached for the back of his neck to find it bleeding, hot to the touch.

"Someone..." he said, his hand falling from his shoulder to land on the floor with a thud. "...keeping them underground...feeding them..."

"He's delusional," Kevin said. Mallory shot him a glance. "What are you babbling on about back there—?"

"Kevin," Mallory said. "Let him rest."

Karl laughed a wretched noise that must have sounded like insanity in his delirium.

"Engineering them..." he said, then again, the laugh. "Breeding them this whole time...for just this...

one...day..."

"Hurry up!" Mallory screamed.

They were the last words Karl heard before the darkness again reclaimed him.

*　　*　　*

The Cherokee grumbled off the highway into the dirt parking lot in front of the clinic, firing gravel behind it, grinding to a halt. Kevin threw open his door and hit the ground before the vehicle even stopped, sprinting around the back of the car to yank the door open behind Mallory. She sat there, hunched over Karl, both of their faces hidden beneath her long, dirty hair.

"Come on," Kevin said, taking her by the shoulder and pulling her out of the way to try to climb into the back seat.

"It's too late," she said, looking up at him. Her face was covered with tears, her pink eyes nearly swollen closed. She tried to forge a smile but her lips just quivered. Looking back down to Karl, she gently stroked the side of his pale face, his cooling sweat now looking more like wax. "He threw himself on top of me...saved me..."

"Come on, Mallory," Reid said softly, his eyes and voice betraying an emotion he generally kept well inside. His right hand slid underneath Karl's head in her lap, his left reaching across her knees under Karl's left arm. "Help me, Kevin, would you?"

The two of them eased Karl off of her lap and rested him gently on his back in the dirt.

"No," she moaned, rolling out of the car and falling to her knees beside the body.

"Come on, Professor Jenkins," Kevin whispered, trying to pull her from atop Karl.

"Get away from me!" she screamed.

"Mallory," Reid said, kneeling in front of her across Karl's body. He gently cupped her chin and brought her shimmering eyes to meet his. "We need to have a doctor look at you."

"No, please…I can't leave him like this."

"Karl would have wanted to make sure that you were fine first. You know that, Mallory."

She looked up over Reid's shoulder to see a pair of nurses hurrying toward them from the open front door of the clinic.

"I know I never told him," she said, lowering her chest down atop his. She wrapped both arms around his now scabrous and cool neck. "I love you, Karl," she whispered, planting a soft kiss on his unforgiving lips.

"He knew," Reid said, now leaning over her from behind. He carefully took her shoulders and started to bring her to her feet.

"Do you think?" she whispered, swiping the back of her hand across her sniffling nose, knowing that once she looked away from his body she would never be able to look at it again.

"I *know*," Reid said, turning her toward him to wrap her in an embrace. "And I'm sure he felt the same."

Mallory's shoulders shuddered in his arms and he felt the warmth of her breath and the dampness of her tears against the side of his neck.

"Necesitamos poner en cuarentena el cuerpo," a dark-skinned nurse said. She and her counterpart were already wearing their sterile precautionary gowns.

"Of course," Reid said, coaxing Mallory away from the body.

Both nurses snapped on latex gloves and donned masks before crouching to lift Karl's body from the ground.

The Infected

Mallory sobbed into his chest when she heard the scuff of gravel as they hefted his weight.

"Cuántos otros se hieren," the other nurse said through her mask.

"Tres," Kevin said, following the nurses, who rushed the corpse toward the doors.

*   *   *

"The doctor suspects a strain of leishmaniasis, which is apparently some kind of disease that eats flesh. It's caused by a bacterium carried by sand flies," Reid said, slumping down beside the others in the waiting area. The chairs were decrepit and there were chicken feathers and manure on the floor from the doctor's other clientele. "I'm conversational in Spanish, but when he starts talking in medical terms I get lost in a hurry."

"That's an infection that attacks the liver and spleen, right?" Kevin asked.

"I think so."

"So are we going to have to get shots or something?"

"No," Mallory said flatly. "Tell him what comes next, Professor Reid."

"They've asked us to accept voluntary quarantine," Reid said.

"And stay here? In this dump?"

"We'll be staying here of our own volition…or they're going to make us." Mallory looked up at him with red where the whites of her eyes should have been. Drainage from her nose ran down over her lips onto her chin. There was an enormous blister on her bottom lip, and another coming in on her cheek. A swatch of blood filtered through the shirt covering her abdomen, another growing on her shoulder.

"Jesus, professor," Kevin gasped, jerking away from

her so quickly that he fell off the chair onto the floor.

"Taken a good look at yourself lately, kiddo?"

He lurched to his feet, looking quickly from one side to the other before running toward the front window. At the right angle, he could see his pale reflection and the boils lining his cheekbones, the swelling under his ribs made them feel as though they were going to crack. Through his own image he watched a green military Jeep pull into the parking lot beside their car. The men who climbed out each had automatic weapons slung over their necks.

"We're going to die here," Kevin said. "You know that, don't you? We're going to die in this shack one way or the other!"

He threw open the front door and lurched out onto the porch.

"En rodillas en el suelo," a voice shouted through a bullhorn.

"Oh God," Kevin said, dropping to his knees and launching his breakfast onto the cement pad before passing out face-first into it.

*   *   *

"I want to see him one last time," Mallory said. Sores were coming in all across her face and arms, her tongue swelling in her mouth.

"¿Puede ver ella el cuerpo?" Reid asked the nurse, who looked at Mallory before averting her eyes.

She nodded hesitantly, looking back over her shoulder, and withdrew a key chain from the pocket of her smock.

"Tenemos que ser rápidos," the nurse said, turning from them and heading down the short corridor.

"She said we have to hurry," Reid said, taking

The Infected

Mallory by the arm and ushering her behind. She stumbled beside him, leaning on the wall as much as him for support. He figured that he was well on the way to whatever she had. Even though he hadn't seen his face, he could picture what it must look like based on the weeping purple sores on his arms.

They ducked to the right at the end of the hallway and stood before an aluminum door that looked like an industrial freezer.

"El cuerpo es adentro," the nurse said, twisting the key in the lock of the long handle before drawing it outward.

The door opened with a pop, followed by the hiss of the seal dragging along the floor. A cold mist hovered in the threshold.

Mallory crumpled to the ground, the base of her skull cracking on the cement floor.

She lost consciousness so quickly that Reid didn't even feel her swoon.

"¡Ayuda!" the nurse screamed, backing away from Mallory, whose head gushed a deep black blood beneath her.

Mallory's vacant eyes stared up at the ceiling, a long last sigh of gasses hissing from her open lips like a propane tank.

"Someone help her!" Reid shouted, dropping to his knees over her and lacing his fingers together atop her sternum. The prospect of sealing his lips over what remained of hers was chilling, but he couldn't just let her die.

There was blood everywhere, burbling through a hole in her cheek and replacing the tears draining from her eyes.

"Nurse!" he shouted, turning back to her. "Help me! Please! Hel — "

Karl stepped through the dwindling mist from the freezer, shivering and twitching, his body moving jerkily like a fawn taking its first steps. His head lolled forward against his chest.

Reid couldn't find his voice, but the nurse screamed at the top of her lungs.

Karl's eyes snapped open, the whites suffused with blood, his head jerking to face the nurse.

His lips curled back from cracked teeth covered by a frozen sheen of blood.

"Dear God," Reid gasped.

Karl launched himself at the nurse, slamming her into the wall and burying his face in her neck. Her scream was cut short by a wet tearing sound. Blood spattered the wall to either side of her as Karl sunk his fingers into the opening he'd created, ripping it even wider. The last of the air from her lungs burbled through the fluids welling in her severed neck, but that was the last thing Reid saw before Mallory jammed her fingers into his eyes and clamped her jaws shut over his windpipe, shaking it back and forth like a dog until she ripped it free with a warm rush of fluids.

CHAPTER 3

Chichén Itzá Ruins, Yucatan Peninsula

"Man, CNN's going to pay a fortune for this footage, you realize that?" Aaron said, lowering the camcorder from his eye. He and Craig, his roommate at the University of Montana, had saved as much money as they could throughout their freshman year so they could spend a week in the Mexican sun on the Caribbean beaches fulfilling all of their adolescent dreams. The night before they'd chased Cuervo with Coronas and ended up partying with a couple of brunettes from South Carolina. They'd slept in and left late, of course, and by the time they'd arrived at the ruins could only get as close to the pyramid as the edge of the jungle.

"There were thousands of cameras out here when it happened. We'd better have something special if we want that check," Craig said. He looked across the meadow at the pyramid. Water flowed from all four doorways of the sacrificial chamber perched at the top, forming waterfalls that descended the staircases and pooling in a small lake from which the pyramid rose like a castle from a moat.

Men and women of every nationality milled about the site, inspecting the chaos from all different angles. The group at the base of the piles of stones they stood atop was speaking in what sounded like German, while another cluster passed by conversing in some Asian tongue. Most of the people had fled to their cars and were speeding through the jungle back to wherever they had come from. They'd seen some people that looked like they'd come under siege by wasps with the swelling all over their faces. Parents had scooped their children from the ground to keep them from being crushed underfoot, though some still wandered the lawn calling out the names of those they'd been separated from.

Aaron brought the lens back to his eye and zoomed in on one of the bodies lying facedown in the grass, the rising water lapping at the woman's legs. He couldn't tell exactly how many dead bodies littered the site like the discarded refuse beside the Yucatan roads, but only a few had gatherings around them. How long would it be before the others were discovered missing? Would their bodies still be recognizable?

Zooming in even closer, he focused on one of those reddish flies as it gnawed at the woman's purple flesh, its fuzzy insect face covered with blood as the pincer worked back and forth, digging deeper into the gooey wound.

They'd managed to duck behind a cluster of stones when the swarm had first exploded from the chamber, being bitten only a couple of times each while they stayed down to avoid being stampeded by the screaming crowd, arising just in time to get a good shot of the cloud of flies as it expanded outward in all directions. Now only a random smattering remained to torment the survivors and feast upon the dead.

"Where do you think all of that water is coming

from?" Craig asked.

"Why would that matter?"

"It's not like they had indoor plumbing in those days. Don't you think it's strange that all of that water is flowing out of the chamber at the top of a two hundred foot stone pyramid?"

"Strange, sure. But not nearly as cash-worthy as live-action footage of people sorting through the piles of the dead looking for their loved ones."

"You're missing the big picture. Look around," Craig said, gesturing with his arms to the entire scene before them. "That guy's down there with a camera. See him? There's another. And another. Half of the people down there are taping with their camcorders, and they're a heck of a lot closer. We're hanging out here as far as possible from the meat of the story —"

"Maybe we should just take what we have and get out of here. The last thing either of us needs is to have to answer a lot of questions for the Mexican police. I barely remember enough from three years of Spanish in high school to order at Taco Bell and we're screwed if we miss our flight."

"That's the day after tomorrow."

"Haven't you heard those stories about the jails down here?"

"We didn't do anything."

"That's right, but neither of us speak enough Spanish to explain that."

"Now you're just being stupid. Think about the bottom line. We could easily make a couple hundred grand with good enough pictures. That pays for all of our undergrad and half of grad school."

"Maybe even a new car."

"Now you're thinking."

"So what? You want to go down there on the lawn

and get some close ups of the bodies then climb up the pyramid?"

"Forget about the bodies for now. We need to figure out where all of that water's coming from. And why. That's where the story is. I can feel it."

*   *   *

The moat had been nearly waist deep by the time they reached the stairs, the dirty water making it impossible to see the bottom. Beneath, the mud had been sloppy and the grass slick, but it had granted enough traction to help navigate the corpses that floated face down, their bodies already beginning to bloat with absorption, long hair floating on the surface like a hydra's heads. It was the bodies beneath, already completely swollen with water that made the going slow, as the feeling of the soft flesh squishing under their bare toes was about the most repulsive thing either had experienced.

When they finally reached the stone stairs and started their journey upward, their legs were nearly numbed from the ice cold water, the hairs on their legs prickled painfully. Freezing water ran down the makeshift waterfall, fortunately chasing away the residual feeling of sloughing flesh. Climbing upward, they passed several other people who shielded their eyes against the sun as they searched from this higher vantage for their lost loved ones, screaming out names that neither Aaron nor Craig could stand to listen to. By the time they reached the top, their feet had long since passed red and gone straight to white from the chill in the running water.

"It's coming from in there," Craig said, pointing through the open doorway into the altar chamber.

"You think?"

Craig let the sarcasm slide and walked through the stone portal into the room. The corridors of light from the four doors still met in the center, their convergence burning like a second sun materialized from the heavens. There was a waterlogged sheet of plywood in the corner, floating atop the standing water amidst the toppled mess of industrial lights and camera gear. There was a square of darkness at the foot of the altar where the water appeared to be the deepest.

Craig looked past Aaron at the large stone sitting off to the right.

"They must have pulled that stone over there out of the floor. I guess the water must be coming from where it was." He found one of the chiseled corners of the massive stone and tossed it with a *sploosh* into the square. "Sounds pretty deep."

"So you think this temple is some sort of big water tower?"

"Maybe...No. You feel how cold this water is? It's nearly a hundred degrees out there. No. This water has to have been underground."

"Where, though?"

"Remember, we stopped at that one little roadside attraction on the way in?"

"The place where we got the Coronas?"

"Yeah, there was that huge pit in the ground with that natural lake at the bottom. What was it called?"

"The sacred pool?"

"Right. The cenote. We walked all the way down that long set of stairs through that cave and there was that sign at the bottom that said something about—"

"The water being so cold," Aaron interrupted. "I follow, but that was like a half an hour's drive away, there's no way..."

"Unless there's another one here," Craig said, turning

and walking back out of the sacrificial chamber onto the uppermost outer level of the pyramid. He looked first across the land to the west. The flooding meadow met with the tangled jungle, which choked the passage to a thin path before opening into a smaller meadow with some lesser ruins. There was more impregnable jungle and then the visitor's center and the huge asphalt parking lot beyond. Only a smattering of cars remained, several tangled in a wreck of twisted metal with crowds surrounding the combating occupants. A line of brake lights led off as far as he could see.

He walked to the southern edge of the platform and squinted against the glare. There were several wider paths leading into the jungle, which parted for more circular fields with various formations of crumbling rock. At the furthest reaches of his vision, he could see a shadowed meadow, and just the far lip of a giant hole in the earth.

"There," he said, pointing.

Aaron sidled up next to him and sighted down Craig's outstretched arm like the barrel of a rifle.

"How in the world would they get the water from all the way down there up through this temple?"

"I don't know," Craig said, nibbling on the inside of his lower lip contemplatively. "Let me see the camera."

Aaron slipped his hand from the strap and passed it to Craig, who brought it to his eye and zoomed in on the hole in the distance. Vines of all colors cascaded over the lip like a waterfall of foliage while red- and pink-blossomed bromeliads grew from the rock walls surrounding.

"I think a better question would be why."

*　　*　　*

The Infected

Their bare feet squeaked on the soles of their flip-flops, only now regaining some semblance of feeling, which was returning with the assault of pins and needles. They'd only passed a couple of people along the path leading to the sacred pool. A child screamed in Spanish for his parents, tears streaming down his face, his skinned knees leaking blood down his shins. There had been another man with sores all over his face and his eyelids swollen shut, screaming at the top of his lungs. He'd stumbled and fallen twice while approaching them, his hands black with bloody mud. There was no one else at the cenote when they arrived and walked to the rails surrounding the enormous pit.

"You were right," Aaron said, leaning over the railing and looking down into the hole.

The mouth of the pit was roughly a hundred feet in diameter, the rocky ledges covered with vines that hung hundreds of feet down into the water like an organic curtain. Where once there had been deep crystal blue water, there was now only a small pond with jagged rocks prodding through the surface. All of the sharp protrusions were still wet, marking the waterline a good thirty feet above its current level. There was a ledge at the base of a set of earthen stairs where people had been able to climb down and swim in the frigid water. Now it almost looked like they would have had to repel from that platform to reach the pool.

"Get a picture of this," Craig said. "Make sure you focus on that line of algae that marks the old height of the pool."

Craig was already starting down the stairs by the time Aaron was done filming. The staircase wound around the circumference of the pit and roughly fifty steps down, the stairs leveled off and widened. There was a hole in the wall to the left, looking out through the veil of greenery at the cenote. Signs were posted to either side prohibiting them from jumping. Even halfway down, the fall would have been lethal. Aaron took about thirty seconds of footage before they continued down the staircase, the rock walls entombing them before finally opening up at the bottom onto the platform they had seen from above. It was made of what looked like adobe and surely would have appeared more stable had it been level with the water table, but without the water it was just a foot-thick piece of pottery supporting them over sharp rocks that looked like a dragon's teeth way down below.

"That's where the water went out," Craig said, pointing down toward the edge of the water. There was a small tunnel in the sloped rock floor that looked almost like a drainage pipe. The water barely covered the lower third, droplets dripping from the smooth roof of the tube. "So that's where we need to go."

"You want to crawl through there?"

"You have a better idea?"

Aaron shook his head and brought the camcorder up, zooming in on the hole in hopes of being able to see what might be on the other end, though all the lens revealed was darkness beyond.

"Well, let's do this if we're doing it," he said, slinging the camera over his shoulder with the strap and crawling to the ledge. He peered over the edge, gauging the distance to a small rock formation about five feet down that looked like stalagmites. Lowering his legs, he braced himself with his elbows until he was able to balance his right foot on the broken top of the sharp rock, carefully transferring his weight until he was able to lean against the wall and step down. The ground was covered with a thin layer of slime, his legs nearly sliding out from beneath him before he found his balance, walking just far enough away to allow Craig to hop down beside him.

"How could they have done this without a hydraulic pump?" Aaron asked, dropping to his rear end so he could slide down the slope toward the bottom.

"I don't know. Reverse pressure maybe? Like you know the tides come in and go out on the moon's cycle," Craig said, shrugging, and followed suit. They slid down the smooth rock, using the stalagmites to guide them to the point where the slant leveled off at the lip of the water.

They walked along the edge until they reached the far side where Aaron slung off the camcorder and dropped to his knees in the freezing water, peering through the mouth into the darkness. The flashing red light that indicated they were recording cast the only faint glare into the otherwise pristine darkness.

"I can't see any light at the end."

"How far can you see?" Craig asked.

"I don't know. Ten feet maybe?" he said, shivering so hard his teeth clacked together. "It just looks like it ends."

"Let me see." Aaron backed away and let Craig kneel down in front of him. He was about to offer what little light the camera afforded when Craig ducked his head and crawled into the hole, his splashing advance echoing dully throughout the cavern.

Aaron leaned down and pressed the record button, now barely able to discern his friend's silhouette from the thick shadows.

"It goes up from here," Craig called back when he reached the end. There was a scuffling sound and splashing as he adjusted his position so that he could stand.

"Can you see where it comes out?"

"There's a faint glow up there. Almost purple."

"What is it?"

"I don't know," Craig said, his voice now significantly muted.

Aaron lowered his shoulders and crawled through the hole, trying to keep the lens focused straight ahead without dropping it into the water or splashing it too badly.

"I think I can reach the top," Craig said.

Aaron heard a grunt of exertion and then the sound of pebbles being scraped from the wall by feet trying to gain traction. After a moment of scuffling, the noise finally ceased.

"What's up there?" Aaron said, peering up through the vent, his voice echoing in what sounded like a large room above.

"You...you have to see this for yourself."

"What is it?" Aaron asked again, maneuvering himself so that he could stand.

"Like I said, dude, you have to see this with your own eyes."

Aaron slung the camcorder back over his shoulder and grabbed onto a pair of rocks on the otherwise smooth wall that almost felt like they'd been designed as handles, water running down the film of slime. When he brought up his right leg to try to gain leverage, his toes went right into a small recess in the wall like a step.

Pulling himself higher, he finally reached the top, grappling with the slick edge until he was able to brace his feet against both sides and climb up.

The room glowed with a phosphorescent aura from bluish-purple specks on the walls. He walked to the closest side, his feet slapping through an inch of standing water, and grazed his fingertips along the surface. Several of the flecks of color flaked off and fell to the ground at his feet. He didn't know a thing about minerals or which may or may not create a lingering aura of phosphorescence, but the whole thing was staggering. It appeared as though the minerals had been ground up and mixed into a paste resembling a cross between concrete and adobe, and painted onto the wall in a thin layer.

A gentle breeze stirred the air in the room, tousling his hair, but, almost like a pinprick leak in an airplane cabin, it pulled the air from the room instead of blowing it in.

"Get that camera rolling," Craig said, startling Aaron out of his trance. He brought the camcorder to his face and tried to get a clear image of the wall. The lens fought for focus, zooming in and out in jerks, before finally producing a weak picture. Static ruled the periphery of the shot, and while each of the glowing specks weren't visible, the haze of color they created was.

"What do you think this is?" Aaron asked, recording his finger chipping a small dust of color away. "How long ago do you think this was done?"

"What do I look like, Indiana Jones? How should I know?"

"Why would it be necessary to have light in a cave?"

"Maybe it was already here in the walls."

"No. Someone painted it on. It chips right off, see?"

"I can't see a thing," Craig said, inching forward into what felt like a large room. He could see the vague outline of the walls like a dome around him, his eyes finally beginning to adjust to the extremely dim light enough to make out the floor under his feet. His right foot struck against something, the resulting sound like he'd kicked over a stack of dry branches. Bending over, he grabbed one of the sticks and held it close to his face. It was smooth like all of the bark had been peeled off and weathered in water for years. There were fine grooves in the surface and knobs at either end.

"Why would anyone be collecting sticks — ?"

Something crawled across the back of his hand, pinching the skin. He let the object fall from his hands, the scent finally reaching his nose. It smelled like the bones his parents would get from the butcher for their golden retriever: that repulsive scent of raw meat that would filter into the carpet in puddles of slobber.

"What?" Aaron asked.

"They're bones."

"What kind of bones?"

"I have no clue. You can see them as well as I can."

"Why in the world would this place be full of bones?" Aaron asked, stumbling into another pile. "Do you think this is some sort of ancient Mayan burial tomb or something?"

"These bones aren't buried, man. They're just discarded on the floor." Craig took another step forward and nearly rolled his ankle on another bone. He managed to right himself before he fell, kicking over another pile of bones. The floor was positively covered with them.

"They used to perform sacrifices here, right?" Aaron knelt and took hold of a bone that felt like a rounded chunk of a broken ceramic bowl. He didn't immediately notice when all of the bugs scurried off of the bone and onto his wrist, but by the time he stood up again, he cast it aside, screaming.

"They're covered in flies!" he shrieked.

Craig kicked through more bones, the piles on the floor growing deeper as he worked his way toward the back of the room. The suction intensified as well, tugging at his shirt like a flag in a stiff gale. He reached out toward the wall with his right hand, the suction so powerful it nearly yanked him off his feet.

"Jesus, man. This has to be how all of the water got sucked out of here. But what's causing it?"

"It's starting to reek in here, Craig. Let's just get out

of here."

"Do you have some good footage?"

"Yeah, man," Aaron lied. At this point he didn't even care. All he wanted to do was get out of there. It was starting to smell like his great aunt's house after she died.

"Should we bring some of these bones with us?"

"Do what you've got to do. I'm just getting out of here," Aaron said

Slinging the camera over his shoulder, he dropped to all fours and crawled along the ground, sweeping his hands from side to side on the smooth wet floor until he found the lip to the hole they'd entered through. It took him a moment to find the footholds, but he was soon lowering himself into the tunnel. When he reached the bottom, he twisted around until he was able to crawl back toward the circle of light. The fresh air blowing in felt absolutely divine, chasing the lingering scent of death from his sinuses. More than anything, he simply wanted to feel the sun on his face, the fresh air in his lungs. That cavern had been a cave of death, almost like he would imagine it might be to stumble into a hibernating bear's den. Why had there been so many bones? If they weren't burying something, then what could they possibly be doing with so many remains unless they were...

"Feeding something," he said aloud.

But what could possibly survive in nearly complete darkness?

Aaron crawled out of the tunnel, opening his mouth to inhale a deep lungful of fresh —

A dirty hand flashed in front of his face, jamming its fingers into his mouth. The fingertips pressed up against his palate so hard he heard something snap inside his head, his neck wrenched back so fiercely that the crown of his head hammered the lip of the maw. He tasted mud and blood draining down his throat as he gasped for air. With a painful tug, the fingertips broke through the roof of his mouth, flooding his tongue and trachea with hot fluid. His body went limp with pain and he was dragged out of the tube. Lying on his belly, his head twisted painfully to the left, the entire right side of his face submerged in the bitterly cold pool, he tried to see who was attacking him.

There was a flash of crimson eyes behind swollen lids. Sores on the face. Muddy hands. The man from the path. Jesus Christ, what was he trying to—?

Aaron screamed in agony as teeth lanced through the side of his neck, releasing a pulsing arterial spray. With another savage bite, Aaron's scream tapered to a hiss, his blood diluting into the sacred pool.

*   *   *

"What the heck was all the screaming about?" Craig asked when he heard footsteps clamber over the lip of the hole. He had a half dozen of the wet bones against his chest, carrying them like corded wood. Granted, he was no biology major and had only narrowly passed anatomy in high school, but he was fairly confident that some of the bones were human. He hadn't the slightest clue what he was going to do with them, but it seemed important to take them. Those scientists on TV could carbon date skeletal remains, couldn't they? "I told you I'd be right behind you."

Heavy, wet breathing.

"Christ, man. Are you out of shape or what?"

Footsteps pounded quickly toward him. He turned in time to see a faint silhouette sprinting directly at him.

"What are you—?"

His breath exploded from his chest as the body

slammed into him with a loud cracking sound that he couldn't be sure were the bones in his grasp or his own ribs.

He tried to scream but there was no air. Panicking, he shoved at the torso atop him, tasting warm breath on his lips, rough fingers clawing into the muscles on his shoulders.

Craig's breath returned with a lurch when teeth met through the soft tissue of his cheek, tearing away a gob of flesh. His screams echoed through the cavern.

Somewhere above, the basking iguanas dove back down into their earthen mounds while disoriented men and women still wandered the site, calling out for their missing loved ones and scratching at the burgeoning ulcers on their skin.

CHAPTER 4

Cancun, Mexico

Ray plopped down in the front row in First Class, right by the window. He'd managed to get himself onto the first flight back to Chicago, and with the way he was starting to feel, he couldn't get stateside soon enough. It certainly didn't take a genius to figure out what had happened. Somehow, they'd unleashed some sort of plague of insects when they'd tapped into that undiscovered chamber beneath the altar. He didn't know how or why, but the last thing he wanted was to be violently ill at some small clinic in the middle of the jungle staffed by doctors and nurses with no experience with modern medicine. If he was going to be sick, he was going to do so back home where he could have the best healthcare that money could buy. Private doctors and surgeons at his disposal. After all, in the United States of America, there was nothing that money couldn't buy.

He looked around at the other passengers up front behind the privacy curtain with him.

Every one of them was looking directly at him.

If he looked half as bad as he felt, he couldn't possibly

blame them. Turning to stare out the window onto the tarmac, he caught a flash of his reflection. His eyes were sunken into deep pits of shadow, his face waxy and pocked with swelling globules of sweat. He felt as though he was expanding from within, swelling like he was being inflated. He ran his fingers through his hair, only to smooth it flat in a puddle of perspiration. Goosebumps prickled from every follicle between purple welts of some sort and he began to shiver.

"Stewardess," he called after the woman walking to the front of the cabin, finding only a fraction of the voice he'd intended.

"Yes," the woman said. Despite her cheerful smile she looked harried. "Is there something I can get you?"

"Blanket," he whispered, tugging at his shirt collar.

She reached into the overhead cabinet and pulled down a light blue blanket. He noticed that she only came close enough to drop it into his lap, then quickly retracted her arm.

"Anything else?" she asked, already continuing toward the cockpit.

"No...thank you," he whispered, leaning to his right against the window and draping the blanket over his torso.

He looked back to the others before closing his eyes. A man in a business suit stared at him like he was some sort of freak, while a matching tanned and accessorized couple watched him with thinly veiled disgust.

Ray strained to get his arm over his head, taking trembling hold of the knob to direct the flume of air down on him. Leaning back against the window, he closed his eyes.

* * *

He awoke with acid gurgling through the lining of his stomach and creeping up his esophagus. Best he could tell, they were somewhere over the Gulf of Mexico as all he could see below was turquoise water flirting in and out through the fluffy white clouds.

"Excuse me," he whispered to the man in the seat next to him, who cringed away from Ray as he staggered to his feet, dropping the blanket to the floor.

Barely able to maintain his balance, Ray fought his way to the bathroom and threw the door open so hard it slammed into the wall beside it.

"Sorry," he apologized to no one, struggling into the small room, closing the door, and flipping the switch to OCCUPIED.

Collapsing down on the seat before he could even pull his pants down, he leaned forward and vomited into the sink. It felt as though he was bringing up whole organs. He was so hot that his skin was painful even to his own touch. One quick glance at the mirror confirmed just how terrible he looked.

The formerly small boils on his face were now several inches wide. The thin film of flesh containing the fluid had ripped away to expose draining red craters similar to how he imagined leprosy might look.

God, it felt as though his blood was boiling...

He leaned forward again, only this time he toppled from the toilet to the floor, pinned between the sink and the seat. His liver lost the fight with the rising toxicity levels in his blood, which raced straight into his brain. His face turned a rich maroon before fading to a bruised color and his eyes rolled backwards.

*   *   *

The Infected

Jason Caisse looked across the aisle at the man beside him, who turned to match his stare. They'd both heard the thud from the bathroom in front of them.

He'd been seriously upset when he boarded and went to his seat to find some guy who looked like he was going through heroin withdrawals or coming down with malaria in the seat beside his, but what was he going to do, go back to coach? At six-foot-six, those seats back there pinned his knees to his chest and he imagined that was how it must have felt in the womb. If he had to pay extra just to have a little room for his legs, he was going to squeeze everything he possibly could out of the First Class experience.

As he had each of the last five years since graduation, he'd met four of his old fraternity brothers from Vanderbilt down at the Riu Cancun to try to relive the debauchery of their youth. This was really the first year where all of them had started to feel too mature to really go crazy. It was somewhat disheartening. Rather than partying in the hotel bar, they'd spent the majority of their time sipping chai lattes and watching CNBC during the day and drinking domestic beer with Sports Center at night. Three of them were already married, and Jason himself was engaged. He imagined that this would be the last year that all of them would come, and wondered if this had actually been one year too many if he got whatever the guy in the window seat next to him had.

The two men looked at each other as though waiting for the other to volunteer to check on the guy in the bathroom, but neither did. The man to his left went back to his *Wall Street Journal* and Jason opened his paperback, merely staring at the pages. After a few moments he began to read, realizing that he was thankful for the time the sick man was spending in the bathroom and away from him. Worst case scenario, maybe the guy had passed out in there. It wasn't as though he could drown in the fraction of an inch of water in the toilet, and the rest would probably do him some good.

Leaning back, he looked up momentarily at the movie playing silently on the screen in front of him before burying his nose back in his book to try to crack *The DaVinci Code*.

*   *   *

He hadn't checked the time, but he could see through the window across the vacant seat next to him that they were already over land. Still the guy hadn't come out of the bathroom. Pink light washed the inside of the plane from the slowly setting sun to the west.

All of the coffee he'd consumed in the airport was beginning to catch up with him now, and it was only a matter of time before he was going to have to do something about it.

"Excuse me," he said to the stewardess speeding past. She held up a finger to him, hurrying to dump the trash she'd collected into the bin around the corner, and then came right back.

"Do you need something, sugar?" she asked. Though she was older, her sweet Southern drawl and recently dyed hair made her seem much younger.

"The guy sitting next to me...He's been in the bathroom for an awfully long time."

She looked past him to the empty seat as though noticing for the first time.

"Maybe he isn't feeling so good."

"He certainly didn't look like he did, but—"

"Feel free to use the lavatory in coach if you like. There'll be a line, but it shouldn't take too long."

"That's not it," Jason said, lowering his voice as he'd

The Infected

drawn the attention of the other First Class passengers. "I think I heard him fall in there."

"So you want me to check on him," she said, smiling, though her eyes couldn't hide her repulsion. "Is he a friend of yours?"

"No...I just...He looked pretty bad is all."

"All right," she said, turning back toward the front of the plane. She slipped behind the wall at the front to check the passenger dossier. After a moment, she emerged again and stopped in front of the bathroom door. "Mr. Thompson?"

She knocked softly.

The stewardess looked at Jason, but he could only shrug.

"Mr. Thompson," she said, knocking harder this time. "Mr. Thompson?"

Still no answer.

"Are you okay in there, sir?"

She flinched as there was a loud bang from the other side of the door.

"Mr. Thomp—"

Another bang from within, the plastic door cracking and bulging outward.

The stewardess retreated from the bathroom door toward the passenger seating, turning to Jason to plead with her eyes for help.

The door exploded outward behind her, but before she could even start to run, the man leapt out of the bathroom, slamming her against the opposite wall. They both dropped to the floor with a thud that made the plane shake. She landed on her stomach with him right atop her, but she couldn't buck his weight.

Grabbing her by the hair, Ray raised her head from the floor, bent it back as far as her spine would allow, then leaned all the way in and tore a chunk of meat from

62

her exposed throat with his teeth.

Blood sprayed the front row of passengers like he'd taken a bite into a ripe orange.

Jason froze, the warmth running down his cheeks.

The whole scene played out before him like a movie, his brain unable to rationalize it enough to trigger his fight-or-flight instincts.

The man who had been sitting next to him thrust his fist into the wound he had opened and yanked out a strap of muscle. He threw his head back like a vulture and choked back the morsel, blood hosing the wall next to him from her carotid. His head snapped down and his eyes locked on Jason's.

The thing that had once been the sick-looking man sitting next to him was now barely reminiscent of a human being. The vessels had burst in his eyes, turning the whites to red, and were sunken deep into the massive black bruises as though pounded there by hammers. The skin was in the early stages of cyanosis: bluing lips and cheeks with everything in between a waxy gray, save for the massive ulcers that looked like acid had eaten away the sickly flesh. Ray's lips curled away from bloody teeth, viscera pouring down his chin. He still wore a polo shirt and khaki shorts, but both were drenched with blood and what smelled like vomit.

Even his movements were no longer remotely manlike. He moved in twitches, almost as though an electrical current fired through his veins. Not robotic movements, but quick snapping movements, like a karate master practicing forms.

He cocked his head at Jason like a raven, then jumped up to his feet, landing still bent at the knees.

Jason screamed and fought to unlock his buckle.

The First Class cabin came to life with terror-stricken cries.

The Infected

Snapping the buckle loose, Jason whirled and sprinted down the aisle toward the tail of the plane, slamming into the man in the suit and sending him toppling over the armrest and into his seat again. There was a shrill scream and he felt something warm and wet slap against his back.

A pair of frightened eyes parted the curtains dividing the cabins, the man's face going pale a heartbeat before Jason plowed right into him. Jason grabbed the curtain, but only managed to rip it off its track, landing squarely atop the other man's chest. Feet stomped near his ears as more First Class passengers trampled him in their hurry to escape. The entire rear cabin exploded into screams. Bodies immediately filled the aisle, stampeding over one another to get as far away as possible.

The man underneath Jason finally drew in a breath and screamed as he was jerked out from beneath, so quickly that Jason flopped right to the floor.

There was a ripping sound and a scream cut short behind him, but Jason didn't dare look back. He forced himself up to all fours and propelled himself forward. Instead of packing in with the others, he veered to the left, stepped up onto a seat, and launched himself five rows back. He righted himself so he could see over the seats between his pursuer and him.

Whatever that man had become was tearing through the passengers like they were dolls. Ray ripped a woman's arm out of the socket while yanking her closer to snap his jaws through her soft neck. He tossed a pretty little girl behind him, her formerly pink dress stained crimson, broken legs bending the wrong way. Blood dotted the ceiling and overhead compartments. His face was awash with it, save for those awful eyes.

A large man stepped in front of his wife and kids to face down the creature while others scurried to get

64

behind him. He raised his fists like a boxer and threw a solid overhand right, connecting squarely with Ray's face.

It sounded like someone took a baseball bat to a rotten pumpkin.

Ray's head snapped sideways, but his left fist slammed into the man's gut. He doubled over and the monster was upon him. Ray drove both thumbs through the tender skin beneath the man's jaw and wrenched his head back with a crack. Before the man could even scream, the thing was crunching on his trachea and tugging his mandible out of the socket. Ray reared back and pounded the man in the center of his face, throwing a mist of blood across the terrified, wide-eyed people cringing behind him.

One man wrenched a child from his mother's arms and threw him at the monster to try to distract him, but Ray caught the boy like a football and crushed his head under his left arm while grabbing the man's wrist and yanking him forward with his right. There was a loud pop and a crunch and the man was on his knees in front of Ray with his broken arm held high.

Another man hurled himself at the creature, but was easily deflected into the seats to the side. He pulled a service revolver from beneath his jacket and pointed it right at the thing, rivers of blood running from his broken nose.

"Air Marshal!" the man yelled.

Ray turned and dove at him. With a deafening explosion in such close quarters, the marshal fired a bullet straight through Ray's forehead.

A plug of gray matter and bone spattered the opposite wall, but he seemed hardly fazed. He just snapped his head back forward and launched a punch hard enough to go through the Air Marshal's face, cracking the glass behind him.

With a whooshing sound like a wind tunnel, the window fractured outward, sucking what remained of the marshal into the hole. He plugged it momentarily before being folded in half and jerked right out into the sky, patterning the windows behind with blood all the way to the tail.

The oxygen masks dropped from above the seats, dangling like so many octopus legs. Those that were close enough lunged for them, strapping the yellow cup over their mouths and shrinking as far away as their tethers would allow.

Papers and magazines filled the air, whipping past the men and women grabbing onto anything within reach to keep from being sucked off their feet with the sudden change in pressure.

The thing spun to face them, the suction pulling blood from the hole in the back of his head as though drinking it through an invisible straw. He grabbed the seats to either side and tried to stagger against the impossible force that brought all sorts of debris, jackets, and blankets to slap him in the face.

Stuffing bloomed from the headrests as Ray gouged his fingers through the fabric to try to stall the inevitable. A man rushed from the cockpit and threw a fire extinguisher right at Ray's head. He flew backwards as though pulled by a string at the waist, his rear end plugging the hole and crumpling him like a fist.

"Everyone!" the copilot yelled, heading back toward the front of the plane. The monster turned and looked at him and he almost bolted for the locked doors of the cockpit again. "Get to your seats and get your buckles on!"

The creature slipped farther back, reaching out to both sides and digging his fingers into the wall, his head now between his knees.

"Hurry!" the captain shouted, sprinting back to his controls.

Chaos ensued: people trampling one another, shoving each other out of the way, throwing punches to reclaim their seats.

"I don't have a mask!" a woman screamed.

A grown man ripped one away from a mewling toddler.

The thing lodged in the window tried to grab at a woman just out of reach. Ray lost what little leverage he had and was sucked backwards through the window; bones breaking loudly to allow him to squeeze through such a small space. Blood followed his body in a stream, spattering against the outside before careening off into oblivion.

The nose of the plane tipped down suddenly, throwing those still in the aisles forward.

Jason used the momentum to catapult him over a few men in front of him. He landed in the clear walkway, sliding through the mess of blood until he was face to face with the flight attendant. It looked like the entire lower half of her face had been peeled upward from her red-muscled jaw like she'd been wearing a mask.

The pull from the window was all-but-irresistible. He curled his fingers as tightly as he could around the brackets bolting the chairs to the floor and climbed back into his seat.

Red emergency lights blossomed from the ceiling to replace the overhead white lights. The scream of their descent replaced the human wails of pain and fear.

Jason buckled himself in and strapped the mask over his mouth and nose.

"Everyone please assume the crash position with your head between your knees," a voice announced over

The Infected

the intercom, barely audible over the wind shear.

Jason looked to his left. The business man's seat was empty, his disheveled body discarded in the corner.

He put his head down, lacing his fingers over the back of his head...and prayed.

CHAPTER 5

Colorado Springs, Colorado

"ETA five minutes," a nurse said, bursting through the break room door and ducking right back out.

"Code gray," the overhead speaker announced.

The staff coming on for the graveyard shift gathered around the small television, watching breathlessly as the live feed showed them what they were about to expect. A passenger plane had crashed on the runway at the Colorado Springs Municipal Airport. While the fuselage had remained intact, the front landing gear had broken and dropped the plane onto its nose, tearing out the bottom and throwing luggage everywhere. Fire trucks hosed down the remainder of the plane despite the lack of flames while passengers slid down the yellow inflatable slides over each wing. The television cut from overhead shots from a helicopter to images from the ground. Red and blue lights flashed everywhere, turning the growing dark back to artificial day. Ambulances raced from the scene after double-loading their cargo.

The first of the sirens became audible in the distance.

"What details do we have?" Dr. Angelica Morgan asked, trading in her starched white lab coat for a powder blue scrub smock. She hung her stethoscope over her neck and hoped the coffee would kick in soon.

"Ninety-eight on board," Marcy Hempstead, the night charge nurse said. "They're still sorting through the casualties, but we're expecting around thirty."

"Thirty?"

"With various degrees of acuity, of course."

"Have they already cleared the lobby and triage?"

"They're in the process now."

"All right people," Dr. Morgan said. "Time to rock n' roll."

*　　*　　*

"Caucasian male. Twenty-seven years old. Multiple facial lacs. Suspected cervical trauma," the paramedic called as she blew through the automatic doors where she was greeted by a doctor and a nurse. She wore her standard-issue navy blues with her hair pulled back into a ponytail.

"Is all of the blood his?" the doctor asked.

Jason strained to look toward the source of the voice, though with the plastic collar tight on his neck, he could only move his eyes. He caught a glimpse of a security name badge that said Morgan. His forehead was taped down to the hard board beneath him with vinyl-covered Styrofoam blocks pressed against either ear.

"I can't imagine he'd have a drop left in him if it were."

"He was butchering them," Jason said, his eyes searching from one side to the other as he tried to get someone's attention. His entire face was crusted beneath a mask of blood. "When he came out of the bathroom...the stewardess—"

"Save your energy," a third voice said, gently placing

her hand on his.

He squeezed it and tried to see her. Marcy had a warm smile that even affected her bright blue eyes, like twin tropical seas against her porcelain skin. Rich black hair was drawn back on her head into a ponytail like a shimmering oil slick.

"He wasn't just killing them," Jason said, his eyes peeled wide. He could tell by her wince that he was squeezing her hand way too hard, but that was beyond his control. "He was ripping them apart. Biting them, tearing their arms out—"

"I need a complete blood chemistry," the doctor said, giving the nurse just enough of a distraction to twist her hand out of his.

"I've got to go back for round two," the paramedic said. "You good from here, doc?"

"What rooms are available?" Dr. Morgan asked the nurse.

"Sounds like a 'yes' to me," the paramedic said. She patted Jason on the foot. "You're in good hands here, buddy. You hang tough."

She whirled and fell away from the cart as they rushed it down the corridor, leaving Jason to stare up at the white ceiling with the fluorescent tubes hurtling past like the dashed white lines on a two-lane highway. Images flashed before his eyes. The man blowing through the bathroom door and tearing out the poor stewardess' throat; ripping that girl's arm out; that thing getting sucked out of the window; the plane crashing and skidding down the runway.

Sparks.

Fire.

Darkness.

He screamed.

There was a loud bang as the head of the bed

slammed into a pair of swinging doors, and then he was through them. Another couple of scrub-clad people were already in there, both wearing matching teal-colored masks. The first stood at the head of the bed as the gurney stopped, the other at the foot.

"On my count," the man above his head said. "One. Two."

They lifted him off the bed by the orange board under him and set him onto another table.

"We need a cross-table c-spine," the doctor said.

The masked woman at the bottom of the bed hurried over to a large cart with a retractable armature and began moving it into position.

Jason started to wheeze. It felt like they'd put his immobilizing collar on way too tight. "We're losing his airway," Angelica snapped, shoving the x-ray tech back out of the way. "Prepare to intubate."

"Look at his neck," Marcy gasped. "It's swelling out through the collar."

"Loosen it."

"We haven't seen the cross-table of the c-spine."

"We won't need it at all if he asphyxiates."

"Yes, Dr. Morgan," Marcy said, carefully holding Jason's neck as still as she could while trying to loosen the collar.

"I need that x-ray!" Angelica shouted.

The tech wheeled the portable machine back into place, lined up a cassette on the other side of Jason's neck, and said, "Shooting x-ray."

Everyone in the room stepped back long enough for the machine to let out a beep, and then moved right back into position as the tech cleared everything out of the way.

"God, it hurts!" Jason bellowed, raising both hands to try to claw the collar off. Had his abdomen grown even larger since they brought him into the room?

"Restrain him," Angelica said, and the man from the head of the bed was fighting against Jason to drag his hands closer to the stirrups to either side of the table.

"He's too strong," the EMT said. "I can't...force his arms down."

His face was flushed with the exertion.

"Get it off! Get it off!" Jason screamed, sputtering blood that drained down his cheeks to either side and into his eyes, which rolled back beneath the fluttering lids. Sores like purple chickenpox arose on his face and arms, expanding before their very eyes. Jerking relentlessly at the collar, the brace finally succumbed with the tearing sound of Velcro. He grabbed the tape and tore it off of his forehead, removing a handful of his bangs in the process. Bolting upright, he threw the neck brace across the room and started clawing into his bulbous abdomen, tearing his shirt and carving bloody grooves with his fingernails.

"Try to calm down," Marcy said, even as she eased away from him.

"Jesus," Angelica gasped, stumbling backwards herself. There was a knot at the base of the patient's ribs like a softball. "I need an aspiration kit."

Jason whirled to look at her, his face as pale as the dead. Sweat bloomed from every pore, drawing lines through the dried blood and the fresh alike. There was a transient moment of lucidity, where the panic and the pain were gone, leaving him only with the fear.

"Help me," he whispered to the doctor, locking his eyes on hers.

Leaning forward, he took her by the sleeve and pulled her closer so she would for sure be able to hear him.

"Don't let me become like him," he begged, his eyes

overflowing with tears. "Please."

"Like who?" she asked, but his eyes rolled back and he collapsed forward, nearly knocking her onto her back as he crashed to the floor, his head hitting the tile with a resounding crack.

* * *

Dr. Morgan inserted the six-inch needle into the bulge of fluid encapsulating the man's liver. He was supine on the table with an artificial airway down his throat like a snake, his head turned away from her so she wouldn't have to see the tortured look on his face or the still-weeping sores.

He'd completely lost consciousness. His pulse oxygen had dropped into the seventies and they'd been forced to put him on a ventilator.

Angelica wore full isolation precautions: a yellow smock with latex gloves pulled over her hands just past the cuffs of the sleeves, an N-series particle-filtering mask, and goggles. Carefully sliding the long needle through the fluid, which seeped up around the site of insertion, she pushed it all the way down until she felt the subtle pop of the parietal peritoneum, the sheath holding the fluid in against the man's liver.

It almost looked as though in the time it had taken her to set up for the sterile procedure that the swelling had gone down significantly.

She drew back the plunger of the syringe, bringing with it an ochre-colored fluid. Repeating the process, she filled three test vials and passed them off to Marcy. They really should have been helping with the other patients from the crash as this one had become catatonic, but Angelica had a hunch that she had to investigate. If she was right, they could all be in serious trouble.

Fluid drained from the puncture site after she removed the needle.

The man's skin was beginning to take on a yellowish cast.

"Would you rush these to the lab?" Angelica asked, sighing as she studied the swelling. She pushed her thumb onto it, leaving a dimple that stayed there far longer than it should have.

"Yes, doctor," Marcy said, shoving open the door with her rear end, the vials bundled together in her hands. "Do you want me to call and see what's taking MRI so long?"

"Please. And Marcy..."

"Hmm?"

"Thanks."

"Anytime," Marcy said, ducking out and allowing the door to swing closed behind her.

Dr. Morgan looked back at the man's belly one last time—had the swelling gone down even more? Where was the fluid going?—and then left him to the nurse's care, hurrying back to join the fracas in the ER.

*   *   *

They were triaging the least critical patients in the ambulance bay before bringing them into the chairs in the waiting area for minor procedures from stitches and splinting to icing and bracing. All of the curtained rooms were in use with the worst of the cases, while those in between were parked on stretchers and in wheelchairs in the hallway. Two had arrived DOA: one from cardiac arrest, the other from blunt trauma to the head. They were still tallying casualties at the scene.

The most disturbing part was that the majority of the patients were spotted with blood other than their own, and Angelica had yet to see anyone with a wound that might have sprayed like that.

She waded through the chaos and overwhelmed personnel, signing off on all sorts of sutures and splints on her way to the front doors, where the chief resident, Dr. Ian Nguyen, was directing traffic as fast as he could.

"Where do you want me?" Angelica asked.

He turned and looked at her almost as though he didn't immediately recognize her. His white lab coat was smeared with bloody handprints and he looked like he hadn't slept in days.

"Room two," he said, turning around again as another ambulance drove into the bay.

The world spun in red and blue.

Angelica blew back through the automatic doors toward her assignment. She was nearly through the lobby when she stopped. Her brow furrowed. Taking a couple steps back, she looked at the patient on the bed in the middle of the room.

The casting nurse sat on a chair at the end of the bed, applying the finishing touches to a blue plastic cast on the woman's left ankle. She was propped up on her elbows so she could see what the nurse was doing. Her brown hair was cut short, hanging longer to the sides in front than the back.

"Excuse me," Angelica said, lifting the woman's shirt so she could clearly see unmistakable abdominal swelling. There was the beginning of a fluid-filled knot like the other man had.

The woman looked at Dr. Morgan, her face crusted with spatters of blood, save for the lines her tears had drawn down through it. She had four black stitches in her lower lip.

"Were you exposed to anything that you know of?"

"What are you talking about?" the woman said,

hysteria quivering at the edge of her voice. "This guy went crazy and started killing people. I saw him take a bite out of some lady's neck. And then our plane crashed. The last thing in the world I'm worried about right now is any goddamned germs!"

Angelica pressed on the swelling with her pen.

"Ow!" the woman cried, slapping the pen out of her hand. "Why don't you go poke someone else?"

Angelica turned and went to the next closest bed. Without thought, she raised the man's shirt to reveal a similar growth. She hurried to the next bed, and the next, each of them spattered with blood and growing a knot in their upper abdomen at roughly the level of their livers.

What in the world was going on here? If these passengers had brought some sort of extremely infectious disease with them, then they were going to have to lock down the hospital and quarantine everyone inside. She needed the results of those lab tests!

She rushed down the hallway into room two, squirting a mess of hand sanitizer into her palms and rubbing them briskly before slipping on a pair of latex gloves from her pocket.

"What do we have here?" she asked, blowing through the swinging doors.

"Forty-one year-old Caucasian female. Severe lacerations to the left lateral side of the neck consistent with teeth marks. Pulse ox seventy-one. BP ninety over fifty."

"She's in shock?"

"Yes, doctor."

"What's her name?"

"Catherine Dougherty."

"Mrs. Daugherty?" Angelica said. "Can you tell me what happened?"

She reached under the woman's gown until she was able to palpate the massive swelling that she knew would be there. The nurse had done an excellent job irrigating the wound on the patient's neck, making it so that each of the muscles and tendons were clearly visible and undamaged despite the ragged edges. Fortunately, the injury was mainly superficial. A patch of skin from her buttocks and she'd be as good as new.

The woman's eyes were fixed and dilated.

She was completely unresponsive.

"Shuttle her along. Manage with a local anesthetic and dressings until surgery can squeeze her in. We've got more acute cases that could use this room."

*   *   *

"Dr. Nguyen?" Angelica asked. The phone at the back of the trauma suite had finally rung in response to her page.

"Make it quick, Dr. Morgan. We're buried up here," the voice at the other end replied.

"I think we need to close down the ER. I think—"

"Close the ER? Are you out of your mind? We're in the middle of a code gray and triaging patients on the street—"

"Listen—"

"No. You listen. The next closest Level I trauma center is seventy miles away. We don't have the luxury of diverting a single patient, so suck it up and—"

"Will you just hear me out, Ian?"

"You're on my last nerve, Angelica."

"I think we have a possible epidemic here."

"What we have is a plane crash."

"Check their livers."

"I give every patient a thorough—"

"Would you just look at their abdomens?"

He sighed into the phone. She envisioned him on the

other end biting his lower lip with his face growing redder by the second.

"What's your theory, Dr. Morgan?"

"A combination of VL and DCL."

"Visceral and diffuse cutaneous leishmaniasis…"

"Look at their skin, Ian. Check out the bulbous swelling at the base of the ribs superior to the liv –"

"I don't have time for this."

She heard a chorus of ambulance sirens across the connection.

"All I'm asking is that we lock the doors and quarantine ourselves until we know for sure."

"And the incoming traumas, hmm? What should we do with them?"

"The worst cases are already here, Ian."

"So I suppose that means no one will wreck their car or go into labor tonight. Has there been a moratorium on people getting shot or having heart attacks?"

"Now you're just being facetious."

"Get your head in the game, Angelica. When was the last time any of us had to deal with a case of leishmaniasis? What's the vector again? The sand fly? Come on, Angie. Are they carrying smallpox as well?"

Angelica fell silent, leaning against the wall and fuming as the doors to the room burst inward ahead of another bed surrounded by medical personnel.

"Just do your job, Dr. Morgan."

"Ian…" she whispered, but he'd already hung up.

The woman on the gurney screamed and tried to throw herself over the side, but the nurses and paramedics managed to force her back down despite her thrashing and shrieking protests.

"Grace Chapman," one of the nurses said, looking up only long enough to ensure Angelica was listening. She fought with the woman's disfigured left arm to keep it down. "Compound fractures of the distal radius and ulna. Multiple chest contusions and altered mental status."

"What about her abdomen?"

"No blunt trauma or suspected bowel perforation."

"I mean, have you palpated her right upper quadrant?"

The nurse looked up at Angelica like it was all she could do to keep from lunging at her throat. She was one of the day nurses who'd surely already worked a twelve-hour shift and now had no prospect of going home anytime soon. Rather than forcing the issue, Angelica stepped forward to the side of the bed and slid both hands beneath the patient's gown, pressing gently upward.

The woman screamed and tried again to break free.

"Of course," Angelica said, pulling back her hands. It felt as though the patient had a breast implant beneath the skin just inferior to her tenth anterior rib.

"Let me go!" the woman yelled. "I just want to go home!"

Her bleached hair whipped across her face as she slammed herself back and forth.

"You have a broken arm and—"

"I don't care! I don't care! I just want to go home!"

Angelica nodded to the nurse, who stabbed a needle into the woman's arm. She struggled a few moments longer before her body finally calmed. Tears streamed from her eyes, smudging tiny spots of blood Angelica had at first thought to be freckles on her dark-tanned skin.

"Please..." the woman whispered. "Don't let me die..."

*   *   *

Angelica snapped off her latex gloves and threw them at the trash can, not even bothering to see if they actually went in. She'd reduced and splinted the woman's broken forearm, but she'd become completely unresponsive. Right now she was unconscious on a gurney in some hallway or other waiting to be casted while a helpless nurse could only monitor her vitals. Like the man earlier, she'd become catatonic without the slightest warning.

This was more than just shock from the plane crash they were dealing with. This was pathological, but no one would listen to her.

Storming out of the trauma suite, Angelica headed straight for the break room. She needed to vent. She needed to cool off. She needed more coffee. But most of all, she needed to get out of the ER, if only for a few minutes.

She'd never felt this powerless in her entire life. It was as though she were merely sitting in the audience at some elaborate play. No matter what she did or how hard she tried, the patient's progression from fully conscious and functional to catatonic seemed to be a foregone conclusion. She could treat all of the surface wounds and breaks, but when it came right down to it, she was completely useless against whatever was causing the rapid degeneration. Even the patient with the open neck had gone downhill quickly after she'd stabilized her and sent her out.

The entire emergency room was beginning to look more like the morgue.

Weaving through the slalom of activity and scattered beds, she threw back the break room door and headed directly for her locker, tears already streaming down her cheeks.

CHAPTER 6

Colorado Springs Community Hospital

None of them saw Angelica enter the break room, let alone noticed her by her locker in tears. They were transfixed by the television. Even the barely restrained chaos around them had ceased to exist momentarily in the face of what they were witnessing. It was as though the entire world were going mad.

"...*live footage from Cancun, Mexico*," a polished announcer's voice said. A CNN logo blocked the bottom left corner of the screen. "*While it may appear to be an apocalyptic vision, I can assure you that what you are seeing is indeed actually transpiring as I speak. Details are sketchy at best, but preliminary indications point toward some sort of mass hysteria.*"

On the screen was an aerial picture of a small airport, complete with the *whoop-whoop-whoop* of the chopper blades. Fires blazed from the windows on the upper level of the concourse, already beginning to consume the roof. Through the swirling black smoke, people ran rampantly first one way and then another. For a moment it looked as though one man tackled another before the smoke again obscured the view. The camera panned down to show the fiery wreckage of a pair of planes strewn across the runway, the fields to either side guiding the crackling flames toward the jungle.

"We've received no word as to why either plane may have crashed or if there are any survivors. All we know with any sort of certainty is that one of them was United Flight 1116 bound for Los Angeles. Currently, we theorize that the planes collided in midair —"

There was a flash of light that turned the image white, followed by a loud explosion.

The camera fought for focus, appearing to zoom in and out on vague gray shapes before finally drawing a bead on the control tower. A fist of smoke curled from where the roof had been, the entire elevated structure ablaze. What looked like a burning man crawled over the broken glass and fell a hundred feet to the concrete below.

The screen cut to an image of an anchorman sitting at a newsroom desk, his notes scattered in front of him. Even though every hair was in place, he looked disheveled. His tie hung askew between the unbuttoned sides of his suit jacket. He wore a look that was a mixture of excitement and fear.

"This is Dominic Cevallos live at the CNN news desk. We're going to take you live now to the streets of Cancun proper. What you are about to see is both violent and gruesome. Please be advised that this footage is not for the faint-of-heart, and small children should be excused from the room now." He paused a moment, either for dramatic effect or to allow parents to rush their children away from the TV.

The screen went black for a full second before a video obviously taken on a handheld camcorder appeared.

"These images were obtained from Mexican television and are being rebroadcast with consent."

The Infected

It looked as though someone was holding the video camera over the railing of a balcony several stories up, focusing it onto the street below.

"You're now looking at the tourist district of Cancun where large hotels line the main road a hundred yards inland from the Caribbean Sea. We're unsure which hotel this was filmed from, but similar footage is appearing all over the airwaves and internet."

Cars were tangled with buses, crumpled in accidents in the middle of the street. A thin cloud of exhaust hovered above like a fog. People ran through it on the asphalt, climbing over the demolished hoods of cars and leaping the wreckage. One would drag down another, knocking him to the street and then pummeling him. It was like watching a prison riot, though completely out of context.

A simultaneous gasp filled the break room as all eyes watched one man yank another to his feet by the arm, snapping it easily at the elbow. He quickly leaned forward and bit the other man on the cheek, tearing away a chunk of flesh. By the time the man clapped his good hand over the bloody hole two more people were on him, slamming him to the ground and opening his neck with their teeth to free a geyser of blood.

Another man ran to his aid, trying to pry the others from atop him, only to have them turn on him and yank his legs out from beneath him. He was easily over-whelmed as he tried to crawl away.

The handheld image shook and then jerked away to reveal a cement balcony enclosed by white rails. Balled glass scattered across the cement. The cameraman whirled to face another man, who cringed in front of a shattered sliding glass door. Hands covering his head, he turned to look at the hotel room behind him. A silhouette slammed into him before he could turn all the way, pounding him to the ground. There was a blur of flailing limbs and the attacker pinned the man's arms beneath his knees, cradled either side of his face, and leaned down as though he were about to kiss him. When the assailant pulled his head back, a strip of flesh flopped from his bared teeth, a spray of blood washing over him.

There was a moment where the camera quivered in the cameraman's hand, as though the eyes behind the lens met with those of the monster ravaging his friend. The thing looked normal, save for the eyes and the expression on its face. All of the vessels in its eyes had burst, bleeding the whites crimson, its pupils swollen to nearly the size of its irises, leaving just a halo of color. Its expression would have looked more at home on the muzzle of a wolf, its lips curled away from a snarl that betrayed an animal nature that was primitive and full of rage.

The camera jerked away from that hideous face and then showed only the floor and the cameraman's feet as he sprinted through the hotel room and out into the hallway.

Everything went black for a moment before the anchor again appeared at the news desk, noticeably paled.

"We've just received reports of similar violence in Tijuana, near the American border."

"Jesus," Marcy whispered, finally able to tear her stare from the tube.

"What the hell is wrong with these people?" Brad Sauers whispered. He wore the only white lab coat in the room as he'd been running sample after sample through various machines in the lab. "It's like they've all lost their minds."

"Group psychosis maybe?" Dr. Avery Martin said. He was a neurosurgical resident, but had been called down in the crisis to sort through the carnage with the rest of them.

"Are you going shrink on us, doc?" Brad asked, remarkably the only person eating. The top of a bag of Cheetos peeked out of his pocket.

"Can you imagine me all touchy-feely?" He partially smirked, which was about as emotive as he got. "And how does that make you feel. Whatever. Who cares? There isn't a problem in the world that can't be solved with a scalpel."

"Remind me not to get a headache around you," Angelica said. She was no longer crying, but even her light application of mascara was streaked down her face.

"...breaking live," the anchor said. "We take you now to La Jolla, California, just north of San Diego. This footage is being broadcast live on the local ABC affiliate."

The CNN logo in the bottom left corner eclipsed a News 7 logo. The rumble of the helicopter blades was immediately apparent, a shaky spotlight reaching toward the ground where there was a half circle of police cars, their lights twirling, blocking the center of the street. Traffic was backed up to either side of the cruisers, people standing outside their cars, but quite positively giving the scene a wide berth. It looked like there was a brawl on the sidewalk in front of a restaurant of some kind. There appeared to be twenty or more people in the fracas, fighting hand-to-hand while police waded in with Billy clubs and riot gear, their fellow officers covering them with drawn weapons from behind the open doors of their police cars. Bodies were sprawled out all over the sidewalk. None of them seemed to be moving, save for the expanding mess of blood beneath them.

"Authorities report that what was originally called in as a domestic disturbance has rapidly escalated into mass violence with somewhere in the neighborhood of a dozen casualties, *though the official number has yet to be confirmed. Crimes of this nature are generally unknown in neighborhoods such as this in the upscale community – "*

Gunfire exploded on the screen, discharge flaring from so many weapons like firecrackers strobing the melee.

"Can we get a closer shot of that?"

As if in response, the camera zeroed in on a cop with a Plexiglas shield raising his baton and cracking it against the side of a man's head. His neck snapped sideways with a splash of blood and teeth a heartbeat before he lurched backwards with an amoeba of blood in the middle of his chest. He staggered in reverse, finally righting himself against another combatant, and lunged back at the officer as if nothing had happened. Tackling the cop to the ground and pinning him beneath his clear shield, he flailed with his arms and legs, smearing streaks of blood across the barrier.

The cop looked up into the camera and opened his mouth to scream just as a hand reached beneath, two fingers slipping into the side of his mouth like a fishhook and ripping the skin back toward his ear.

The camera turned sharply away as if the cameraman had lost his nerve, now showing only the sidewalk a half-block up the street where another group of people were sprinting not away from the chaos, but toward it. The lens drew back, but followed the shadows out of the darkness and into the light where they charged straight into the scrum, knocking people over. One of them, a balding man with an otherwise frail-looking frame, bit right into the neck of one of the officers. When he pulled his head back there was blood all over his face and a fleshy morsel hanging from his teeth. The cop smashed his left hand over the wound, though the blood poured unimpeded through his fingers, and pressed his service weapon to the bald man's forehead. With a flash of muzzle flare, he blew the back of the man's cranium onto the restaurant window. As if by delayed reaction, the bald man was thrown backward into the glass, shattering it and littering the entire area with shards.

No sooner had he struck the table beyond the window than he was back on his feet and rushing the officer.

Still holding the messy wound on his neck, the cop took aim and fired once, twice, hitting the bald man in the upper chest and then the left shoulder before the man was again upon him, slamming him to the ground.

"Damn," Brad said. "Did you guys see that? He was attacking that cop with his teeth for God's sake!"

"I counted three GSWs at close range," Avery said. "The first one alone should have dropped him like a stone."

"Drugs?" Marcy offered.

"I don't care what you're on. If someone blows your cerebrum out the back of your head, you die. Period. Even a blank at that range would be lethal."

"Then what's your theory?" Angelica asked.

"I don't even know where to start. I've never seen anything like—"

"Code yellow," a panicked voice announced over the intercom. "Code Yellow to MRI."

Avery looked to Angelica, their eyes locking.

"Security crisis?" he asked. "In MRI?"

"My patient!" Angelica snapped. "Marcy? Did we already send our guy up?"

"About fifteen minutes ago."

"Oh God," Angelica gasped, dashing for the doorway.

*   *   *

Chris Behrents, the MRI technologist, was standing outside the examination room with his back to the far wall. He was just staring across the empty hallway into his control room, his face a ghastly shade of pallor, his eyes unblinking.

"What's happening?" Angelica called to him the moment she squeezed through the opening elevator doors. The clicking of her heels echoed back at her from the stark white hallway.

Chris didn't even look at her. He held himself against the wall so tightly that he appeared incapable of moving.

There was a loud bang and Chris flinched like he'd been shot.

Avery, Brad, and Marcy rushed down the hallway behind Angelica.

Four security guards appeared through the fire compartment doors on the other side of the MRI room, sprinting straight at them.

They all converged on Chris as another loud bang came from the room.

"What's going on?" Angelica screamed, taking him by the shoulders and shaking him until he finally turned to look at her through vacant eyes.

He opened his mouth to speak, but nothing came out. Slowly, his eyes turned back across the hallway to the control room.

Bang!

Angelica spun and raced into the control room. There was a counter in front of her with a computer monitor and a keyboard between an industrial printer and a cheap stereo. All sorts of images filled the screen, the majority of which were ovular slices of gray brain as though the crown of the skull had been chopped off and she was looking right down into it.

Bang!

The Infected

She looked up to the enormous window separating the control console from the actual magnetic chamber in time to see the long off-white MRI table slam into the glass. It made a loud cracking sound as though it were going to break, but just shook in its frame.

Reflexively, she closed her eyes and threw her arms up in front of her face.

The glass vibrated with the crackling sound of the seal wearing away.

She braved a peek through her crossed arms. The man she'd been treating downstairs stood across from her on the other side of the half-inch pane, looking directly at her. He cocked his head first to one side and then to the other like a predatory bird. All of the veins in his eyes had exploded, leaving the whites no longer visible beneath the shimmering blood, which drained down his cheeks like tears.

Angelica could feel the others crowding into the room behind her.

There was the snap of a holster being opened.

"What's his name?" she asked, unable to wrench her stare from him.

"Caisse," Marcy said. "Jason, I think."

"Mr. Caisse," Angelica said, bringing her arms from in front of her face and holding them out to either side. "I'm Dr. Morgan, from the emergency room. Can you tell me what's going on in there?"

His eyes flicked from one of them to the next like a serpent.

"Mr. Caisse?"

His stare locked in on Angelica again.

"Can he hear me?" she asked, turning to face Chris.

"N-no," he finally said. "Jesus. Would you look at his eyes?"

"How do I turn this on?" she asked, tapping the small

microphone at the end of the bendable metal stand.

Chris leaned past her and toggled a switch beneath the counter.

"Mr. Caisse?" She heard her voice weakly from the room beyond. "Jason?"

He lunged at the glass, slamming both fists against it over and over until the skin ruptured and he was swiping bloody arcs all over the glass.

"Do you want us to handle this?" one of the security guards asked.

"Not yet," Angelica said, leaning back toward the microphone. "Can you tell me how you feel? Where does it hur—?"

He pounded the glass again, harder this time. Flesh peeled away from bone as he hammered the pane between them, but he didn't appear affected in the slightest.

"Mr. Caisse?"

There was now so much blood on the glass that she couldn't see what he was doing until the MRI table slammed into it again.

"Try not to hurt him," Angelica said without turning from the window, where she could vaguely make out the man's silhouette through the smudged mess.

A thunder of footsteps raced out of the room behind her, around the wall and to the entrance to the exam room.

"Keys," one of the guards called.

Chris followed them to the door, the keys jangling in his trembling hand. There was a clatter as the lock was breached, and then Chris's footfalls as he hurried back into the control room.

The bolt slid back into the door with a thud.

"Hands in the air!" the same guard shouted. "You move an inch and I'll—"

The Infected

There was a bang on the console window and the side of the security guard's face pressed through the blood, smearing away a clean patch.

Angelica stumbled back into Avery at the sight of the terror in the man's eye.

There must have been an inordinate amount of pressure forcing him against the glass as she watched his zygomatic arch snap, flattening his cheekbone and making it look like his eyeball was about to spill out.

She watched helplessly as there was a flash of blood-skeined teeth and the security guard finally pried himself away, smothering his right hand over the tattered remains of his ear.

"He bit me!" he shrieked. "I can't believe he bit me!"

Another guard stepped right behind Jason, jamming the barrel of his pistol into the back of Jason's head.

"Freeze mother—!"

Jason whirled and knocked the gun out of the man's hand, grabbing him by the wrist and jerking him forward so fast that he went down to the floor.

The other guards threw themselves at Jason before he could attack further, pinning him to the ground beneath their amassed weight. His arms fought free, trying desperately to grab hold of anything, but a baton rose from the fray, followed quickly by another. There was a loud crack and then another. Another.

"Don't kill him!" Marcy screamed into the microphone, knocking Angelica out of the way in her hurry. "Stop it! Please!"

One at a time, the security guards rose, spattered with blood, shoulders heaving with exhaustion. Jason lay on the floor between them, the back of his head looking like a shattered ceramic bowl filled with spaghetti sauce.

"Oh God," Marcy gasped, dashing out of the control room toward the entrance to the inner chamber.

She'd barely taken her first steps into the room, the floor slick with spurts of blood, when Jason slapped his hands to the floor and staggered to his feet.

The group of guards could only stare in disbelief as the man rose, swaying like a drunk. Blood poured from his smashed nose and past broken teeth. He stumbled forward, barely able to raise his arms enough to grab onto the un-tucked shirttails of the female guard. She pushed at his chest, but he pressed through her defenses until he held her tightly. He leaned in, opened his mouth, and —

Marcy saw gray matter fly out of the side of his head in a jumble of cranium fragments and blood long before she heard the report of the gun.

She turned away, but not quickly enough to keep from seeing the body topple sideways into the wall, draining blood like a rain gutter.

The security guard still stood there, holding out the smoking barrel of the gun as though he were no longer in control of his arm. His eyes were wide, unblinking, his pupils narrowed to dots.

"You did what you had to do, Mark," one of the other guards said, slapping his buddy on the shoulder.

Mark still stood there with that blank look on his face, the discharge dissipating in front of him.

"You didn't have to kill him," Marcy whispered.

"Don't you dare go all bleeding-heart on me," the female security guard said. Hot blood still dripped down the side of her face from her sandstone-brown hair, past her neck, and into the collar of her uniform shirt. Her name badge read: Sarah — Hospital Security. "He would have killed me if Mark hadn't blown his head off."

Marcy turned and stormed out of the room, burying her face in her hands.

"You did good, newbie," Sarah said, helping Mark to

finally lower his arm to his side. The service weapon fell from his limp hand and clattered to the floor. "Probably better pick that up, kid. Don't want that—"

He whirled and raced to the side of the MRI gantry donut, vomiting all over the wall and the floor.

* * *

"It's one of those things you have to see to believe," Chris said. He was sitting in front of the console and doing everything in his power to keep from looking through the bloody window as the police cameras flashed beyond. "I printed out a copy of his vitals since even I didn't think it was possible."

He held out the EKG slip for Angelica, but Avery intercepted it.

"Flatline," he said, tossing it aside. "The electrodes must not have been in contact with his skin."

"That's what I thought at first," Chris said, "but I went in and checked them myself. They were attached just like they were supposed to be."

"Did you think to check his pulse?"

"What do you think I am, an idiot?"

"Relax, Chris," Angelica said, placing a reassuring hand on his shoulder. "And how about you try a little tact, Dr. Martin?"

Chris sighed.

"I checked his radial pulse first. Nothing. Then I checked his carotid. There was no pulse whatsoever. Not weak. This guy was dead."

"Obviously you don't know what you're looking for."

Chris leapt out of the chair and slammed Avery up against the wall, both fists knotted in his surgical scrub top over the button-down shirt and tie.

"You arrogant prick! Do you just assume that every-body else is stupider than you?"

"More stupid," Avery said with a devilish smirk. "Everyone else is *more stupid*."

Chris bared his teeth and bounced Avery off the wall again.

"You two knock it off," Brad said from where he leaned against the back wall, the first words he'd said since before the incident.

"Tell me Chris," Avery said. "Did you enjoy your employment here at the hospital while it lasted?"

"You can't fire me."

"I can make it happen just like that..."

He brought his fingers up to snap, but Chris caught them and tightened them in his fist until the knuckles cracked.

"Not the hands! Not the hands!"

"Enough," Angelica said, wedging herself between them. "This all stops right now or so help me, I'll see that both of you face the ethics board."

Chris nodded his acquiescence and went back to the control console. Avery looked as though he was preparing to get in the final word, but Angelica's expression stopped him cold.

"I was just having a little fun with him," Avery said, leaning back more comfortably against the wall to massage his fingers.

"Were you able to scan any images?" Angelica asked, pulling a chair over so she could sit beside Chris at the controls. Avery placed a hand on either chair-back and leaned over their shoulders so he could see the screen.

There was another flash of light from the exam room as an officer photographed the bloody window.

"Yeah," Chris said, pulling the keyboard closer. "I was in the middle of the brain scan when he coded."

"Show me."

He tapped a couple keys and then scrolled the mouse across the screen, clicking through a series of submenus.

"I'm telling you...You aren't going to believe this."

After a moment, a series of images appeared. The pictures were in various shades of gray. One featured a profile picture of a head and neck, the brain and spine clearly visible as though the person had been chopped in half and turned sideways. There were two more pictures of horizontal slices, one a cross-sectional shot of the lower portion of the head at the level of the eyes, the other lower, as evidenced by the rows of teeth.

"Look here," he said, pointing to the side shot. "See how this upper portion of the brain is so light? This is consistent with a lack of higher brain functioning."

"These were taken during the flatline?"

"Yeah...Now look at this." Chris pointed to the screen with the tip of a pen. "See this black area back here? This is the hindbrain, or what we think of as the 'primitive brain.' This rounded area is the cerebellum, and this bulge that looks like a backwards P is the medulla oblongata and the pons."

"We don't need an anatomy lesson," Avery said.

"Let him finish," Angelica said. And then to Chris, "Why are these areas so much darker?"

"It means that they're not only functioning, but they're doing so at a much higher level. It's almost as though they're being stimulated electrically."

"Impossible," Avery said.

"Prove me wrong, doc," Chris said, sliding back away from the console.

Avery produced a pair of glasses and seated them right at the tip of his nose, staring down at the screen.

"You can scroll through the slices sequentially," Chris said.

"I know," Avery snapped, rapidly moving from one image to the next like a cartoon flipbook building the head. "There has to be another explanation."

"What would happen if only the hindbrain were functioning?" Angelica asked.

"All of our higher functions are contained in the cerebrum. Speech, emotions, taste, logic, reason. Our hindbrain controls our primal impulses. Essentially, it triggers our feeding and drinking reflexes, just the basic biological tools to keep us alive. I like to think of a shark as the ultimate expression of the hindbrain. It's an animal that kills without remorse, eats until it's sated—regardless of whether or not it's consumed its entire kill—and then just moves on to the next cycle of feeding. Without the cerebrum to temper the mindless hindbrain, we'd be at the mercy of our most basic instincts.

"But I've never seen a human brain damaged in such a way that one is even remotely functional without the other. Usually, lack of higher functioning leaves the patient in a vegetative state, not sentient like this guy was. Hell, not even conscious.

"Your readings have to be wrong."

"Like I said. I checked them my—"

"Code Yellow to the ER," a voice announced over the speakers. "All available hands please attend."

"Time to go," Angelica said, leaping from the chair and heading for the door, where she nearly ran headlong into Marcy.

"What's going on?" Marcy shrieked.

"Hurry!" a frantic voice shouted over the intercom, followed by a crash.

"You don't think—?" Brad said, taking the first hesitant step forward.

"We don't have time to," Angelica said, sprinting toward the elevator.

CHAPTER 7

Colorado Springs Community Hospital

The three security guards who'd been walking through the incident in the MRI room with the police reached the elevator before the doors closed, cramming in with the rest of them.

"Come on, come on," Sarah muttered, willing the doors to close.

Static crackled from the receivers on the security guards' hips.

"We'd better get hazard pay for this," Mark said.

"Just try not to kill anyone else," Marcy whispered.

"Look, lady—"

"No you look! We can't help them if they're dead, and that's the only reason any of these people came here in the first place."

"How do you think you could have done anything differently?"

"I wouldn't have shot him in the head to start."

"He was going to kill all of us in there!"

"He could have been subdued."

"Bullshit."

Michael McBride

"You didn't give us a chance."
"Next time, you're welcome to—"
Ding.
The sounds of chaos assaulted them through the opening doors. Orderlies and nurses raced past down the hall. There was screaming. So much screaming.

Drawing their batons, the guards led the charge down the hallway to the right into the emergency room, which had become a mosh pit of activity.

Gurneys were overturned in the main thoroughfare, their patients crawling or scurrying deeper into the hallway by whatever means they could. Racks of laundry and supplies were scattered across the floor as though a semi had blown through. In the center of the cyclone of activity was one woman, screaming, windmilling her arms, fingers curled to claws. She held everyone surrounding her at bay with the sheer fervor of her rage.

One of the doctors lunged for her, but she caught him across the side of the face with her fingernails and drew blood as easily as if with razors. The man clapped his hand over his cheek and fell away, hurrying toward the nearest exam room and a box of gauze. Several others hit her at once, knocking her soundly to the ground, her head ricocheting from the floor with a crack. They piled atop her as she fought to get out from beneath, her jaws snapping at everyone within range. She latched onto a man's ear and tore off a bite to the tune of his pained wails. He lifted his hands to cover his bleeding ear, giving her the chance she needed to rip a chunk of flesh from his forearm. Throwing himself from atop her, he crawled away, bloody arm cradled to his chest, crimson streaming down his neck from what remained of his ear.

The woman struggled back to her feet, spinning and leaping at one of the hesitant bystanders, knocking her onto her back on the floor while gnawing a mouthful of

99

skin from her neck.

Mark reached her first after forcing his way through the stunned crowd, appearing behind her as if by magic with his baton raised. Swinging it with all his might, he hammered her across the back of the skull so hard that the stick broke in half with an explosion of splinters. He held the stump of the club in front of his face in disbelief as she leapt from atop the other screaming woman and charged him.

Sarah lowered a shoulder and rammed her from the side, knocking her against the wall. By the time the woman flopped to the floor, Sarah was already bringing the baton down on her head.

There was a wet thump and the woman screamed, her voice resplendent with rage rather than pain.

Thump!

Thump!

"Stay down!" Sarah shouted.

It looked like the entire left half of the woman's head had been caved in by the repeated impact, blood pouring out from beneath a ragged tatter of flesh and tangled hair.

The woman raised her eyes to look at Sara, her head wobbling as though her neck were barely able to support its weight.

"Don't even try it," Sarah said, cocking her right arm with the staff held high.

With a smile full of broken teeth, lips smashed and swollen, the woman tried to get to her feet, only to receive the blow from the baton squarely across the bridge of her nose. She sputtered blood and collapsed forward.

It wasn't until she finally flopped to the ground, her ponytail trailing behind her head, that Angelica recognized her as the woman from the stretcher who had yelled at her earlier for poking her.

Angelica started walking, finally spurring her feet to motion as she'd been frozen, watching the scene unfold before her. Shoving through the mob of medical personnel, she hurried to the woman's side.

Her back lurched convulsively, as though she were still trying to get to her feet despite the fluids that poured unimpeded from her head.

Angelica knelt and palpated just beneath the woman's right ribs. It was still swollen, though to nowhere near the same degree. While it had formerly been squishy and pliable, it was now more solid than the flesh surrounding it, almost as though she'd grown another bone. Angelica slid her hands to the woman's neck and felt the carotid pulse, which was still strong. Pulling a pen from her pocket, she raised the woman's hand and poked her fingertips in succession, waiting for the twitch of her reflexes.

There was no reaction, so she poked harder, pushing deep into the skin.

Still nothing.

She dropped the woman's hand and went back to her head. Though her face was pressed against the floor, the woman was still doing her best to look at Angelica from the corner of her eye, her jaws snapping like a rabid dog.

There was so much blood.

The woman had noticeably paled, her skin stark white in contrast to the drops and smears of blood. She began to gulp at the air like a fish, signaling the end was imminent. It sounded like she was breathing through a straw in a glass of milk, gurgling, bubbling, and then finally, with one last wheezing exhalation, she went still.

"I need a crash cart!" Angelica yelled.

No one moved. They all just stood there, watching her kneel over the body, her bloody, gloved hands shaking.

The Infected

"Someone grab a crash cart!"

"Doctor..." Marcy said softly from behind her, placing a hand on Angelica's shoulder. "There's nothing—"

"Fine. If you won't do it for me, then at least get the hell out of my way."

Slapping Marcy's hand from her shoulder, she bulled through the sea of bystanders toward the large red metal cart at the back of the nurse's station. She was sobbing, shoulders heaving, but all she could think was that she needed the cart and she needed it right that second. The woman on the floor was dead. She knew that deep down, but she couldn't bring herself to face the reality of the situation. The facts were incomprehensible. She had seen two formerly stable patients go out of their minds and start attacking everyone around them. Neither appeared capable of feeling anything resembling pain, but rage was certainly still well within their range of expression.

She grabbed the handle of the cart and tried to jerk it away from the wall, but it wouldn't budge.

"Someone help me!"

Throwing herself back and forth, she yanked on the cart to no avail.

Angelica screamed and dropped to her knees, burying her face in her hands.

"There was nothing you could have done," Marcy said, crouching beside her and bringing the doctor's head to her shoulder. "She had altered mental status and—"

A shrill scream trilled from down the hallway, followed by panicked shouting.

"What's happening here?" Angelica whined, looking up in time to see several people charging directly at her down the hallway from the surgical suites.

She recognized one of them as a surgical tech, his

masked face freckled with blood. Another man staggered several paces behind, blood flowing from the hand he held to his chest.

There was a crashing sound past the bend in the hallway and a cart of surgical supplies slid across the floor and slammed into the wall, scattering steel implements all over the tile. Before the tools even came to rest, a woman in a hospital gown sprinted around the corner, a scalpel ripping her foot open from her pinky toe all the way to her heel, but it didn't even faze her.

Another gowned man turned the corner, hot on her heels.

Half of the woman's face was stained a rust color from the Betadine prep, the contents of her neck still held in by a clear Tegaderm patch like transparent skin. Both of her eyes were nearly black with blood, the excess trailing down her cheeks. Her arms and legs were a ghastly gray not so dissimilar to the faded blue hospital gown. She drew away from the man as he was hobbled by the fractured length of femur poking out through the skin above his right knee, his lower leg already discolored with crusted blood. His eyes matched hers, as though every vessel feeding his orbs had burst simultaneously, making it appear from the distance like someone had driven both thumbs into his sockets.

The surgical tech blew past Angelica as Marcy fought to drag her to her feet.

Mark dove into sight, his shoulder catching the woman on the outside of her left knee and wrapping his arms around her legs, which crumpled beneath his weight. She fell forward, bouncing her forehead off the tile, the majority of her mass toppling sideways and landing atop Mark.

The man with the bone through his leg leapt over the two of them, landing without slowing and not losing a step on the surgical tech.

The woman screamed and slashed Mark across the face with a clawed hand, opening up four bloody seams on his cheek. He howled and scrabbled away, the woman seizing the opportunity to get to all fours and lunge after him.

Sarah appeared from the screaming crowd, a gun pressed to the side of the woman's head. She pulled the trigger without hesitation, spraying blood and gray matter down the hallway.

The woman simply slumped forward, her rear end in the air, into a puddle of her own fluids.

The ding of the opening elevator went unnoticed, but there was no missing the repeated report of gunfire as the officers who'd been investigating upstairs announced their arrival in the ER. Circles of red appeared on the man with the broken leg's chest a heartbeat before he was lifted from the ground and launched backwards. He hit the ground with a thud and slid through his spilled blood until he crumpled against the wall.

Screams of terror replaced the gunfire as what seemed like the entire room stampeded toward the front doors at once. They crammed into the bottleneck, trampling each other in their rush to freedom.

Angelica could see Dr. Nguyen on the other side of the glass wall trying to keep his staff from fleeing, only to be unceremoniously knocked onto his rear end.

In all of the excitement, the blur of motion had been readily apparent, but now that there was only a fraction of the staff in the open lobby, the stillness was overwhelming. There were no mangled cries from tortured patients on the beds filling the room. No sobbing. No one shouting for their nurses. It wasn't until that precise moment that Angelica realized that nearly every patient in the room was dead.

Michael McBride

She'd never seen anything like it. That entire section of the hospital had become a morgue.

"They're all dead," Marcy whispered, voicing what they were all thinking.

"They can't be," Avery said. "What in the name of God could kill so many people so quickly?"

"I suspected visceral leishmaniasis," Angelica said.

"It couldn't kill this quickly, especially not asymptomatically."

"I palpated subcutaneous abdominal masses on at least four of them."

"How large?"

"Maybe ten centimeters."

"Ten centimeters. Are you serious? Why didn't you report it?"

"I told the chief resident."

"Nguyen?" Avery said, shaking his head. "That guy's just about as useful as a man's nipple."

"I'll give you a moment to recant, Dr. Martin," Dr. Nguyen said from behind him. Avery hadn't heard the smaller man approach, but he didn't particularly care either.

Avery smiled.

"You think that just because you're standing there I'm going to take back what I said? You ER docs are all the same. Blood, guts, and glory, with the emphasis on the glory. All you really do is direct traffic."

"That's right, Avery. I'm a glory hound. I bust my ass eighty hours a week so I can feel like a super hero. You know where you can stick it."

"I've had enough of your posturing and egos for one day," Angelica said. "We've got a serious problem here."

"And what would you suggest?" Nguyen asked.

"I suggested that we lock down the hospital, but it's obviously too late for that now."

The Infected

"So this is all my fault now? Why don't you both just gang up on the only doctor here taking responsibility for any of this?"

"Stow it, Ian."

"You're bordering on insubordination, Dr. Morgan."

"Take charge then! If you want to be the martyr, then climb up on your cross. Otherwise, we need to figure out exactly what's going on here."

* * *

Angelica studied the body, scrutinizing every inch of the woman's flesh. There were several abnormal markings that would indicate that her skin was eroding in ulcers, but there weren't any abnormal growths, save for the large knot over the woman's liver.

Her repeated efforts to drain it had been to no avail as the viscosity of the peritoneal fluid had become so thick that she just couldn't pull any out. It was like sap in there. She could force the needle all the way in, but for the life of her, she just couldn't free a drop of fluid with the syringe.

There were now close to a dozen police officers milling about the emergency room. Some took pictures while others marked the locations of where the bodies had fallen and where the spent casings were found. The hospital security force hung back and watched, their authority usurped, but more than that, this was now well beyond their area of expertise. They were trained to prevent the escalation of conflict, to disarm combatants, and to hold patients still long enough for restraints to be applied. Multiple homicides were well outside the scope of their training, though the looks on their faces were easy enough to read. They wanted to be out there working on the investigation; taking depositions and exploring the crime scene, not standing idly by.

Sarah flipped the snapping latch on her pistol open and closed nervously. Try as she might to look at anything besides, her eyes kept flicking back to the bodies on the floor. They were only that moment being scooped into body bags.

Mark crouched beside her, bringing an unlit cigarette to his mouth and letting it dangle there for a few moments before pulling it away. Angelica guessed he was nearly in shock, but she didn't have the time to tend to him now if they were going to figure out what in God's name had killed all of these people. All she could do was pray that whatever these passengers had brought back from Mexico wasn't extremely contagious. With all of the exposed employees now out there in the city, their grid of containment was non-existent.

If whatever disease they carried was viral, then it could easily be spread through the air, but if it was bacterial, it would take contact, more than likely by body fluids. That could be their one saving grace. It was extraordinarily unlikely that these people would be out on the streets swapping fluids, at least not in large numbers.

Angelica was stymied. Her training in pathology was limited at best. It was her job to identify the signs and symptoms of a malady and make the proper diagnosis. Failing at that, she treated the symptoms. But she'd never in her life seen anything even remotely resembling this massive swelling at the base of the ribs. She'd encountered leishmaniasis on more than one occasion, but never to this extreme, and only the cutaneous strain. The visceral leishmaniasis bacteria was infrequent at best, though far more severe. And transmission from one person to another took time and rather intimate contact. She couldn't fathom how it had been passed to every surviving member of the plane crash in the few hours it had taken to fly from Mexico…

She remembered what she'd seen on TV. Was it possible that all of these people had been exposed while they were down there and had only now become symptomatic?

"Where did the plane originate again?" she asked, tossing the sterile tray and collection vials into the trash can beside her in disgust.

"Cancun, Mexico," Ian said. He was studying another body a dozen feet away and trying to keep from looking toward the front doors where a pair of uniformed officers were holding a crowd of reporters at bay across a line of police tape. Angelica knew he'd have to make a statement soon enough, but he didn't want to look like a complete moron. He needed answers, or at least some inkling of what was going on before he got anywhere near the bright halogens and flashing red lights of the live broadcast cameras. Their situation would lose a large amount of its network appeal if he could stall past the ten o'clock news. "It was a direct flight headed for Chicago."

"Where did the plane come from before that?"

"I don't know. What does that matter anyway?"

"If whatever pathogen was already on the plane—?"

"Let the investigators worry about that. You just help me figure out what the hell we're dealing with here. Besides, I've got calls in at every emergency facility on the Yucatan Peninsula. Eventually one of them has to call back."

Angelica turned her attention back to the corpse in front of her. She knew better than to try to argue with the chief resident. He'd not-so-subtly dismissed her speculative line of thinking. Once they identified the sickness, she could deal with the cops and let Ian go back to being the public face of the hospital.

She couldn't help but ruminate over the riots she'd seen in Cancun and San Diego. The similarities to their current situation were staggering. Uninhibited violence. Seemingly as random in its origin as it was brutal in its ferocity. Bloodshed. Animalistic combat.

The world was overdue for a global pandemic, something along the lines of smallpox to substantially thin the herd. She'd at first imagined that SARS would prove to be such a disease, and then the bird flu. Maybe they'd finally stumbled upon it after all.

Angelica pressed her gloved hands to either side of the woman's trachea, feeling for her lymph nodes and any abnormal swelling. She poked with three fingers all the way down the neck before pulling the right arm away from the body enough to reach up into the armpit to check for swelling in the axillary glands. Starting closer to the body, she felt all through the armpit until she was beneath the shoulder—

She jerked her hands back.

There was no possible way...

Slowly, she reached forward again, pressing just the first two fingers of her right hand into the soft tissue, looking for what she thought she had just felt.

"Angelica," Ian said from somewhere in the room, but she didn't dare make the slightest sound, even to shush him.

She isolated the brachial artery and pressed it flat. Dear God, she could feel blood moving in there. The woman had a pulse.

"Help me!" Ian shouted, punctuated by the clamor of surgical steel dropping from a toppled table.

Angelica turned, the corpse's pulse still tapping on her fingertips.

"Get him off! Get him off! Son of a—!" His words

broke into a scream.

The man Nguyen had been studying on the gurney, the man who had only moments prior been clinically dead, was now sitting up in the bed. He'd managed to grab Ian before the doctor could flee, seizing him from behind by either side of the head. The man opened his mouth as wide as it could stretch, revealing gums already beginning to gray. Like a bear trap snapping shut, he bit down on the top of Ian's head, teeth ricocheting back from the bones with a clatter. Over and over.

Clack.

Clack.

Clack.

Ian's scream became the shrill wail of terror.

His eyes were wide between the man's thumbs across his brows and the forefingers pointing to his nose as he jerked forward and back, trying to wrench his head out of the man's impossibly strong grasp. The top of his head had opened in several superficial arches, the sides peeling apart to dampen his close-cropped black hair with blood. Rich red covered the suddenly-living man's face past his nose and over his eyes, so he just closed them and went back to gnawing on Ian's head.

"Let him go!" a deep voice shouted.

Angelica was frozen. Every impulse in her body screamed for her to run as fast as she could, but her feet felt like they were rooted in cement.

A hand closed on her arm.

She looked down at the source of the pressure: a hand, the nail beds blue with cyanosis, gripped her upper arm.

The woman's eyelids slid back like twin slugs, revealing pupils the width of a pencil's lead in the middle of aqualine irises. She twitched, her head snapping back, her spine forming a contorted rainbow on the gurney.

Her pupils suddenly widened, nearly eclipsing the irises. Forked blood vessels struck at the thin ring of color from the whites like lightning bolts, then burst and spilled their contents out onto the surface of her eyes. The woman blinked furiously, trying to clear the sheen of blood, which now drained down over her temples.

Angelica screamed, but the sound was lost beneath the explosion of gunfire.

Blood patterned the white tile leading up to her feet as the bullet careened off the wall beside her.

She couldn't stop screaming as she pried at the woman's fingers, finally able to rip her arm free. Sprinting in the opposite direction, she didn't even see the woman fall off the side of the rolling bed as she tried to get up.

Ian threw himself onto the ground in front of her as the man who'd been gnawing on his head hit beside him, sliding on his side toward the woman, who was now about to gain her feet.

"Don't get up!" an officer shouted, pointing a smoldering barrel at the man where he lay.

Another handful of uniforms raced toward their fellow cop, ducking around the nurse's station, from behind the curtained rooms and out of doorways.

All Angelica saw was a flash from her left as she sped past the officer and through a haze of gunpowder smoke. She clapped her hands over hers ears at the sound of the discharge, still screaming as she ran.

She didn't know where she was going. All she knew was that she had to get out of there. Her mind couldn't find a way to rationalize what she'd seen. Both of those patients had been dead. There was no arguing that simple fact. There had been no pulse, no heart activity. They had been dead. Dead, dead, de—

Avery appeared from around the bend in the hallway

a moment before she slammed into him. She saw the startled expression on his face, and the next thing she knew her hands slapped the floor just in time to keep her forehead from hammering it. Her right shoulder drove the wind from Avery, who rolled out from beneath her, gasping for air.

"Get up!" Angelica screamed, grabbing him by the arm and jerking him to his feet as she climbed to hers.

He wheezed in a deep inhalation, but resisted her.

He'd been in one of the trauma suites preparing to remove a dead man's occipital bone to inspect his hindbrain with his own eyes when he'd heard the first shot. Now, as he rolled onto his side and looked past Angelica into the ER, he wished to God he'd run in the other direction.

Ian scurried toward them on all fours, a flap of scalp peeled back from his exposed cranium right at the vertex. Another man jumped to his feet and started running after the chief resident, but a group of policemen opened fire on him, knocking him in several different directions before he was finally tossed off his feet with a splash of blood from the bullet that tore right through his neck, nearly decapitating him.

Another woman rose behind the man before he even hit the ground, lunging at the closest officer and grabbing him by the shirt. She spun him between her and the other officers, their volley of bullets tagging him repeatedly in the back.

A flume of blood spouted past his lips as she tossed him aside and dashed at the other policemen. One bullet tore through her right shoulder, barely staggering her, before she pounced on a cop who didn't even look old enough to shave yet. He screamed as she drove him to the floor, right up to the point where she buried her face into his neck and crunched through his trachea. The last of his oxygen hissed from the impromptu stoma while he pawed at it, trying to hold his opened neck closed with both hands. Blood pumped out faster than he could even hope to hold it in, filling his lungs and burbling past his lips.

With that severed section of windpipe still bouncing from her clenched jaws like a fat noodle, she dove at the officer to her right and hit him at the ankles. He managed to lower his gun to her head in time to get off one good shot that tore off her right ear before he was sprawled across the ground.

"Behind you!" Avery shouted over her shoulder. Until that point, Angelica hadn't seen the still-gowned patients running through the emergency room toward the police from behind.

One of the cops turned, but a much larger man had already thrown himself through the air, striking the unsuspecting officer right in the chest and slamming him to the ground. When the man looked up again, his beard was sloppy with blood, his gown a Rorschach design of agony, and the officer was screaming something unintelligible through a mouth now ripped all the way back to his left ear.

Angelica felt a tug on her shoulder and screamed.

"It's me, Dr. Morgan," Marcy said, catching Angelica's right wrist before she could hit her when she spun. "Come on."

Though Marcy's voice was level, tears spilled from her wide eyes and she was a single shade of pale this side of the grave. Her scrub top was torn from her left shoulder all the way to the pocket on her left hip, revealing her undershirt, both of which shimmered with fresh blood.

"What happened?" Angelica gasped, feeling for a wound on Marcy's chest. "Are you all right?"

The Infected

"They're everywhere," Marcy said, her face expressionless. "What's going on?"

"They're all coming back to life."

*   *   *

"We have to get out of here!" Angelica shouted. From where she now stood, she could see the front doors twenty yards away beyond the nurse's station. For the first time ever, the desk was unmanned. No one stood at the computer terminal accessing records. No one tended to the phones or reception. No attending checked off the assignment board, full to capacity with the names of patients and their locations. There was no bored-looking security guard standing by the front doors. Only the patients. Three more ran at the group of cops, now firing wildly from the ground as they'd become overwhelmed by the sheer numbers and ferocity with which they were attacked.

Three appeared from the hallway to the left of the automatic doors and dashed out into the night.

There was a sound like thunder, but the officers outside were only able to get off that single shot between them. Spotlights from the cameras stationed in the ambulance bay veered from the front of the building before being cast aside entirely in the cameramen's hurry to flee. Newshounds from the papers to the television stations screamed as they tried to run away.

"We can't go out that way," Angelica whispered.

A polished reporter with a golden crown of hair was slammed up against the front glass wall from the outside, her suit ripped to ribbons, the gashes on her opened chest smearing on the window.

Angelica looked away before she was forced to witness anything more, turning back to the left where there were no longer the sounds of struggling and gunfire.

The bearded man's gaze shot upward from his kill, his crimson eyes trapping Angelica's. The corners of his lips curled back from a snarl filled with blood-drenched teeth. Clumps of flesh clung to his ratty beard from where his face had been buried in the neck of one of the unmoving officers a moment prior.

He leapt over the body toward her before her mind even triggered her survival reflexes.

She whirled and ran away from him, dragging Marcy along. They nearly ran over Avery, who had managed to help Ian to standing with the chief's arm slung over his shoulder.

"Run!" Angelica screamed, narrowly dodging them.

Avery looked back and saw the man charging directly at them. With his face contorted with rage and dripping with blood, the man didn't look even remotely human.

The others had arisen from the mess of savaged flesh in the puddle of blood to follow the bearded man in pursuit of a fresh kill.

Avery's first impulse was to throw Ian aside and sprint as fast as he could, but for whatever reason, he wrapped his right arm tighter around the other doctor's waist and turned back toward the hallway.

Two large wooden doors stood sentry at the end of the hall, separating the emergency room from the general portion of the hospital. They were smoke-compartment doors, designed to contain a fire to either side to keep it from spreading wildly throughout the facility. In case of a fire they would be automatically locked magnetically.

Angelica blew through the doorway first, the door already closing behind her by the time Avery reached it. Grabbing the handle, he jerked it open and looked back over his shoulder. The bearded man was maybe ten feet behind and closing fast, several more right behind him.

"Pull the fire alarm!" he shouted, throwing Ian through the doorway. Marcy grabbed Ian before he could hit the ground, bracing him so that the chief resident fell only as far as his knees.

Avery clasped the inner handle and pulled the door shut behind him, leaning back and gripping the knob in preparation of what he knew was to come.

"Pull the alarm!"

There was a bang from the other side of the wood, causing both of the side-by-side doors to shiver in place, nearly knocking Avery backward and stealing the knob from his grasp, but he managed to hold on.

"For the love of God, pull the—!"

A high-pitched alarm drowned out his voice.

There was a loud *thunk* of the magnetic locks engaging in the doors.

He stepped back, watching the handle shake violently, the doors swaying ever-so-slightly forward and back as they were attacked from the other side. But they held.

They held.

Avery turned to see Angelica step away from the fire alarm.

"Thank you," he said, though even he couldn't hear his own words.

The white fluorescent tubes overhead snapped off, replaced by the red emergency lights. At first he thought it was just his eyes adjusting to the sudden change in luminescence, but now he was sure that he could see several more people charging at them from the far end of the hallway.

He spun in a quick circle.

"The stairs!" he yelled, grabbing Angelica by the shoulder and shoving her toward the door on the left side of the hallway, adorned with a blue placard depicting a white staircase.

Angelica jerked the door open, the movement at the distant end of the hall finally catching her eye. She turned back to Avery, her teary eyes wide with panic, and helped usher Marcy ahead of her, moving as if in slow motion as she struggled to help Ian up the stairs.

Nguyen had his left arm over Marcy's shoulder, using her as a crutch. Angelica raised his right arm and ducked beneath, hoping to give them the balance they so desperately needed to move faster. Rivulets of blood rolled down Ian's face from his hairline, draining around his eyes and nose, made even brighter red by the emergency glare.

Avery slammed the door shut, significantly muting the piercing siren, and started hurdling the stairs two at a time, passing the others on the first landing, bending around to lead them up another flight of stairs to the second floor.

The door exploded open behind them, the handle pounding the concrete block wall, allowing the siren again into the acoustically-amplified stairwell.

Avery knew they weren't going to outrun anyone while towing the anchor that was Ian. He could sprint faster — after all, he'd run track as an undergrad — and let the others be dragged down like gazelles on an African savannah. Survival of the fittest. But then he would be alone. Alone in a hospital crawling with the recently deceased, who had now become victims of their own genetics, their hindbrains feeding them only rage and the primitive desires to hunt and kill.

Alone.

He threw open the door leading to the second floor.

"Hurry!" he shouted, bracing the door open with his back and reaching for the others.

The Infected

Marcy hit the landing first, leading Ian and Angelica through the doorway as Avery shoved them from behind. Once they were through, he pulled the door shut and turned the frighteningly inadequate-looking lock on the handle.

"Keep going," he said, unable to take his eyes from the latch.

He flinched when something collided against the door from the other side. The knob began to rattle.

The fire compartment doors had sealed on this floor as well, barring them from heading back toward the patient rooms at the front of the hospital. Only radiology was back there in the corner of the hospital where they now found themselves trapped.

Angelica sprinted ahead of Marcy and Ian, opening the main doorway that led into the department reception and waiting room. Marcy slipped past and deposited Ian on the first chair she could find, immediately straightening her back against the incredible pain from bearing the doctor's weight.

Walking backwards through the doorway, Avery listened to the pounding from the stairwell growing louder and louder over the dimmed wail of the alarm.

Angelica slammed the door shut as soon as he was all the way into the waiting room and twisted the lock on the knob.

"What do we do now?" she asked, trying to maintain some semblance of control while all she wanted to do was curl up in a corner and pray to awaken from this nightmare.

"Is there a back staircase?" Avery asked.

"That was the only one I know about on this wing."

Avery ran through the lobby into the back area where a hallway stretched to either side. At the far left was the diagnostic area: three x-ray rooms and a fourth for fluoroscopy. Directly ahead were three CT scan rooms, and all the way to the right were the nuclear medicine and ultrasound rooms. There would only be a couple of diagnostic technologists on this late to handle the emergent patients for both x-ray and CT. An ultrasound tech was probably on call, and the MRI tech was down the hall.

All of the lights were out, save for one room at the far left end.

They were alone in there.

And there was no other entrance…or exit.

"There's no way in back there," he said, hurrying back into the waiting room. Doubling over, hands on his hips, he tried to catch his breath.

Beside the only entrance was an enormous fish tank, darkened by the timer for the night cycle. Several large saltwater fish floated like shadows against the wall behind, large coral structures poking from the gravel like an underwater forest. To the left of the door was the front desk, the area behind bathed in shadow. Rows of chairs lined the walls and the center of the room beside wooden tables stacked with magazines. Only the faint red glow of the back-up lights penetrated the darkness, forcing it back into the corners.

"Help me get these chairs over here against the door," he said.

"We should call for help," Marcy said. "Dr. Nguyen isn't looking so good."

"As soon as we barricade the door you can call anyone you want, but we have to block this entrance first."

Avery grabbed the armrest of the gray vinyl chair closest to the fish tank and dragged it away from the wall, bringing the three chairs beside it along as they were apparently soldered together as one long unit. Pushing it up against the door, he raced back for the next closest cluster of chairs.

Marcy helped Ian up from the seat and did her best to support his weight as he limped over to the front desk, easing him to the floor to lean his back against the tall counter.

"Do you really think these will be able to hold them out?" Angelica asked, grabbing the other end of the string of chairs and helping Avery scoot it across the tile to brace the others.

"You have a better idea?"

Angelica shook her head.

"Then just help me drag everything we can find — "

Bang!

They both stopped and looked at the door.

There was a moment of silence.

Angelica turned to Avery, the color draining from her face.

The doorknob shook back and forth, rattling like a diamondback's tail.

Bang!

They both flinched and raced toward the next line of chairs.

"Hurry! We need to get this one up on the others," Avery called.

Gunfire from the hallway. It sounded like so many bombs going off.

"Oh God," Marcy gasped. She leapt from Ian's side and ran around behind the reception desk. She grabbed the phone and dialed 911.

"I can't lift it high enough," Angelica grunted.

"Yes you can."

"Avery, I can't — "

"Just do it, Angelica."

She sobbed as she heaved, struggling to get the chair legs high enough to —

"Is anyone in there?" a man's voice shouted from the other side. "Security."

"Thank God," Angelica said, dropping the chairs back to the floor. "Help me move all of this stuff back away from the door."

"We don't know if they're infected," Avery whispered, taking her by the arm before she could tug at their barricade.

The doorknob rattled as it was turned frantically from the other side.

"We don't know that we're not," Angelica snapped, dragging the chairs away from the door.

Avery had just begun to help her when he noticed the blood seeping under the door, spreading into a widening pool around their feet.

"Don't step in it," Angelica said. "We don't know how this is spread and we can't risk it. Marcy?"

"I've been sitting here on hold." She sounded like she was ready to start pulling out her hair. "This is a real emergency and all I can get is this stupid recording."

She raised the phone to throw it, but caught herself as she thought better of it.

"Stick the phone in your pocket and find a spill kit."

Marcy didn't even look over her shoulder as she headed back toward the examination rooms.

"Where's all the blood coming from?" Angelica yelled through the door.

"There were two of them," the guard called back. "They were trying to break down the door and I...I..."

"Are they dead?" Avery interrupted.

"Yeah."

"Are you sure?"

"I just told you that's where all the blood's coming from."

"Have you touched it?"

The Infected

"Jesus, God. Just let us in."

"We need to know that you aren't infected."

"Hurry and let them in, Avery," Angelica said, reaching for the knob.

He swatted her hand away.

"Have you come into contact with the blood?"

"We're standing out here soaked in it. You want to know why? Because I just shot the hell out of the two guys trying to knock down the door to get in at you. So why don't you open the door right now before I start shooting holes through the goddamned wood to try to get—?"

There was a click as Angelica disengaged the lock.

She swung the door inward to reveal three silhouettes standing against the red glare in the hallway about four feet away. On the floor in front of them were two mangled carcasses absolving themselves of what looked like gallons of blood. One's head opened like a Muppet, the handgun blast nearly ripping his skull in half. There was nothing left of the other one's head except for the chunks of brain and cranium stuck to the front of the door around a good dozen bullet holes.

"Hurry up and get in here," Angelica said, holding out her hand. "Just don't step in the blood. We don't know how this disease is spread yet, so try to avoid coming into contact with it as much as possible."

"Lady," one of the guards said. She recognized him as the one who'd killed her patient in MRI. He stepped forward, allowing her a better glimpse. He looked like he'd been bathing in blood. His hair was slicked back and his entire face was crimson, except for his eyes. The only dry spot on his clothing stretched from beneath his kneecaps to his ankles. "I think we're past the point where stepping in it is going to make a difference."

He walked over the bodies crumpled in the doorway,

122

his smoking sidearm gripped tightly in his right hand, his index finger still beneath the trigger guard. His expression was similar to Marcy's, as though somewhere in the middle of the storm of insanity he'd found a calm in his head, the eye in a hurricane.

"Thanks," the female guard whispered to Angelica as she stepped around the piles of rent flesh, her own gun held down toward the floor, issuing thin wisps of smoke. Her eyes darted to Angelica's, then back to the floor as she tried to daintily step around the blood while not tripping in the tangle of limbs. The entire left side of her face was covered with blood, her navy blue uniform now black with it.

Brad stood behind them both, his lab coat no longer sterile white, but a Jackson Pollack canvas in myriad shades of red. He stared down at the mess of bodies as though he'd never seen anything like it.

"Come on, Brad," Angelica said as patiently as she possibly could.

He looked at her only briefly before gazing back down at the carnage.

"Brad…" Angelica said, stretching her arm out toward him.

There was a loud crash as the stairway door at the end of the hallway was thrown outward and slammed into the wall. Two shapes emerged at a sprint, already turning down the corridor toward them.

"Now!" Angelica shouted, yanking Brad's tentative arm. His toes caught on one of the bodies, sending him sprawling to the floor. Still pulling on her arm, he tried to scrabble out of the warm mush and over the heaped remains, the last of their fluids finally draining from the ruptured arteries.

Angelica looked up and choked on a scream. They were coming down the hallway so fast…

The Infected

"Come on, Brad! Come on!"

Avery reached past her and grabbed Brad's arm farther up by the shoulder, tugging so hard that Brad let out a yelp. She saw a blur of black from the corner of her eye and then it felt like someone had clocked her upside the head with a tire iron. Wailing, she dropped to her knees. It wasn't the severe throbbing of blunt trauma that she'd expected, but rather a searing pain in her inner ear. Pawing at the ringing orifice, she drew her hand away, expecting it to be dripping with blood, but there was nothing on her trembling hand.

There was a tug on her shirt collar, toppling her onto her rear. She was being dragged away from the door, away from Avery as he helped Brad over the pile of corpses, and away from Sarah as she fired repeatedly into the hallway.

She hadn't been hit. The gun must have discharged right by her ear.

A rather rotund woman's head snapped sideways as a bloody slash appeared across her temple where the bullet grazed her. Another bullet pounded her chest, a flower of blood blooming from her left breast. Still she charged forward like a rhinoceros, dirty clumps of bangs hanging over her bloody face, flesh jiggling beneath the gown as she thundered ahead. There was another woman beside her, this one much more lithe. She wore tight jeans, though her upper body was bare but for a black bra and a spattering of dried blood. Her muscles tensed beneath her taut, tanned skin, her face a rictus of pain. Long black hair trailed behind her like the mane of a thoroughbred. A bullet took a fleshy bite out of her shoulder, but it didn't even slow her down.

"Barricade the door!" Angelica screamed, but she couldn't hear anything but the tapping of gunfire over the ringing that was expanding inside her ear, trying to pop like a balloon.

Avery slid Brad through the mess, the momentum carrying him over by Ian.

The smaller woman reached the doorway first, but Mark stepped up and fired on her at close range. She bucked backwards, hitting the floor on her back and sliding in reverse. Her momentum hadn't even stopped before she was pushing herself back up to her feet in a smear of her own fluids.

Avery slammed the door and lowered his shoulder against it, bracing for the imminent impact.

"Lock the door!" he shouted, the collision from the outside knocking him back several inches.

Mark and Sarah threw themselves against the door beside him before it could open, forcing the lock to turn.

Avery was already dragging chairs against the door by the time they turned around.

Angelica rose, her equilibrium off-kilter from the inner ear trauma, and staggered up to the others to try to help shove the lines of chairs toward the door.

The banging from the other side grew frenzied as the women repeatedly hurled their bodies against it.

*   *   *

Avery slumped to the ground beside her, his undershirt completely saturated with sweat. He'd cast aside his scrub top long ago, and his shirt and tie during the heavy lifting. They'd managed to pile five rows of chairs against the door, bracing them with all of the end tables. It wasn't much of a solution, but it was all they had to work with. Besides, they couldn't possibly have to stay in there all that long, could they?

"Are you okay?" he asked, swiping the sweat from his brow and wiping it on his slacks.

The Infected

"I think so," she said. Her hearing had returned, but along with it a ferocious pain that felt like a rusted railroad spike had been pounded through her ear. "I'd kill for some ibuprofen though."

"I'm sure we can round some up." He tried for a smile, but had to settle for a reassuring hand on her shoulder. He was completely exhausted; mentally, physically, and emotionally. Though the fact that he couldn't understand what was happening weighed more heavily upon him than the other stressors combined.

Marcy still sat on hold with 911, slouching in the reception chair as far from the door as the cord would permit.

The banging had intensified outside; a constant drum roll of pounding fists and bodies throwing themselves against the wood. Every now and then there would be a loud crack as though the door were preparing to give way or the clatter of wooden legs from the chairs as the whole stack shivered against a particularly violent blow. They were lucky though, as all of the doors and walls in the radiology department were lined with varying thicknesses of lead to prevent the escape of radiation. Even factoring in that additional support, there was no way that they would be able to withstand such an assault indefinitely. They kept waiting for the people outside to tire, but either whenever one did another rose in his stead or they had endless reserves of energy. Either line of speculation led only to despair.

"You guys have got to check this out," Mark gasped, appearing from the hallway at the back of the lobby.

"What's wrong?" Angelica asked, rising to her feet on weary legs.

"You wouldn't believe me if I told you."

"Try me."

"Just come on, would you?"

Angelica headed for the back area, stepping over Ian's legs. He was still propped against the counter, chin resting on his chest. They'd found enough gauze and tape to cover his wounds and some steri-strips to draw the edges of the lacerations closed, but it was a pathetic substitute for stitches. He'd have some nasty scars when all was said and done, but his hair ought to cover them. It was better than bleeding to death anyway.

She spared him a cursory glance, noting the blood on his collar was crusted, the skin beneath pale, though reasonably well disguised by his Asian skin. They had to keep him upright to staunch the bleeding as the wounds would have continued to weep unimpeded were he to be left lying down. He hadn't been conscious since the application of the Betadine, the pain driving him firmly into the embrace of shock. She really needed to check his vitals and made a mental promise to do so as soon as she came back into the room.

Following Mark into the back area, they bent to the right and headed all the way down the hallway and through the next to the last door on the left. They passed through a small chamber that served as the nuclear medicine injection room and into the larger office beyond. There was a long counter running the length of the wall in front of them, a computer terminal at either end, and an enormous window above that looked out over the side parking lot and Maple Street to the north.

There was a patch of grass fifteen feet down, a small knoll sloping away from the building to the sidewalk where a pair of people crawled past what looked like a third, lying flat on his face, arms sprawled out to either side. One bled from a gash to the side of the face, holding a palm to it as she crawled up the street, unable to support herself well enough with just that one arm to keep from dropping repeatedly onto her skinned face.

The Infected

She collapsed one final time, only this time she didn't get up. The other figure crawled over next to her, lifting her shoulders just enough to roll her, cradling her head in his lap. He rocked back and sobbed up into the night sky.

"My God," Angelica gasped. "We need to help them."

"There's nothing we can do for them," Mark said.

"What are you talking about? I'm a doctor for Christ's sake."

"No," Mark said, taking her by the elbow. "Just watch…"

A car stopped in the middle of the road, headlights staring down the vacant street from between the looming elms that enclosed the street like a tunnel. The interior light came on when the driver's side door opened, framing the silhouette of a man with a baseball cap who couldn't have been out of his twenties. He shouted something and then ran toward the sidewalk. Before he was even halfway to the injured couple, they appeared from everywhere. One stepped out from behind a tree trunk as another crawled out from beneath a parked car. Several more just materialized from the darkness, racing right at him.

Angelica held her breath and watched the man's brief moment of indecision. He tried to stop, but his inertia carried him forward several more feet. He looked at the couple, and then back to the open door of his car.

"Run!" Angelica screamed, leaning across the counter and banging on the glass.

He looked up at the window briefly, and in that split-second wore a look of sheer terror.

Turning, he bolted back toward the car, but they were upon him in no time. One leapt over the hood of his sedan and barreled into him like a linebacker, hitting him squarely in the chest and driving him to the asphalt. Five more descended upon him before he even caught his breath.

Angelica averted her eyes from the flailing fists and claws.

"I told you," Mark whispered. "There's nothing you could have done."

"We let it happen."

"They'd have gotten us too."

"You don't know that."

"You don't think so? Take a look out there, doc, and tell me what you see."

She turned back to the window and looked down at the street. There had to have been close to a dozen of them down there, silhouetted in the light of the Volvo's open door. Standing there. Watching. The mangled remains of the Good Samaritan at their feet, they stared right up at the window.

"They can't possibly see us…Can they?"

Those dark statues simply stood there, transfixed by the sight of the window.

Angelica watched them as long as she could bear before lowering her stare to the sidewalk. The man who had been sprawled out, lifeless, was no longer there, and the woman who had collapsed before her eyes rolled out from beneath the unmoving body of her former beau and took a giant bite from his cheek.

"We're all going to die," Angelica whispered, easing back from the window.

When she looked back to the middle of the road, everyone was gone.

Yet she could still feel their eyes scouring her from the darkness.

"We're all going to die."

JUNE 21ST

CHAPTER 8

Colorado Springs Community Hospital

Avery held one of the magnifying glasses they'd found in the radiologist's reading room to Ian's face while Angelica steadied the flashlight on the chief resident's rapidly paling skin.

"You're sure he didn't have this ulcer earlier tonight," Avery said, gently prying at the edge of the purple wound that had grown to the size of a dime before they'd even noticed it on his cheek.

"Positive."

"It looks..." he said, bringing his eye right to the lens and then pulling it slowly back. "It almost looks like the flesh is deteriorating as I watch. Look."

Avery passed the magnifying glass to Angelica and took the flashlight, directing the beam onto the sore as Angelica knelt and inspected the wound.

"Can you see how the connective tissue is melting away from the epithelium?" he asked, leaning right over her shoulder. "It's almost behaving like he was exposed to a corrosive substance, an acid maybe, that's just lique-fying his skin as it eats deeper and deeper."

"It's a form of cutaneous leishmaniasis for sure," she said. "I've only seen it in person once or twice, but the signs are unmistakable."

"Then what's the vector?"

"The sand fly."

"We don't have any of those around here, do we?"

"You see this kind of thing a lot in impoverished third world countries. I saw it on soldiers who'd recently been in Iraq, though their sores were nearly healed by the time I treated them."

"So they will heal then?"

"Given time, yes," she said. "It's an infection caused by the leishmania bacterium, but it's only superficial. They eat through the skin until the white blood cells eventually overcome them and start to heal again. This ought to leave a nasty scar, but that should be the worst of it. Have you felt his liver yet?"

"No," Avery said, kneeling beside her and setting the flashlight on the ground. He placed his right hand on top of his left and pressed just beneath the lower border of Ian's tenth rib on the right side.

Ian groaned and pinched his unconscious eyes against the pain.

Avery looked at Angelica with a puzzled expression, and then pressed a little harder.

Ian's eyes snapped open and he slapped Avery's hands away.

"Stop it," Ian whimpered before his eyelids lowered again.

"What's causing the liver to swell like that?" Avery asked, scooting away from Ian and again directing the light toward him.

"I'm pretty confident that's a different strain of leish-maniasis that attacks the liver, though I haven't heard of the two acting in conjunction before. It's as though one opens the skin to provide access for the other, which immediately overwhelms the liver."

"That only explains the sores and the swelling. What the hell is causing them to come back to life? Why are only their hindbrains active?"

"I was hoping that you might be able to answer those questions. You're the brain specialist."

"I've never seen anything like it."

"Let's break it down into its simplest terms. The skin is the first line of defense from any sort of invading organism. The cutaneous leishmania bacteria eat through the skin to provide access to the deeper tissues and the bloodstream."

"Then once they reach the blood, they're taken right to the liver," Avery said. He paused to gnaw his lower lip contemplatively. "The liver's function is to filter toxins from the bloodstream. So if this visceral leishmaniasis overwhelms the liver, it can't filter out the toxins..."

"Is it possible that some form of toxin could also have infiltrated the blood?"

"And passed through the liver since it's no longer able to remove it?"

"Well?"

"It's possible, I suppose. We would just need to figure out what kind of toxin would—"

"Hey!" Brad called from the hallway behind them. "I think we figured out how to get out of here."

*   *   *

There was a small map behind a plastic shield in the hallway, showing the emergency exits from the department in case of a fire. Sarah gestured to it beneath the red glare from the emergency lights.

"This is where we are now," she said, pointing to a

large red dot placed in the middle of a hallway with various skeletal rooms branching from it like looking at a blueprint. "I figured there has to be some sort of emergency exit in this department. I can't imagine they'd make it so that if the fire doors were sealed no one could get out. Look here."

"Is that an elevator?" Angelica asked.

"Yeah, but with the fire alarm triggered, all power to the elevators has been cut off. But if you look right here next to it, there's a staircase—"

"Then what are we still doing here?" Avery interrupted. "Let's get out of here before they figure out how to get in here to get us."

"The problem is we'd have to go back out into the main hallway."

"And we already know they're right outside the door," Mark said.

"So you're saying that all we have to do is get past the ones banging on the door and head down the stairs?"

"They're everywhere out there," Brad said. "You saw what they did to that guy down on the street."

"So we're back to being trapped in here. I thought you said you'd figured out a way for us to get out of here."

"I have," Sarah said. "We go up."

"And then what? Jump down and start running? You're out of your mind."

"No," Angelica said. "I see where she's going with this. If we can barricade ourselves up on the roof by the helipad, then surely at some point we'll be able to get a hold of someone who'll be able to send a helicopter to pick us up, if a flight-for-life chopper doesn't land up there in the meantime."

"Okay," Avery said. "So we're going to need to get past the ones in the hall, and any others that may be in the stairwell or on the roof. What do our odds look like?"

"We need to be able to see how many are out there in the hall before we blindly charge out there. For all we know, there could be dozens of them."

"Or just two."

"Right. I've got three more rounds in my magazine. Mark?"

"Four."

"That only gives us seven shots. We'd be lucky if that brought down the two we assume are out there. Any more than that and we're screwed."

"So how are we going to figure out how many of them are out there unless we open the door?" Avery said.

"I'm not sure yet, but there has to be a—"

"Hello?" Marcy gasped, her trembling hand barely able to maintain its sweaty grasp on the phone. "Is this 911?"

"She got through," Brad nearly shouted, taking in a deep breath as though he hadn't been allowing himself to breathe at all. "It's only a matter of time now. Once they dispatch their SWAT team, we are so out of here."

"What do you mean?" Marcy said. "There are people out in the hall trying to kill us! We've already seen them tear through the entire emergency room and—"

Everyone crowded closer to her in hopes of hearing the voice on the other end through the receiver.

"No," Marcy said, a tear pinching from her right eye. "We're locked in the radiology department." There was a moment of silence. "For now, but—"

"They aren't coming," Mark said, steeling his jaw. His hand clenched the butt of his pistol, nervously trying to find the perfect grip.

"She didn't say that," Angelica said.

"She didn't have to."

"A television?" Marcy said. "You can't be serious.

We're trapped in here with all of them trying to break down the door and you want us to...No. Please. I'm sorry. Can you just...?"

Marcy stared at the handset for a moment before it slipped from her hand and clattered to the floor.

"That's not a good sign," Avery said.

"She said...she said to turn on the television."

"Does that mean they aren't going to send someone out here?" Brad asked, his voice rising with each syllable. His breathing now came rapidly, bordering on hyperventilation.

"She said they'd get someone here as soon as possible—"

"That's good, right?" Sarah said.

"—but since for the moment we're safely locked up here in the department, we're not a high priority. She said they're stretched so thin it could be morning by the time they had a free officer to come by."

"Morning?" Brad gasped. "We could all be dead by morning! How long do any of you think those walls are going to hold? Even that door? They can't do this! There should be a SWAT team standing outside this building already and..."

Angelica placed her hand on his shoulder as his words trailed into sobbing. He buried his face in his hands and leaned back against the wall, sliding down into a heap on the floor.

"Then we're on our own," Sarah said. "He's right. If we just wait around in here, then eventually they'll either wear out and forget about us...or they're going to find a way in. I, for one, don't intend to be here to find out."

Her unblinking eyes reflected her grim determination.

"Then we're going to need to figure out how many of them there are out there," Avery said.

*   *   *

"Sarah will be the easiest since she's the smallest," Mark said, hopping down from atop the x-ray table where he'd slid back one of the panels in the ceiling.

"There's no way those ceiling tiles will support even her weight," Avery said.

"If she stays right here above the table, she ought to be fine. There's extra support for the track the x-ray machine runs on."

"Does it run all the way out over the hallway?"

"I don't know. It's too dark to see that far."

"Have any of you stopped to think that if we can crawl through the ceiling over them that they could easily be able to do the same?" Marcy said.

"The actual floor above should have lead shielding to prevent the x-rays from coming up into an office or patient's room or whatever's up there. I'm counting on the fact there ought to be some sort of barrier right above the wall that serves the same purpose."

"Then how is she supposed to see down into the hallway?"

"All we need is a small gap, just big enough for her to be able to see through," Mark said. "If she gets up there and can't see anything, then we've only wasted our time and we'll have to figure something else out."

"But time is what we need most right now."

"Then we'd better stop wasting it," Avery said, climbing up onto the table, which was raised as high as it would go. Mark followed suit, standing so that he was facing Avery with the gaping hole directly above them.

"I suppose that's my cue," Sarah said, climbing up between them. She paused to look up into the darkness and drew in a deep inhalation.

The Infected

Avery presented her with his laced fingers, stooping just enough to allow her to step up onto his hands. She grabbed onto his right shoulder and tested his grip with a couple bounces before taking Mark's shoulder as well. Avery heaved her upward as Mark grabbed for her free foot, cradling it as best he could while raising her into the rafters.

She grabbed onto something out of sight and pulled herself up, breaking the tile beside the one they'd removed in the process.

"Hand me a light," she called down.

Angelica passed the one she was holding up to Mark, who held it as high as he could until Sarah reached down and took it. A small arc of light spilled out from the gap where the tile had been, growing fainter by the second. They could hear her crawling around up there, the occasional tile bowing beneath her carefully transferred weight.

Sarah eased forward, the circle of light settling on what looked like a metal sheet ahead of her. She swung the light from side to side as she drew closer, grappling with the steel armature mounted in the darkness beside her. It was apparent the rails didn't run all the way to the wall, but if she was exceedingly careful, she thought she should be able to lean from the edge of it to the wall separating the room from the hallway beyond. Shoving aside massive braids of wires, she reached the end of the metal framework, bracing her left knee on the steel and her right on one of the support joists, she leaned forward until she was able to balance on the parallel joist and lower her chest to it. From her vantage, she could see where the ceiling met the impromptu wall, but she wasn't close enough to be able to tell if she could see down into the hallway or not.

"Shoot," she whispered, inching forward until she

was able to reach the next wooden slat ahead of her. Carefully setting the light down on the flimsy tile beside her, she grabbed the wood with both hands and pulled herself forward, transferring her weight from her knees to her chest and sliding until she could only rest her ankles where her knees had been. Taking back the flashlight, she directed it toward the wall separating her from the ceiling above the hallway, but there didn't appear to be any cracks at all.

"I can't see anything," she called back, but only heard muffled voices in response.

Straining, she reached all the way to the top of the lead barrier with her right hand, slipping her fingers between it and the floor above, and pried it downward. She was surprised to find it pliable, and simply folded it all the way down until she'd created a gap large enough to lean through.

The banging from beneath her was now deafening.

Carefully, she pulled up just the corner of one of the tiles and slid it back, barely far enough for her to see a sliver of the hallway. The red light from below drew a diagonal slash across her right eye.

They were everywhere down there. There had to be at least twenty of them. If she craned her neck, she could see that two of them continued to pound on the bloody door, hurling their bodies against it and clawing into the wood with now skeletal fingertips. The others simply milled in the hallway, impatiently pacing like so many caged animals. Most were now covered with splotchy purple ulcerations, opening sickly on their faces, arms, and feet, leaving bloody smears on the floor and on the walls.

Seven bullets, she thought.

There was no way they were going to get out of there alive.

The Infected

They were all going to die.

Sarah reached for the tile to drag it back into place, bumping it just slightly.

The frenzied movement in the room beneath her halted and every head snapped up to look at her.

"Jesus," she gasped, sliding the tile back into place.

All of their eyes had been full of blood, draining down their cheeks. Their faces had been fixed in tortured contortions of rage and agony. Teeth bared, whatever flesh-eating disease they carried making short work of the straps of skin connecting their cheekbones to their jaw-lines, they stirred to life beneath her. The banging intensified as she could now feel a barrage of fists pounding the walls to the point that the wooden joists beneath her shook.

"Get me down!" she screamed, throwing her weight backward. Her right foot broke through one of the tiles and she barely managed to grab onto one of the planks before she fell straight through to the examination room beneath.

She felt arms wrap around her leg before she lost her grip and fell atop a heap of humanity on the floor.

"They're everywhere!" she screamed, throwing herself from atop the bodies that had taken the brunt of her fall.

"Calm down," a voice said, but she couldn't. They were going to die, *they were going to die*.

"How many?" Avery snapped, grabbing her by the shoulders and shaking her to draw her eyes to his. "How many of them did you see?"

"Seven bullets," she whispered.

"Snap out of it, damn it! How many of them did you see?"

Sarah's wide eyes jerked from one side of the room to the other as though unable to settle on any one thing.

"Sarah!"

Finally, she blinked and all of the blood drained from her face.

"At least twenty," she whispered. "Maybe more."

"Twenty?"

"That I could see. For all I know there could be hundreds of them down there."

Avery released her shoulders and took a stumbling step back.

"We're going to die in here," she whispered.

*   *   *

Ian stirred long enough to slump from against the wall of the front desk to his right, spewing a mixture of blood and bile onto the floor before toppling face-first into it. With trembling hands, he tried to raise himself from the ground, but all of his strength had deserted him. Even the normally simple task of breathing was taking the majority of his focus and effort. It felt as though his lungs were filling with fluid, and based on the wheezing and gurgling he could hear over the ferocious pounding on the door, he was quite confident that was the case.

Wounds bloomed all over his body, though as his sight began to fail him, he could only feel the infection eating through his flesh like there was a magnifying lens focusing the sun on his skin. The pain in his abdomen was like nothing he'd experienced before, as though his liver were swelling to the point that it threatened to pop.

He pinched his eyes shut against the staggering pressure building behind his lids and prayed for death.

The vessels in his eyes ruptured as one, flooding a skein of warmth across his eyeballs, dripping to the floor.

With a belch of rotting gas and a flurry of tight muscular contractions, his prayers were answered and he was finally released from the pain.

Alone in the waiting room, with the dead trying to force their way through the door and the walls.

Alone.

CHAPTER 9

Colorado Springs Community Hospital

Sarah closed the bathroom door and leaned against it, thankful for the momentary reprieve from the chaos and the banging and the hardly-restrained panic that was rising within them all. She slumped down to the floor and started to cry, wiping the tears away, smearing the red stains on her cheeks. She had to try to be strong. Even in the face of what would surely be her death. Each breath tasted different, knowing it could potentially be her last.

There was a little voice at the back of her head, gnawing into her brain like a filthy rat, whispering that if death was a certainty, she should face it on her own terms, though whether that meant closing her teeth on the barrel of her gun or throwing the front door wide and going out in a blaze of glory she wasn't sure. For the most part, all she wanted to do was curl up on the floor, close her eyes, and make the entire world go away.

"Oh, God," she moaned as she felt the contents of her stomach surge up her esophagus.

She crawled to the toilet, threw back the lid, and

spewed a splash into the bowl. It was several minutes after she had drained her gut before she stopped heaving.

They were going to die.

Forcing the thought from her mind, she staggered to her feet and leaned over the sink to throw some water in her face. She splashed the cold water into her eyes and all over her cheeks until she could feel it running down into the collar of her uniform.

They were going to die.

She raised her eyes to the mirror, catching her own bloodshot stare from beneath sopping brows. Dried blood still ringed her face, crusted into her hairline, scabbed in the curves of her ears.

They were going to die.

There was a red splotch beneath her right eye. Raising her index finger, she gently poked it and had to bite her tongue to keep from screaming aloud. She brought her face right up to the glass and used both hands to try to pull the skin tight so she could get a better look at it. Blood wept from a pinprick hole in the center, the edges seeming to deteriorate as she pulled those festering lips apart.

"Please, Lord," she whimpered, smearing the blood away.

There was another ulcer starting to form at the left corner of her mouth.

Whirling, she found the soap dispenser and hammered it repeatedly until she filled her palm and covered the countertop with the white ooze. Slopping it on her face, she scrubbed at it with her fingers, working it into the skin until the pressure was nearly unbearable. She could feel the sores growing wider with the furious effort, droplets of soap somehow reaching her tongue.

They were going to die.

She turned on the water as hot as she could bear and

splashed it on her face, still scrubbing as hard as she could. The skin was red and abraded, the ulcers angry and crimson and spitting blood bubbles from the holes in the middle.

Grabbing a handful of brown paper towels, she scoured her face until it was dry and she felt as though she'd peeled the entire top layer of skin off.

She looked at herself in the mirror again.

They were going to die.

Staring deeply into her eyes, focusing on the blue irises to keep from looking at the expanding wounds rising on her face, she pulled her gun from the holster and unloaded the magazine. Without looking, she slipped the top bullet from the magazine and set it on the counter in front of her before slamming the magazine back into the pistol.

She was going to die.

Tearing off a couple pieces of paper towel, she pressed them over the sores like a man using tissue to blot his shaving wounds, grabbed the lone bullet, and slipped it into the front right pocket of her pants.

*   *   *

"If it was that easy for Sarah to look over the wall, why haven't they climbed over from the other side? The ceiling's maybe what, nine feet up?" Angelica whispered to Avery. They were trying to keep the conversation between just the two of them so they hung back, down at the end of the hallway between ultrasound and nuclear medicine.

"I don't know. Without higher brain functioning, it's possible that they're unable to grasp the concepts of creative problem solving. I'm not comfortable waiting around until they figure it out though. We need to decide how to get out of here right now."

"And then what? Where are we going to go?"

"I can't imagine these things are everywhere."

"You saw the news before all of this started. This kind of thing was happening all over the world."

"It physically can't be everywhere yet. If your leishmaniasis theory is correct, then the only way this can be spread is through physical contact. I'm confident there aren't any sand flies around here, so the infected patients must be serving as the vectors themselves and harboring a reservoir of the leishmania bacteria. It would have to be transmitted via bodily fluids. Come to think of it...didn't most of the patients come in with blood on them?"

"Yeah. Dried blood. Most of them didn't appear to have any open wounds on them either."

"So we know the cutaneous bacterium is capable of eating through the flesh. It would stand to reason that even topical contact with the epithelium would be acceptable for transmission, allowing the visceral bacterium to enter the blood stream. If properly quarantined, we could stop the disease quite easily."

"You want to go out there and round them all up?"

Avery grimaced. "You're being counterproductive, Angie."

"So what's your theory then? Hmm? The disease eats through the skin and disables the liver so that something else, another bacteria maybe, can overwhelm the brain. What kind of agent could possibly do that and lead to such insane altered mental status?"

"A toxoplasma perhaps?"

"You're grasping at straws and you know it."

"I've read studies about children exposed to toxoplasmas who experience uncontrolled rage and violent tendencies. There was even one kid in Texas or something who actually bit off his mother's ear."

"That's not what I mean, Avery. Where could these people possibly be exposed to toxoplasmas?"

"That kid ate some cat crap out of his sand box."

"Toxoplasmodium?"

"That strain certainly isn't the most virulent, but that's why it's so important not to let little kids play in the litter box, or even allow the cat to be near a newborn."

"So, if this were some sort of aggressive type of toxoplasmodium, could it be responsible for what's going on out there?"

"Violence and rage...Definitely. The inability to differentiate between food and non-food sources? Sure. But what we're missing here is whatever is actually killing the cerebrum and only leaving the hindbrain. As it is now, what we're describing is something that would have to have been genetically engineered. There's no way I would buy that this was random exposure. Even if one of these flies happened to carry both strains of leishmaniasis, it would have required exposure to tainted cat feces on top of that. And then all of these bacteria would need to have been concentrated to such a degree as to allow them to spread through the host's body so quickly."

"Biological warfare?"

"Please, Angie. When we've got things like anthrax at our disposal this seems positively primitive."

"You don't have to be a jerk about it."

Avery opened his mouth like he was about to fire back, but hesitated.

"Sorry," he said, looking away. "I don't like...I don't like the feeling of not knowing."

He sighed.

She took his hand and gave it a gentle squeeze.

"Neither do I."

She allowed her hand to linger within his longer than

she had intended, until the point that he raised his eyes to meet hers. Releasing his hand, she looked away.

"So what do we do now?" he asked. "The cutaneous leishmaniasis will eventually run its course and then heal. How about the visceral?"

"I'm not sure."

"And there's only one way I can think of to effectively shut down the hindbrain."

"What's that?"

"By separating it from the rest of the body."

"Jesus," she whispered.

Both jumped as a piercing scream echoed from down the hall.

*   *   *

Brad sat just inside the waiting room. There was something comforting about the fish tank in the corner, or maybe it was simply that so long as he didn't have to converse with the others, see the fear in their eyes and hear the panic in their voices, he could escape the reality of the situation. The pounding on the door and the shaking walls a dozen paces from him were simultaneously terrifying and reassuring. So long as he could hear the beating of their fists and physically see that the door and walls were intact, then he knew he was safe. And sitting where he was allowed him to be the first to see if either were compromised. Besides, it was better than having to watch them out the windows as they dragged down people on the street and butchered them remorselessly.

He forced the thought out of his mind as he could still clearly see the man who had stopped to help the people on the sidewalk being ripped into human confetti.

Scratching at the itch he couldn't quite seem to sate,

he pulled his bloody fingernails away and was just preparing to look at them when he saw movement from the corner of his eye.

He turned to face it, but it had only been Dr. Nguyen falling onto his side from where he'd been sitting up. The man had been so quiet that Brad had forgotten he was there at all.

"Are you okay?" he asked, pushing himself from the floor to his feet and walking over to where the chief resident had crumpled onto his face with blood spilling out of the corner of his mouth.

Brad knelt and pressed his fingers to the inside of the man's wrist, but couldn't find a pulse. Dropping the hand, he pushed beside Ian's trachea and finally felt a weak thumping.

"Hey," he called back over his shoulder.

The pounding on the door ceased.

They must have heard his voice.

He was preparing to call out again when the banging began again in earnest, more fervently as though the mere sound of his voice had worked them into a frenzy.

Staring at the door and watching the metal frame shuddering against the assault, he didn't immediately notice when Ian's pulse stopped gently tapping his fingertips.

"Are you okay?" Marcy asked, peeking around the corner from the hallway. She managed to fill her pockets with all of the painkillers she could find in the department, which was kind of like going grocery shopping at a hardware store. She'd been able to find nothing more potent than lidocaine to treat the pain and a small handful of band-aids and tegaderm strips.

Brad looked up at her briefly before turning away. A meek sob crossed his lips as he suddenly realized with complete and utter certainty that it was only a matter of time before the door gave way and opened the flood-gates. He didn't want to die. Not in here. Not like this. He was barely out of school, only now beginning his life, the prospect of death was something he hadn't even begun to ponder yet. He spent his time thinking about saving up for the down-payment on a nice luxury condo, about trading in his Stratus for a Lexus, about—

The doctor's pulse started again, stronger this time, throbbing against his fingers.

He looked at Ian's face. The doctor's eye slowly made its way to the corner so that he could look up and see Brad. The iris quivered in the blood, creating ripples like a stone breaking the surface of a placid pond.

"Holy crap," Brad gasped, stumbling backward and tripping over his own feet, landing soundly on his rear end.

"What?" Marcy asked, having just turned to head back down the hallway.

Ian raised his head from the pool of black blood. Brad could see the huge ulcers that had eaten through the man's face, revealing even the bone beneath in spots.

"Help!" he called, louder this time, but he could barely hear it in his own ears over the furious barrage of punches and kicks from the hallway. "Help!"

Marcy took a single step into the room before seeing what was happening, and stopped dead in her tracks, screaming.

Brad rolled over to all fours and tried to lunge toward her, but before he could even push off, he felt a sharp tug on the tails of his lab coat, jerking him away from the examination rooms. Landing flat on his back, he found himself staring straight up at Dr. Nguyen, whose cooling blood was soaking into Brad's hair and clothes from the floor. He kicked at the tile, trying to propel himself away from the doctor, who bared his teeth like some feral beast,

the muted red emergency lights glimmering on the skin
of blood over his incisors, but his wet feet only squeaked
on the vinyl tile, unable to gain traction.

"Get away from me!" he wailed, raising both hands
above him to fend off the coming attack.

Marcy staggered backwards, shaking her head and
screaming.

The thing that had once been Ian snatched Brad's
right hand and yanked on it, lowering its head at the
same time. Before Brad could even guess what was about
to happen, he felt teeth tear through the meaty flesh of
the webbing between his thumb and index finger. He
screamed as blood poured from the wound, which only
excited the thing more. It wrenched him to his feet by his
arm and snapped at him. Brad barely had time to jerk
away, offering up his shoulder instead of his neck. It bit
down on his deltoid, latching onto it even through the lab
coat and the shirt beneath. It shook its head back and
forth like a dog fighting for a bone, ripping at the skin,
but unable to procure a clean bite.

Brad screamed and threw himself away from the
creature, landing on his stomach and shimmying through
the open doorway into the back hall. Marcy had retreated
until her back was against the wall at the far side of the
hallway, her legs still moving as though trying to force
her screaming form through the plaster. Clear down to
his right he could see a pair of shadows.

"Help me!" he screamed.

In that one fleeting moment, his eyes locked onto
Angelica's.

Hands clasped his ankles and dragged him back into
the lobby, leaving a smeared trail from the wound in his
hand.

"No!" he wailed. "Please! Please! Just leave me
alone!"

The Infected

His breath exploded from his lungs as a great weight slammed down on his back. Knees ground into his lower back, pinning him to the extent that he could only raise his head from the floor to scream.

Sharp pain in his neck.

He tried to reach for it but only ended up fanning at air.

The crack of bone.

Marcy's shrill screams.

Blood gushed from around the seal of the thing's lips on Brad's neck as it broke its own teeth in the process of chewing through Brad's cervical spine, slurping in both blood and cerebrospinal fluid alike. A chunk of vertebrae lodged in its throat, forcing it to release its meal to try to choke down the bone like a hawk.

A wash of blood splashed the floor behind it before the report of gunfire boomed in the small room. Fragments of cranium and sloppy morsels of brain slapped the door in a pattern around the blackened wood where the bullet was now lodged. Another flare of muzzle fire and a deafening boom, and the top half of Ian's head vaporized into a cloud of matter. His body toppled backwards, his back bending like an agonized rainbow, blood draining from what remained of his head.

Brad's screams trilled from beneath the echo of the report, but none of his appendages flailed to try to push him to his feet. Only his lips moved around his pained cries, his eyes blinking away the spatters of blood draining from his temples.

Avery threw himself to the floor beside Brad and pressed his hands into the gaping wound on the back of the man's neck, trying to simultaneously staunch the bleeding and gauge the extent of the damage. The bite was even deeper than he would have imagined. The spinous processes of the third and fourth cervical vertebrae were entirely gone, exposing the vertebral canal where the spinal cord would have been, had a large section of it not been torn out. He could still feel the grooves the teeth had left in what remained above and below.

"His spinal cord's been severed," he said, frantically looking around the room, trying to find something, anything that he could possibly use.

Sarah walked over to where Ian's body lay on the floor and nudged it with the toe of her right boot. Only more blood spilled out of what remained of the cranium. She looked down at the tendrils of smoke still rising from her hot barrel.

"Only one bullet left," she whispered, though no one could hear her over the intensified pounding from the hallway. It was almost as though those things on the other side of the door could smell the blood like sharks tasting it in the water and it was working them into a wild tumult.

Brad sputtered a mouthful of blood through the tail end of his dying scream, gurgling like water in a cooler, and then was completely still.

Sarah turned to watch the light fade from his eyes, leaving only a dull shine in the right eye to lifelessly watch the floor.

Avery pulled his hands out of the man's neck with a slurp and flung the sloppy fluids onto the floor.

"Oh God," he said, raising his bloody hands in front of him, only that second realizing exactly what he had done.

"Avery?" Angelica said, raising a trembling hand and taking a step toward him.

"Move!" he shouted, dashing right through her arm and into the hallway where Marcy had slumped to the floor with only her wide eyes visible over her hands. He paused long enough to look quickly in both directions before sprinting to his left toward the open door of the bathroom. He cranked both handles on the hot and the cold and shoved his hands beneath the firm stream, frantically rubbing them together and watching the blood dilute, running along his forearms and swirling down the drain. "Gotta get it off, gotta get it off. Get it off!"

He slapped at the soap dispenser repeatedly until he completely filled his palm with soap and then smashed his palms together, rubbing them so hard that the tendons stood out in his forearms. Curling his fingers to claws, he carved at the upper layer of his epidermis, trying desperately to peel it off along with whatever contamination may have already begun to leech through his tissue.

Even after the water and the rubbing had removed all of the soap and blood from his bright pink skin, he continued scratching at it until bloody abrasions opened from his wrists along the backs of his hand.

"Avery," Angelica said, gently taking him by the right biceps and pulling his hand out of the water. "You got it all. Opening the skin can only make it worse."

He looked up at her with tears streaming down his face.

"I didn't...didn't even think."

"You did what you were trained to do, Avery. You did the right thing."

"Did I?" he said, staring down at his trembling hands, at the crescents of skin packed under even his short fingernails, at the droplets of blood welling to the surface in small dots where he had gouged through his own flesh.

"Avery..."

"I'm a dead man, Angie," he whispered.

"You don't know that. It's possible that the infection..." Her words trailed into silence metered by the rhythmic pounding of fists on the walls.

He shook his head and slipped past her into the hallway.

Closing her eyes, her chin fell to her chest, loosing the tears that had been clinging to her chin.

CHAPTER 10

Colorado Springs Community Hospital

Mark stood in the nuclear medicine office, staring blankly down at the ground. There had to be fifty of them down there now, all standing in the middle of the street in front of the poor guy's car, which still sat in the middle of the road with the driver's side door wide open. No longer did they try to hide in the shadows to bait their prey. They just stood there, still as the night around them, staring up at him through the window. Though he couldn't see their eyes in the shadows draped across their faces, he could feel their weight upon him. He couldn't bring himself to tear his gaze from them for fear that if he did they'd be even closer the next time he looked.

He'd heard the gunshots, but had waited through the tense moments following before deciding whether or not they were going to need his assistance. The prospect of having to kill again was more than he could bear. He should have called in. That's what he should have done. He would still be sitting at home behind his locked doors in his apartment watching whatever the hell was on TV and wouldn't be standing here now covered in the blood of the people he'd been forced to kill. Deep down, he knew it wasn't his fault. He hadn't killed them in cold blood, but that didn't mean they didn't still haunt him. The man in the MRI room, the patients downstairs and in the hallway…

He opened his hands and inspected them. Dried blood formed lines in the fissures of his skin, lining his knuckles and palms as though traced by a pen. He licked his thumb and scrubbed at a particularly thick area of crust like a scab, wincing as he exposed not the unmarred skin beneath as he had expected, but instead a small crater that reminded him of a fresh burn after peeling off the blister. It was deep and red, the edges lined with the layers of skin like the strata of the earth bordering the highways cut into the sides of mountains.

Closing his eyes, he let his arms fall to his sides. When he opened them again, the mob of people down on the street were now closer, milling on the sidewalk and on the lawn nearly beneath him, still staring up at him.

"What are you waiting for?" he whispered, slapping at his cheek where it felt as though something had just bit him. Smearing away the blood, he picked at the source of the pain, cringing as he felt not a swelling, but a small pit, which he had widened with his fingernail and was now draining down his cheek.

His shoulders were shuddering before he even knew that he'd allowed the tears to break through his defenses.

Snatching his gun from the holster, he pointed it out the window at the people down there, swinging it side to side and flinching as though preparing to fire, but none of them so much as moved. They simply watched him intently like magpies from a telephone line.

He howled and thrust the pistol back into the holster.

"What are you waiting for?" he screamed, yanking the computer monitor off of the table in front of him, cords whipping from it like the stingers of a jellyfish, and throwing it at the window. It shivered and shook, a crack forming like a starburst, but dropped the monitor back onto the desk. The clear plastic screen within spider-webbed from the point of impact. "Just get it over with!"

"What's going on?" Sarah shouted, turning the corner into the room.

Her breath stilled in her chest as he drew his gun and pointed it at her with a shaking arm.

"Don't come any closer!" he screamed.

"Mark..." When she looked into his eyes, all she could see was terror verging upon madness. "It's me...Sarah..."

"Take another step and I'll blow you back to hell!"

He readjusted his sweaty grip, the barrel of the gun swiveling wildly.

"Mark...I'm not going to hurt you."

"We're all going to die here tonight. Don't you get it? They're going to kill every last one of us!" His voice rose into a high-pitched wail with the final words.

"Mark...Lower the gun."

"They're everywhere, Sarah. Everywhere!"

"I know, Mark. I know. But you're wrong. We are getting out of here. You have my word."

"I don't want to die..." he said, the barrel tipping down toward the floor, "...not like that guy down there did."

"I know, Mark. Neither do I."

"They ripped him apart, Sarah. Can you see what's left of him down there? He's just bones scattered along the street in a mess of his own blood."

"Put the gun down and I'll make you a deal," she said, producing the lone bullet from her pants. "You see this?"

He nodded, though his brows lowered in confusion.

"I want you to lower your gun and pull out one bullet. Okay?"

He still just stared at her.

"Stick one bullet in your pocket. I'll have one in mine. Here's the deal. If it even starts to look like there's a chance we're going to…you know, what happened to that guy down there, this bullet in my pocket will be for you, and the one in your pocket will be for me."

"You mean…" he said, the light of insanity finally dimming in his eyes. "You do me and I do you."

"That way it will be quick and neither of us should feel a thing."

Mark studied her face a moment longer, searching her eyes for the resolve that he lacked. Slowly, he lowered the pistol and ejected the magazine. Prying the first bullet from the top, he held it up and stared at it, the tip glinting with the crimson glow, and then looked at Sarah.

She nodded and replaced the bullet in her pocket, her eyes never leaving his.

He followed her lead and shoved the gold casing into his pocket.

"Do we have a deal then?" Sarah asked.

Mark simply nodded and turned back to the window, though by now he had to lean across the counter and nearly press his face to the glass to see them staring up at him from the lawn directly below.

*　　*　　*

"We have to be sure," Angelica said.

"With his spinal cord severed like that, even if he did come back to life, he wouldn't be able to move. Only his cranial nerves would be functionally innervated."

"But his heart could still beat."

"Possibly," Avery said, looking at the backs of his

161

hands every few seconds as though checking a watch that wasn't there.

"Those sores on his face and arms are still expanding."

"Just because he's dead doesn't mean that the bacteria are."

"That's my point, Avery. If they're still alive and eating his flesh, then whatever process may occur in his body to bring it back to life could be happening as we speak."

"What do you propose then? Should we use one of the few bullets we have to blow a hole through his skull...just in case?"

"Do you have a better idea?"

"Maybe," Avery said. "But first I have to know..."

Angelica waited for him to finish, but instead he just stared down at Brad's body.

"Know what?"

He looked at her as though he hadn't initially meant to speak aloud.

"Something's bothering me about they way they're acting."

"Who? The others?"

"No, those...things out there."

"How so?"

"Listen," he said, but all she could hear was the tireless hammering of fists on the wall across the lobby from where they stood.

"All I hear is them trying to get in."

"Precisely."

"I don't understand."

"Down in the emergency room...they attacked the police and tried to get us."

"I was there, Avery."

"Don't you see? If my theory was correct and they

were simply victims of their own instincts purveyed through their hindbrains, then why aren't they attacking each other? Why are they only going after those of us…" He swallowed and chased the thought from his mind as soon as it formed. "…who aren't infected?"

Angelica hadn't made that connection until now, but it was a powerful observation.

"So you think they have some way of recognizing each other as something other than a food source."

"By all rights, they should be ripping each other apart out there in the hall instead of trying to get in at us. There has to be more to it than I originally speculated."

"You compared them to sharks before. What keeps sharks from attacking each other?"

"If the others sense weakness or can smell blood on one of the other sharks, then they would attack it the same as a wounded swimmer or seal. In that way they're indiscriminant killing machines."

"So what are we missing?"

"Maybe…" he said, pursing his lips. She could see the wheels turning behind his lowered brow. "Maybe, like sharks, they can smell blood."

"But they're all full of blood. That doesn't explain it."

"I mean, what if they can smell something in the blood?"

"Even then, Avery, I doubt their olfactory senses would be capable of smelling blood. I can't even smell it, and I'm around it all day. Not unless there's some sort of infection…"

She stopped.

"What?"

"The infection. They can smell the infection in the others."

"You think?"

"It would stand to reason, wouldn't it? I can tell you

163

if a patient's septic before I even walk into the room. I can smell it in the hallway. Gangrene has an unmistakable scent. So does necrosis. I'll bet they can smell the infection. Even in the wild, a coyote won't eat a dying prairie dog."

Avery turned and looked at the bodies sprawled across the floor in the middle of a rapidly drying puddle of their own fluids.

"There's only one way to find out," he said, walking over to what remained of Ian's body and dropping to his haunches like a baseball catcher. He brought his face down until it was only inches above what remained of the chief resident's head: the fractured mandible minus a section of chipped teeth leading back to the jaggedly broken cranial base, which now served as little more than a reservoir for congealing blood and brain matter.

Closing his eyes, he drew a deep inhalation through his nose. Maybe they'd waited too long, as all he could smell was decomposition. Festering flesh in the process of dissolution. Could it possibly be as simple as that?

"I don't think it's the infection that they smell, but rather...death. You know what I'm talking about. You can't work in a hospital long without becoming intimate with the smell of death. That putrid reek of ammonia from urine crystallizing in the body. The gasses seeping out of every orifice as it deflates. Cellular decay begins immediately, and...I don't even know how to describe that. Like food rotting in a dumpster. The smell of the pus that seethes from a diabetic's black toe."

"Does it even make a difference at this point? They're waiting for us outside of every exit, and it's only a matter of time before they break through the door to get in at us."

Avery stood and walked to her, offering his hand to help her to her feet.

"Have a little faith, would you?" he said, flashing a hint of a cocky smile.

*   *   *

Mark and Sarah were sitting in a pair of rolling chairs in front of the lone functional computer monitor when Angelica and Avery walked through the door. Marcy crouched in the corner, whimpering. What looked like news footage flowed in jerks on a window in the middle of the screen. The voiceover sounded like it was coming from underneath the table where presumably the computer tower was seated.

"What are you guys watch—?" Angelica started.

"Shh!" Mark whispered.

"...*as far north as Minneapolis, Minnesota where people are cramming into the streets even at this late hour. Live footage from the local Fox affiliate confirms that this bizarre and violent behavior fits the same pattern we have been witnessing all over the world to various degrees tonight. Again we take you to London where Fox correspondent Walter Matheson is standing by to brief us on the details of what the Crown is already calling 'The Great Pandemic.' Walter?*"

"*Thank you, Ron,*" the man said in a thick British accent. The feed was hindered by the modem connection, which allowed the audio to come through just fine, but the images were jerky and often frozen. The Tower of London stood behind him against the midday sun, poking through dingy gray clouds. It appeared as though he was standing on the balcony or roof of some high structure. "*Prime Minister Lester Badgett just wrapped up an impromptu press conference at an undisclosed location in a building secured by heavily armed Royal Guards. He confirmed that the Queen has already been airlifted to a safe location, while members of Parliament have been gathered in an emergency session to enact precautionary measures, which they fear may already be too late."*

The screen showed a lane packed with people, thundering through the narrow corridor like the running of the bulls in Pamplona. A rolling tide of humanity, they washed over anything unfortunate enough to be in their way. The image froze on a man's wild-eyed face as he slammed into another poor soul from behind, biting right into the nook of the man's neck.

"Oh, God," Angelica said. The man had the same bloody red eyes and a sore on his cheek large enough to see his molars through.

The image cut to a building in the distance, the flames rising from its roof twice the height of the building itself.

"...International Airport, where the first of the outbreaks were documented. Reports are still being disseminated, but early eyewitness accounts, which were immediately discounted, indicate that roughly twenty infected people appeared from nowhere in the international terminal and savagely attacked anyone they came across. Preliminary indications suggest that the origin of the flight carrying the diseased passengers was somewhere in Mexico, though that has yet to be officially confirmed, and may remain that way until enough fire personnel are available to bring the blaze under control. Emergency services are spread far too thin battling out-of-control fires all over the city and..."

"We need to get out of here," Marcy said, rising to her feet and regaining some semblance of control over her tears.

"Where are we going to go, huh? They're everywhere!" Mark yelled, tearing his fingers through his hair. He moderated his tone before continuing. "There's nowhere left to go..."

"I suspect that this virus will eventually run its course," Avery said. "I have no idea how long it may take, but ultimately their bodies will simply have to give out. With the bacteria attacking their skin, liver, and brain, it's only a matter of time."

"Time appears to be what we're lacking," Sarah said, nodding to the window where the ranks of the infected staring up into the window had nearly doubled in the last half hour.

"If it's only affecting humans, then what we need to do is find an area where there aren't any others around. I'm guessing that if we were to make it into the mountains, not only would we not be surrounded by these things, but we'd also find towns that are completely unaffected.

"If we're correct, and this disease originated in Mexico and arrived on the crashed flight from Cancun, then only major population centers with international airports will experience this phenomenon before it runs its course."

"All that's great, doc," Mark said, "but look around you. It's not like we can even walk out into the hallway, let alone across the parking lot to our cars so that we can drive to the interstate and—"

"What happened to the idea of getting up to the roof and being airlifted out of here?" Marcy asked.

"That's a pipe dream," Sarah said, shaking her head. "I can't think of any way we'd be able to get past all of them out there to get to the stairs. We'd be dead before the door even swung closed behind us. And especially with only three bullets—"

"I thought there were seven," Angelica said.

"I used four on that ER doctor."

Angelica was about to say, "But you said you only had three bullets to begin with," but bit her tongue as she couldn't be sure which one had said they had three bullets and which one had said four. Either way though, she'd only heard two shots...

"...*where the governor of California has officially summoned the National Guard to Los Angeles where violence and bloodshed are rampant in the streets. A safe haven has been established inside the Staples Center where police are fighting off wave after wave of rioters hell-bent on breaking through their barricade. This picture you are seeing now is live. The smoke hovering around the building is the residue of the tear gas the officers used to try to ward off the first assault, but have now resorted to using live rounds after even the rubber bullets were unable to stymie the advances of citizens who appear to be infected with some sort of flesh-eating virus.*"

"I think I may have figured out how we can get past them," Avery said.

All eyes were immediately upon him.

"What are you waiting for, a drum roll?" Sarah said, standing and turning to face him. "Out with it already."

Avery nodded and lifted the chair she had been sitting on only a moment prior, pointing the wheels and the metal X they were attached to toward the window.

"What are you doing?" Marcy shouted, but he was already swinging the chair with all of his strength at the crack Mark had created with the monitor.

There was a dull thud and the window shivered in the pane, but before it came to rest Avery was swinging the chair again. The window exploded outward, dropping enormous jagged shards of glass down onto the people beneath.

He leaned over and looked down at the crowd, which appeared oblivious to the sharp diamonds of glass poking out from their heads and shoulders like armored plates from a stegosaurus's back.

"Why did you do that?" Sarah screamed, taking him by the front of the shirt and shaking him. "That was the only thing standing between us and them. What if they decided to—?"

"Do you want to get out of here or not?" Avery snapped.

Sarah's chin jutted forth and her eyes narrowed, but she said nothing.

"Someone help me," he said, turning and heading back into the hallway. By the time he reached the lobby, he could hear two sets of footsteps following him.

He turned to his left into the lobby, which was now beginning to smell like rotting meat, and walked right up to Ian's corpse. Taking him by the wrists, he dragged the body backwards until Angelica and Marcy appeared in front of him. Each of them cast him only a cursory glance before taking one of the physician's ankles and heaving him from the floor. They carried him down the hallway, his limp neck allowing what remained of his head to bounce, slopping piles of blood and brain onto the floor for them to navigate.

Avery backed into the nuclear medicine room and through the small injection chamber into the work area.

"Help me...get him up on the table," he said, groaning as he raised the shoulders just high enough to clear the edge of the counter.

"What the hell are you doing?" Mark nearly shouted, scooting his chair backward from where he was still focused on the news. "Jesus Christ, man. Do you want us all to get whatever he has?"

"Just help me shove him out the window, would you?"

"Yeah," Mark said, realizing that the farther the body and the infection residing within were from him, the better off they would be. Let those things waiting down there tear the doctor limb from limb, it's not like he was even still in there. "I can do that."

Angelica and Marcy brought his legs up onto the

counter and barely had time to catch their breath before they were again shoving the body over shards of broken glass to the edge of the counter where the air hardly stirred in the still night.

"On three," Avery said. "One…"

"Aw, hell, just do it," Mark said, lowering his shoulder and leveraging his legs to push Ian's torso out into the night. It balanced there momentarily before sliding away from them. Ian's feet rose from the table and pointed at the ceiling only long enough for the remains to slither out the window.

Avery heard a wet thump like a cat might make against a speeding bumper as he leaned across and looked down at the grass.

The corpse had knocked several of the people down there to the ground. Those still standing continued to stare up through the window as those that had been pinned beneath crawled out from under the corpse like a wet blanket. It now lay there in their midst, surrounded by the infected who seemed oblivious to the fact that it was even there as they walked across it and shuffled atop the ribcage vying for position to see the fresh meat above.

"…unrelated news," the newscaster's voice said from beneath the table, "spotted reports are coming in from all over the southwestern United States from Texas to California claiming that the skies are filling with flies."

"Let's get the other one out of here, too," Mark said, already brushing past Avery and into the hallway.

"No," Avery said, stopping Mark in his tracks.

"Why the hell not?"

"We still need it."

"For what?" Angelica asked, but she already knew.

CHAPTER 11

Colorado Springs Community Hospital

"You're out of your mind," Sarah said. "They're going to butcher you like all of the rest."

"I don't think so," Avery said, wrapping the final layer of duct tape around his right ankle to hold the formerly sterile blue booties to the pale blue examination gown he had wrapped around his leg.

"What if you're wrong?" Angelica asked.

Avery looked up at her, but didn't respond. She could only see the crescents of his eyes through the small slits torn into the gown wrapped around his head like a robber's mask. Silver duct tape ringed his face, wrapping all the way around from the bridge of his nose to his neck where it sealed the connecting point to the bright yellow isolation gown that covered his chest and arms. Two pair of surgical gloves had been pulled over each hand past the wrist and over the cuffs of the gown where they were sealed together with more tape. The bottom of the smock was taped around his waist like a belt, connecting it to the ordinary gowns they'd used to hide his legs. A spiral of duct tape wound down toward both ankles like the stripe on a barber's pole.

171

The Infected

"Goggles," he said, rising to his feet.

Marcy handed him the pair of plastic isolation goggles, while Angelica went behind him to help seat the rubber strap. The lenses covered the slits that shielded his eyes, the rubber seam fitting firmly against his face.

"Are you sure you want to go through with this?" Angelica whispered into the bulge on the side of his mummified head.

He turned and looked at her. She could see the fear in his wide eyes, but he managed to nod.

Angelica lifted another yellow isolation gown from the back of the chair where she had draped it, pulling it on over her arms and chest. She turned her back to Marcy and waited for her to tie it for her before strapping a green mask over her mouth and nostrils and pinching the metal over the bridge of her nose to hold it in place. Avery handed her two pair of latex gloves, which she pulled tightly over her hands until the ends were nearly to the middle of her forearms, holding the gown in place.

Mark and Sarah stood in the doorway between the lobby and the back hallway, trying to see what the others were doing, but at the same time trying to stay as far away from Brad's body as they possibly could. While both wore looks of sheer revulsion, they clung tightly to the specter of hope that Avery's plan might actually work, voicing silent prayers within their heads.

"Last chance to change your mind," Angelica said.

"If this doesn't work," he said softly, averting his eyes, "you know what to do, right?"

She looked back over her shoulder to Mark, who gave a single nod and double-checked the safety on the pistol.

"Yeah," she whispered, rubbing the back of her arm over the bridge of her nose so that he wouldn't see her tears.

"Don't you dare miss," Avery called back to Mark,

glad that the others couldn't see his lips quiver as he tried to fake a smile, if only for himself. "Don't get it on your skin, Angie."

He sat down on the floor next to Brad, looking nervously at the body. The lips were already beginning to blue, and though the skin had taken on a gray cast, the ulcerations on the man's face were still continuing to grow. Thankful he was covered to the point that he wouldn't be able to smell the bacterial advance and the resulting decay, the evacuated bowels and the festering in the abdomen, he lay back beside the dead man and looked up at Angelica, who had now donned a surgical cap and goggles. He imagined that must have been how he looked to his patients as they gently succumbed to the wiles of the anesthesia.

In one hand she held a wedge-shaped gray sponge about eight inches square, in the other a pair of scissors they'd procured from the radiologist's reading room. Both items shook in her grasp.

He watched her take in a great breath and close her eyes to try to steady her nerves.

"Please just do it," he whispered, closing his eyes.

Marcy took several long steps backwards to keep from being spattered.

There was the soft sound of Angelica's approaching footsteps, followed by the silence where he could only assume she was kneeling across Brad's body from him. Holding his breath, he waited for what he knew was to come. A slight whistling sound preceded the loud *thuck* he knew all too well. It was the sound of steel ripping flesh, though not the gentle hiss of a scalpel parting pliant skin, but the sickly wrenching sound of a surgeon venting his frustration on the body he was unable to save, of the mortician opening a cadaver with all of the grace of a blind man with a hatchet.

The Infected

"Please hurry," he whispered, no longer able to deny the terrible stench that leeched beneath the fabric into his nostrils.

He heard the slurping sound of her inserting her hand into the wound and wriggling around her fingers until she was able to open it wide enough to slide the scissor blades in beside her hand. The hinge on the blades whimpered as she opened it, positioning it for the first cut. Metal scraped metal, followed by the sound of tearing raw meat. She grunted as she pulled on the lip of the maw to help the scissors along. The long clean strokes weren't working so she had to resort to short, choppy cuts, ripping more than slicing, until he heard something sloppy slither to the floor with a slap.

More slurping as she dunked the positioning sponge into the open abdomen, squeezing it to fill it with the welling fluids spilling out of Brad's gut. When the sound stopped, Avery braced himself for what was to come, biting his lip as she expelled the fluid from the sponge, pouring down on him in a thin stream as though he were being urinated upon.

"Jesus," he heard Marcy say from down past his feet, her footsteps leading off into the hallway.

There was light pressure on his chest as Angelica began to run the sponge over him, painting him with the man's death-blood. He could only imagine it; thick and resplendent with corpuscles, the faint green hint from the expunged gallbladder, the brown taint from the wrung liver.

He made a muffled gagging sound as he felt it leeching into his clothing and nuzzling up to his skin, cold and damp like the belly of a serpent.

More slurping sounds as she thrust the sponge back into Brad, sliding it beneath the layer of fat and filling it atop the coils of intestine.

He heard the tap-tap-tap of the blood dripping between his body and Brad's and then another wash of it splash down onto his stomach before she started spreading it around again.

Mark retched, followed by the quick slap of his hand over his mouth and his footsteps heading back down the hallway.

"Let it end," Avery whispered as he forced his mind to wander to a fantasy where he was being anointed with oils like an emperor, rather than drizzled with blood in what could be the final moments of his life.

*   *   *

"Ask him if he's ready," Sarah called back over her shoulder toward the displaced tile. Again, she was poised at the edge of the ceiling preparing to peel back the lead shielding above the wall to look down at the hallway. There was a lot more light this time, coming through the panel directly beside and behind her, where she had fallen through before. It was the same muted red glare, but her eyes had finally adjusted to it.

"Are you ready?" Angelica shouted from the examination room down the hallway.

"Yeah," Mark called back from his post in the threshold between the hall and the waiting room. "Let us know when we have enough room to do this."

"They're all set," Angelica said to Sarah, and then as calmly as possible: "You can do this."

Sarah locked eyes with Angelica through the ceiling. She couldn't tame the shaking in her hands. Finally, with a nod, Sarah ducked back up into the ceiling and took hold of the lead sheet where she had peeled it down before.

She closed her eyes and tried to regulate her breathing as she silently voiced prayers she thought she had forgotten long before.

With a measured sigh, she swallowed her thumping heart and bit her lower lip, summoning her strength for what was to come.

In one motion, she yanked the lead foil down and propelled herself forward until she felt the wall snag her breasts, pried the ceiling tile from the square aluminum frame, and slid it to the side. Her entire head and shoulders hung out over the hallway.

They were everywhere down below, pacing up and down the walls pounding on them like great apes testing the weaknesses in their cage. All eyes snapped in her direction at once and she screamed.

Those eyes.

Fresh blood shining on those orbs as though their eyeballs had been replaced by rubies crammed into bruised and bludgeoned sockets.

Before she could even draw in another breath to replenish her scream, they were sprinting at her. They moved with a fluid grace that was almost serpentine, as though the muscles moved independently of the bony framework. Their speed was staggering. One moment they were twenty paces down the hall, and the next they were right beneath her.

"Are they all down there?" Angelica shouted up to her, but Sarah could hear nothing above her own screams. The bodies beneath her leapt up and swatted at her as though she were a piñata dangling there for their amusement. One slapped a bloody hand on her wrist and the terror drove her out of her right mind, sending her into a screaming fit where she couldn't even control herself. As soon as one scream ended another started.

All she could see were flailing arms with ragged, slashing fingernails and snapping jaws like so many dogs. Split lips were peeled back from cracked and missing bared teeth. Rust-colored clothes hung in tatters from the bodies that were now beginning to look as though the sores were consuming the flesh between.

"Sarah! Can they go now?" Angelica yelled, but she knew there was no way Sarah could hear her over the screaming. She sprinted back out the doorway into the hall. "She can't hear me!"

"What do you mean?" Mark called back.

"She's panicking. I don't think she can tell us if they've all come to her."

"Did you hear that?" Mark turned and said to Avery, who stood at the lobby door leading out to the hallway. All he could focus on was his right arm through the tangle of chairs, grasping the doorknob with his blood-crusted glove. His heart pounded harder than it ever had in his life, but there wasn't enough oxygen reaching his brain. He felt as though he might swoon, the floor teetering beneath him to either side as though he stood on the fulcrum. Black and red spots blotted his vision and though he could see how tightly his hand clenched the knob, he couldn't feel it.

Marcy stood behind him, prepared to lunge forward and hurl her weight against the door to help keep it from opening unexpectedly.

"Come on," he said, his voice faltering. He cleared his throat and yelled it this time. "Come on. Let's do it. Now. Before I can't."

He heard the pounding of Mark's approaching footsteps and the metallic clatter of chair legs being wrenched apart. Flicking the lock on the door, he held it a moment longer, willing his frozen legs to move. His breathing grew short and ragged and he bit down on his cheek so hard that he released a swell of blood.

Like he had practiced it in his mind, he yanked the

177

door open and stepped out into the hallway, closing it tightly behind him and leaning back against it. The hallway directly ahead of him was empty, but he could see all of them down the hall to his right, leaping toward the ceiling where Sarah dangled. Her hair fell down over her face so that he couldn't see her features, contorted by terror. All he could hear were her screams.

Oh, God. Oh, God. Oh, God.

He looked directly ahead and to the left. There was the service elevator, and beside it the doorway that surely led to the staircase that would go to the roof and freedom. Every fiber of his being screamed for him to run while he had the chance. Ten yards and he'd be to the door. He could fly up the stairs and be on the roof before any of those things noticed that he'd even entered the hallway, let alone passed through it.

He'd be damning the others to their fate, though, and he knew it. Even if he could somehow force his trembling legs to run, he would be signing the other four's death certificates.

Grasping the knob with his left hand, his back flat against the door, he turned it to the point that he knew all he would need was to lean backwards and he'd be through it. He balled his right hand into a fist and knocked twice in rapid succession, paused, and then knocked twice more.

"Get her back in!" he heard Mark shout from the other side of the door. He turned to look at Sarah. She was now swatting at them, her fingers curled to claws and slashing at their skin, though it didn't even appear to be slowing them down.

In a single stilled heartbeat, she raised her head and stared directly at him down the hallway. Their eyes locked. The unadulterated fear in her eyes froze him to the bone and suddenly the situation felt real in a way it hadn't before.

"Oh, my God," he whispered aloud, recoiling at the sound of his own voice.

Sarah disappeared back up into the ceiling as though she'd never been there at all and Avery found himself standing alone in the hallway, frighteningly exposed.

The people down there still leapt and snatched at the empty air, though one by one, their frenetic activity ceased until they stood there in a crowd, staring silently up into the rafters.

It was all Avery could do to keep from closing his eyes as the first of them turned to face him. The skin around its right eye appeared to have melted away, the weeping wound shedding tears of blood down the exposed cheekbone and the gritted teeth visible through the dissolved skin on the mandible. He felt his mouth opening to scream so he bit down on his lower lip. Blood spilled out into his mouth and a tatter of nipped flesh dropped onto his tongue, but he managed to keep from screaming. His heart rate accelerated to the point that it felt like a hummingbird lodged in his ribcage, and the breathing through his nose was coming way too fast and in short bursts that could only lead to hyperventilation.

Sarah still screamed from somewhere behind the wall to his right.

The cluster of bodies down the hall began to peel apart. A pair shuffled to the wall directly beneath the hole where Sarah had been dangling above and began pounding on it with their fists so ferociously that Avery was sure their bones had to be broken. Bloody smears covered the wall between them. Sections of drywall had been pounded into craters against the thicker lead lining in the lower portion of the wall. Tatters of bloody flesh hung from where they'd snagged in the seams like used dishrags.

179

The Infected

Avery could feel the clothes tightening on him, constricting as the blood dried.

They were coming toward him now. A wall of bloody humanity stumbling down the hallway. Several broke off and began beating against the wall as the handful that remained walked directly at Avery.

Please, he prayed, pinching his eyes as tightly shut as he could. *Please let it be quick.*

He waited in the darkness in his own skull, expecting to feel teeth sinking into the soft tissue of his throat or hands yanking him in different directions at the same time. He could smell them all around him, every bit as pungent as the innards he had been smeared with. Their footsteps slapped the floor all around him and shoulders bumped into him, nearly causing him to scream.

A fist struck the door beside his head and he could feel it give against his back just slightly. He knew Mark and Marcy were leaning against it from the other side, but they would only be able to stand against their assault for a few moments.

Avery forced himself to open his eyes. There was one directly to his right, thrashing against the door, pounding its fists to pulp that drained down its wrists from its swollen and bruised palms. Its bloody eyes were focused intently on nothing more than the wall in front of it where one fist struck right after the other. He could see the fine mist of blood flying from the exertion, freckling the right side of his goggles. There was another only inches to his left, throwing punches against the door beside his head. Its metacarpals were so fractured and displaced that they stood through the skin on the back of its hands like spikes, yet it continued to beat them against the unyielding wood.

His plan was working just like he'd hoped. Maybe if given enough time they'd be able to see through his ruse, but he wasn't about to give it to them.

He rattled the doorknob in his left hand, cranking it twice to the right, and then twice to the left. Mark's hand closed around it from the other side, his back still leaning against the door and his legs braced in front of him.

Avery felt Mark bang the door with his elbow from the other side and began the silent countdown in his head.

Five.

Dear God, they were all around him now.

Four.

Avery released the doorknob and looked directly into the inhuman eyes of the creature to his left.

Three.

He tried to take in a deep breath to steady his nerves, but he couldn't even make himself breathe.

Two.

Reaching out with trembling hands, he wrapped his fists into the bloody hospital gown on the man's chest.

One.

Throwing himself backwards and bringing the creature to him, he met with the resistance of the door and screamed. Time stood still in that moment as surprise registered on the thing's face. Its eyes only inches from Avery's, he saw a spark of understanding before its lips drew back from crimson-coated teeth. Astoundingly strong fingers closed around his ribs to either side, trying to claw through the duct tape to find him beneath.

The door swung open behind him and he felt himself falling, bringing the monster with him. He managed to stagger a few feet in reverse before their momentum sent them sprawling to the floor. The world flashed by all around him in a whirlwind. Angelica flew by from his left and helped Mark and Marcy force the door closed again.

The Infected

Avery's breath exploded from his collapsed lungs as the other man's weight came down atop him. The pressure from his ribs rose to his throat, intensifying to the point that the red blotches swarmed his vision. A small hand entwined in the thing's bloody hair and yanked its head back before it could snap its bear trap jaws closed on his neck.

Marcy screamed from somewhere out of sight.

A length of steel flashed in front of Avery's eyes, hammering the thing atop him right in the center of its raised face, cracking its nose to the right—

A burst of light and the smell of burnt gunpowder.

Blood and bone exploded outward in all directions, slapping Avery's goggles before he could even raise his hands to cover his ears against the resultant bang.

Sarah's hand swung away with the crown of the man's head as everything beneath patterned the walls. The thing's lower jaw worked up and down, as though trying to speak, never encountering the resistance of the teeth in the upper jaw, which had been turned into projectiles and embedded in the drywall.

It toppled forward atop him, spilling a rush of blood onto the floor beside his ear as though poured from a bucket.

Avery felt his mouth open beneath the cloth and tape, but couldn't hear himself scream with his returned breath, the sound of gunfire still ringing in his ears.

He saw a boot and then the thing fell off of him and to his right. Scurrying away, sliding in the fresh mess of blood, he looked back to the lobby door. Angelica and Marcy still had their backs to it, their torsos popping away from the wood with each blow from the other side, but at least Mark had managed to turn the lock again before rushing to the piles of chairs to drag them back in front of the door. As soon as there was a sizable stack,

Angelica threw herself from the door and helped Mark slide the blockade back into position, allowing Marcy to slip out from behind at the very last second.

Avery turned to Sarah, who still held the top of what had once been a man's head by the hair in her left fist, the smoking pistol in her right. Her face was stark white in contrast to the deep red of the thing's blood spattered all over her. It appeared as though she'd retreated to somewhere deep inside, away from this nightmare, leaving only her body standing there with the expanding puddle of blood spreading around her boots.

"... you...Avery?" Angelica's words faded in and out of the ringing. "I said...all right?"

Avery nodded and tried to sit up, but all of his energy had deserted him and he collapsed back down to the floor.

"I was right," he whispered as the sound of banging fists bludgeoning the walls chased away the ringing.

"He's definitely fine," Angelica said, rolling her eyes.

"Is it...Is it going to be enough?" Avery asked.

"If not," Mark said. "It appears as though we have an unlimited supply."

CHAPTER 12

Colorado Springs Community Hospital

Avery dragged the chair across the lobby, standing on it to punch through the ceiling tiles and then drag the fragmented board back to the floor. He repeated the process over and over until he isolated a sufficiently sturdy beam in the ceiling.

"Toss me the belt," he said to whoever was listening without taking his eyes from the ceiling. When he felt something touch the palm of his lowered hand, he gripped it and brought it up in front of his face.

It was a firm leather belt, but even something that strong might not have enough tensile strength for what he had planned. He looped the end through the buckle once and then strained to reach over the two by four with the end again, passing it to his free hand. Pulling it down until he had enough slack to work with, he tied the ends together, jerking the leather tight against the base of the wood with each successive knot. It was already starting to unravel a little, but once they attached the weight, that ought to serve to tighten it more.

He looked to where the others were standing at the mouth of the rear hallway. Muted gray light crept along the floor from the only window all the way down the hall to the right. It seemed the sun had finally deemed them worthy of its celestial presence.

Mark sat on one of the chairs against the wall, wrapping the duct tape around his ankles to seal his booties in place. He already wore the goggles, and had to repeatedly tug at the light blue cloth covering his face above the silver tape over his mouth to keep the eye slits open.

"Are you ready?" Avery called to him.

Mark walked back to where Angelica was taking advantage of the light to help wrap Marcy into her makeshift contamination suit. There was only so much tape remaining, so none of the others had the liberty of using the extreme amounts Avery had used. A band around their mouths and noses; one around their necks to seal the union of the gowns. Wrists were wrapped over snug white gloves and they wore a single belt of tape around their waists. A wide spiral led down their legs to hold the wrapped fabric in place, terminating in a single circle around the ankles. Even cutting back as they were, Avery worried that there might not be enough tape for five of them.

"Here," Mark whispered, passing the tape to Sarah, who hung back from the others, still clothed in her security attire. She was already drenched with blood, and though none of them wanted to be the one to say it, there was probably no point in taking the time to bind her up like the rest of them. Avery had already noticed the ulcers opening on her cheeks, and while they still looked like little more than superficial lesions, he knew it was only a matter of time. He could see in her eyes that she knew as much too. There was a quiet sense of reservation about her as though she was now only going through the motions.

For whatever reason, she hadn't been able to drop the top of the thing's head, which she carried around like a handbag.

"Grab his legs," Avery said, pointing to where the body lay on the floor between them. "We don't have a whole lot of time to do this. His blood's already beginning to cool and soon enough it will start clotting."

Mark grunted as he hefted the legs from the ground and dragged the corpse through a smear of its own blood, dropping it again to the floor by Avery's chair. He grabbed one of his own and scooted it across the tile with the sound of wrenching metal, shoving it right up against the one Avery stood on.

Neither of them spoke as Mark brought the ankles to his chest and wrapped his arms as tightly around them as he possibly could. Avery transferred his right foot to the second chair to help balance it, opening the loop by the buckle wide as he could. Kicking at the chair, Mark finally raised his foot high enough to balance atop it, and after several bounces, yelled as he lifted the body and climbed onto the chair at the same time. Avery grabbed onto one of the legs with his left arm and helped lift it, baring his teeth against the strain beneath his blood-crusted mask.

Wobbling from side to side, they tried to steady the corpse between them while maintaining their own balance, finally succeeding in raising it to the point that Avery could slide the loop of the belt around the right ankle.

"Got it," he growled, every muscle in his body aching.

Mark hopped off the chair down to the floor and collapsed onto his rear end, his shoulders heaving as he tried to replenish the spent oxygen.

Avery jumped down to the other side and kicked the chairs out of the way.

The body swung between them by one ankle like a deer strung from a tree by hunters. It twirled in slow circles, the loose leg folding at the knee, the limp arms drawing circles in the air a foot above the floor. The gown had apparently been so thick with blood at some point that it was now dried to the man's body, congealed into his chest hairs despite the best efforts of gravity to yank it down over his head.

"Scissors," Avery said, trying not to look at it.

Blood drained from the open esophageal hole like a hose, spilling out from where once the upper half of the head had been, spreading into a widening puddle on the tile.

"Whoever's ready, get underneath it," he said, tightening his grip on the scissors and stabbing them as hard as he could into the lower abdomen when it again swung toward him. The whole corpse shook with the impact, tossing spatters of blood in every direction. Wrapping his left arm around the loose leg for leverage, he jerked the scissors back out, a flume of brown-tinted fluid spouting out behind. He opened the blades as far as he could while still keeping his fingers in the handles, and slashed downward from the initial puncture, tearing through the flesh. With one final whack from the scissors, he ripped the skin all the way down to the top of the abdomen where it snapped off the xiphoid at the end of the sternum. Casting the blades aside, he brought the backs of his hands together and slipped them deep into that ragged maw until he was able to grasp the skin and fat, and yanked them away with a sound like carpet being torn from water-damaged floorboards.

The loops of bowel folded out over his hands and

stretched toward the floor in convoluted loops held together by tightly-stretched ligaments and peritoneum. Slowly, the thin sheath of connective tissue began to tear at gravity's urging, freeing curls of small intestine to slop to the floor. A rush of blood reeking of sepsis and infection splashed down around his feet, washing back up over his shoes.

Mark and Marcy just stared down at the warm lake forming beneath the body, forcing themselves to keep from looking at the eviscerated corpse spinning between them, flashing an empty abdominal cavity where all they could see were two kidneys dangling in front of the lumbar portion of the spine, exposed from within like so many human building blocks.

"Hurry up," Avery shouted. What he'd done affected him on such a primal level that he would have welcomed the release from the acids seething in his guts were it not for the mask over his face. He was a surgeon. In his hands was the power to control life and death. When he stood at the head of the operating table, power coursed through his veins. He was omnipotent, unerring, doing things that only gods could dream of doing. Yet here he was, having stripped God of all His divine mystery, tearing apart his creation with no more care than were he gutting a fish.

As he stared down at the festering mess around his feet, what bothered him the most was that he felt no remorse.

"Oh for God's sake," Angelica said, strapping the last of the tape around her ankles and crawling forward between the dangling arms. She lowered herself to her belly and slid back and forth, wiping it from her gloves onto her face, spreading it over her mouth and cheeks, before flopping over onto her back and wriggling through the diseased mire. A fold of bowel popped under her weight, squeezing out excrement like brown toothpaste.

She crawled out from underneath the body and slipped a couple times before finally gaining her feet. Without looking at the others, she smoothed her palms across her entire body, rehearsing her anatomy in her mind to ensure that she didn't miss a single inch.

Mark slid under the body as the last of the viscera flopped to the ground, leaving only a gentle trickle dripping from the swollen tongue.

He followed Angelica's example, sprawling first on his stomach, and then rolling over onto his back, retching against the smell that was like so many snakes trying to slither up his nostrils and down his throat. With a hideous belch that had surely filled his mouth with bile, he crawled out and scurried up against the reception counter where he fought to choke the vomit back down.

Before Marcy could even fall to the floor, Sarah slid under the thing's head as though she was trying to beat a tag at second.

"What are you doing?" Angelica screamed, hurrying to the smaller woman's side and grabbing her beneath the arms.

"I'm as good as dead anyway," Sarah said, throwing herself away from Angelica. "Look at me! The stuff's already eating through my face and I'm covered in infected blood. I'd be just wasting time by putting on all of that gear."

Angelica didn't know what to say, so she backed a step away and kept her eyes focused on Sarah's.

"All I want," Sarah said, tears budding from the corner of her eyes and draining through the blood on her cheeks. She had to sniff and swallow to again find her voice. "All I want…is to not have to die in this room."

Crawling out of the bloody mess, she spread it all

The Infected

over her body with her left hand, while seating the crown of the skull from the corpse atop her head like a cap. The short dark hair was flattened with blood, ribbons of it trailing down through the mussed blonde.

Marcy dropped to all fours and ducked beneath the arms, doing what looked like the breaststroke in the vile-smelling fluid, smearing it over her face and head while trying not to cover the plastic lens of the goggles. She felt as though with each unit of blood that soaked into the clothing that a portion of her humanity was being stripped away. Deep down, she felt like an animal, wallowing in her kill so that the other animals would smell it on her, fear her. Right now the only thing she truly feared was herself. What else would she be willing to do to survive?

She rolled onto her back, flopping from side to side like a trout on a bank, and then pushed herself out from beneath it. Standing, she held her dripping arms away from her body and eased away from the corpse, turning her back to it.

Avery rolled in the smudged remainder, hoping to merely freshen his coating, until the fluid was dry and crusted on the floor, and then stood.

He looked from one face to the next, trying to find the slits of their eyes through the blood-pocked goggles.

"Let's get this over with," he said, heading directly toward the tangle of chair legs and seats separating them from the pounding on the other side of the door, the frame shivering with each blow.

*   *   *

With their blockade moved to the center of the room, the only thing that stood between them and the living dead was two inches of lead-lined wood. The metal framework had rattled a half-inch from its moorings, and it wouldn't be long before the whole works collapsed inward.

Avery was closest to the door, with his back pressed against the wall, his right arm stretched across the wood, grasping the handle. The others were bunched to his left, waiting breathlessly, packed as closely together as possible so they could remain behind the door when Avery threw it open.

"Everyone ready?" he whispered. "Remember…wait for my signal. We want as many as possible to rush past us before we head out there…Just in case."

He could feel their eyes upon him, feel the terror radiating from them in waves.

The door now wobbled with every blow, knocking his hand from the brass knob now swathed with blood.

"I'll open the door on three," he whispered, finally tearing his eyes away from them so they wouldn't be able to see his fear. "One."

The remaining two counts ticked off in silence, metered only by the throbbing of the wall against their backs. Avery pulled his hand from the knob on three and twisted the lock, hesitating as his shaking hand fought for traction on the smooth knob, finally cranking it to the right.

The door exploded inward, hammering him in the right shoulder and pounding him into the others as racing bodies funneled through into the room. In no more than the time it had taken them to catch their breath, the room was positively crawling with the infected. The fax machine and phone were smashed behind the counter. Chairs were slammed into walls and hurled through the air. One struck the fish tank, shattering the glass and sending a hundred-fifteen gallons of water splashing to the floor.

The Infected

Mark pressed forward into the others as he felt the cold water slap onto his back and drain down his legs.

"Oh shit," he whimpered, imagining the blood washing off his back. "I've got to get out of here!"

He sprinted around the others and ducked out the front door, slamming into one of them and sending it careening to the side.

"Wait," Avery whispered, trying to grab his arm as he raced by.

He glanced back at the room where several of the things were still tossing aside chairs and end tables looking for them. They raced back and forth through the hallway at the back of the department, flashing through the doorway with wild bloody eyes.

Grabbing Angelica by the hand, he broke into a sprint, hauling her around the door and across the threshold into the hallway. He tried to listen for the others' footsteps behind him, but all he could hear was his heart thumping in his temples and his harsh breaths dampening the inside of the mask. Angelica's hand ground his knuckles together as she held far too tightly.

A quick look to his right confirmed that there were a few still attempting to beat their way through the walls. Their eyes shot toward them, hopefully only drawn by the sudden movement.

Avery felt his heart sink when the infected stopped their incessant pounding and took off after them.

"Faster!" he screamed, turning back to the hallway where Mark was ducking behind the door. His footfalls pounded back at them from the hollow cement corridor as he hit the stairs.

Avery swung Angelica through first, bracing the door on his back as he ushered the others past. Marcy and Sarah raced by and he ducked around the door. Through the closing crack he could see them charging down the hallway, even more racing out of the radiology lobby.

They weren't going to make it.

The lock was on the outside of the door so there was absolutely nothing standing between them.

It should have worked, he thought as he leapt the stairs two at a time. *It should have fucking worked!*

There was no reason that he should have been successful when he tried it before but not this time. They'd done everything the same. Maybe there hadn't been enough blood to coat them as thickly as he'd been the first time, but other than that he couldn't think of anything they'd done differently.

None of it mattered now anyway. They were six floors…twelve landings from the roof and there was no way they were going to outrun their pursuit.

The door slammed open behind him, echoing like gunfire in the darkened confines.

Angelica screamed at the sound, spurring her already tired legs to fly up the stairs that much faster. She could barely see Mark's silhouette against the darkness ahead of her, rounding the landing five steps above. He was already gasping for air, his footsteps barely leaving the ground. The sound of thudding feet from behind was like a stampede. She had no idea how many people were behind her, though it sounded like hundreds.

"Go!" Avery's voice called up from below in the darkness. "They're right behind me!"

Marcy screamed in response, urging herself upward so quickly that she could barely keep hold of the railing. She could no longer feel Sarah's presence beside her, but she couldn't even force herself to look back over her shoulder.

Sarah slowed and finally stopped on the landing between the third floor and the fourth. Doubling over, she braced her hands on her knees to suck at the air, which she could feel entering her mouth through a hole in her cheek, chilling her teeth and tickling her tongue. She couldn't bring herself to run any farther. A momentary calm settled over her and she pulled her gun from the holster and the lone bullet from her right pants pocket. Ejecting the magazine, she placed the bullet in the top and with a click, slammed the mag back in and chambered the load.

"What are you doing?" Avery shouted, grabbing her by the arm as he dashed past, but she didn't budge.

"Just keep going," she said, shrugging out of his grasp.

"They're right behind me! You need to—"

"Go!" she shouted.

He couldn't force her to go against her will or she'd be condemning them both. All he could do was start running again and hope that she changed her mind at the last second.

"Sarah!" Mark called down from above at the sound of shouting. He turned and nearly collided with Angelica, stepping to the side just in time to keep from sending them both toppling to the ground.

"Come on!" Angelica screamed, grabbing him by the elbow.

"We can't go without her."

"There's no time to argue."

"I'll catch up."

"No you won't."

"Please," Mark said, lowering his voice. "I can't leave her…"

The thunder of footsteps grew deafening, pounding like the drumbeats of cannibalistic natives.

Angelica released his elbow and was helpless but to watch his shape turn and run in the opposite direction, bounding past Marcy and down the stairs.

The *snick* of his magazine being slammed into the weapon echoed in the stairwell.

"Hurry," Angelica said, grabbing Marcy by the hand and hustling her up the stairs. The darkness seemed to grow thicker with each advancing step, their legs heavier.

Avery didn't even see Mark racing down the stairs until he was already past him.

"Sarah," Mark called.

"Get out of here!"

"You can't stand against them with one bullet."

"And how much better do you think we'll do with two?"

"It's me they're after," he said, alighting beside her on the landing. "I think the fish tank washed the blood off my back."

Footsteps pounded on the landing ten stairs down, the railing groaning against its moorings as they made the turn beneath.

"I'm already infected, Mark."

"Run while you can."

"It's too late for me."

"We had a deal," he said, taking her by the hand.

They were so close now their ragged breathing was audible over the thunder of their tread.

"Are you sure?" she asked, raising the pistol and pointing it straight at his head.

He merely leaned forward and placed his forehead against the tip of the barrel in response, offering his to her.

She matched his gesture, both of them standing a paltry foot from one another.

"Now," she whispered as the wave of bodies washed over them. Fingernails tore into flesh and teeth snapped shut through human meat.

Ba-Bang!

The Infected

Avery turned at the sound of gunfire two flights down. He could no longer hear the sound of rushing footsteps, but rather the scrabbling sound of chaos highlighted by ripping fabric and tearing flesh.

"Jesus," he whispered, his legs finally kicking into gear again.

He ran upward with only the thumping of twin footsteps above joining his own.

*   *   *

Angelica threw open the door to the roof, stumbling into the morning light and nearly falling on her face from sheer exhaustion. She managed to grab onto the railing leading up the sloped surface to the helipad, staring up along the concrete walkway into the sky above the city. She'd been up there hundreds of times before to unload patients from the Flight for Life choppers and rush them down into the emergency room, but she'd never been this glad to see it. Still holding Marcy's hand, panting, the two stumbled up the slant and onto the flat surface. There was an enormous yellow circle painted in the center with a smaller X in the middle.

She turned in time to see Avery burst through the doorway. He slipped through the closing door and slammed it shut with his back.

"Help me find something to barricade this with!" he shouted.

Angelica spun in a circle, looking for anything at all they could lean up against the door, but there was nothing. There were several large air conditioner units, but she feared that even if she knew how to disconnect them, by the time she did they'd need a mop to gather enough of her to bury. Large metal pipes, faded to a dingy rust color, stood from the roof, running into

Michael McBride

various machines that looked more like small sheds.

They'd made it this far only to die up here.

"There," Marcy said, pointing to a large cement planter filled with various perennials just above the door and to the right against the railing. There was a small bench and a standing ashtray beside it.

All three converged on the waist-high circular planter at the same time. Grabbing onto the raised lip, they were able to twist it back and forth until it started to move. Progress was maddeningly slow, but eventually they were able to wriggle it around the end of the railing onto the smooth concrete where they could slide it more easily down the slanted walkway until they reached the door. Shoving it as far as it would go, Avery stepped to the side and tried jerking on the handle, but the door wouldn't even budge. They would have the leverage from the inside, but he knew this was a stall tactic at best anyway.

There had been no sound of footsteps following them up the stairwell after the gunfire. If his theory was correct and those things had been able to smell one of them, then they must have finished off whoever it had been. His mind rehearsed the variables that might have led to one of them being able to be tracked, but he needed to focus on the present. They were on the roof with no form of communication device. No food. No water.

No hope.

He walked past the others up the incline and around to where the planter had been. Lifting one end of the bench, he raised it until he could flip it back over the railing and onto the planter below. The iron frame bent over the enormous cement container, cracking it in the process and loosing a stream of dirt like sand from an hourglass down its side. He tossed the ashtray down into the jumble as an afterthought.

"What now?" Marcy asked, shielding her eyes

197

against the rising sun and looking out over the city.

"I don't know," Avery said, walking toward the western edge of the building, his shadow stretching up over the three-foot retaining wall and off into the nothingness. Bracing his hands on the round rail that ran inches above the wall, he stared out over the city.

Downtown rose from a ring of deciduous green like fingers breaking through the ground, a body clawing out of the grave. A black cloud of smoke hung over it like smog, shifting just slightly at the behest of the wind to reveal the amber glow of flames. The Holly Sugar building, taller than all the rest, was now a column of charcoal preparing to crumble back to the earth. Against the serene backdrop of the blue Rocky Mountains, framing the bald pate of Pikes Peak, the whole vision was surreal, an apocalyptic vision stolen from the dreams of a madman. The city stretched to either side against the foothills lining the mountains, interspersed with clusters of green. The smaller bungalows of the downtown area gave way to larger and newer homes winding into the hills. Smoke rose in pillars sporadically across the plains from neighborhoods and shopping centers alike. Flashing lights from emergency vehicles dotted the landscape, though he couldn't hear a single siren. He could only vaguely discern the outline of the highway, but there were no sparkles from the rooftops of cars speeding toward their destinations, only tangles of wreckage issuing more smoke into the gray sky.

"Is it possible that the whole city is infected by now?" Angelica asked, mesmerized by the stillness, the only movement belonging to the churning towers of smoke joining with the thickening clouds overhead.

"How long did it take for it to infect the entire hospital? Maybe a couple of hours?"

"There still have to be tens of thousands of people

who haven't come in contact with any of the carriers."

"I'm sure…and right now they're probably holed up in their basements watching the world fall to pieces around them on CNN."

He leaned over the rail and looked all the way down at the emergency bay in front of the hospital. The usually busy streets were empty, save for the full measure of cars parallel parked to either side of the road and a handful locked together in random snarls of twisted metal. A news van had been toppled on its side atop the curb, the extended satellite dish on the roof having smashed through the front window of a pizzeria. A herd of people dashed across the street and disappeared into the parking structure. Another tore through the middle of the park. He watched long enough to see a single woman step from around the side of her house, only to be run down out of sight, her dying scream trilling in the silence.

"Hunting parties," he whispered, raising his eyes again to the horizon.

"I don't want to die," Marcy whispered.

Angelica and Avery looked to her, but could offer no solace.

CHAPTER 13

Colorado Springs Community Hospital

Sweat drained down her face beneath her mask, twirling along her neck and welling at the base of her spine. Her palms were wet beneath her gloves, the moisture making her upper thighs cling together. More than anything, she wanted to strip out of all the extra layers, but that would surely mean her death. So she sat, leaning against the only slightly elevated roof to the north of the helipad, clinging to what little shadow arced down, dehydrating like a tomato on a sunny ledge. She licked the sweat on her upper lip, but it was only momentarily satisfying as the salt worsened the feeling of being wrung like a dishrag.

Angelica rose from her haunches if for no other reason than to let as much sweat as she could race down her legs to her feet, bringing with it a momentary cooling sensation.

At least on the roof they were privy to what little wind stirred the sweltering day, though it wasn't nearly enough to keep the expanding blazes from filling the sky with smoke and ash. She coughed under the mask, wishing she could rub her eyes, and walked over to where Avery was standing at the southern end of the roof, staring down upon the city below.

"See anything yet?"

Avery turned to look at her, the fabric around his eyes a deeper blue with his saturated sweat, the bottom of his goggles filling with it.

"Look down there," he said, pointing toward what looked like several small apartment buildings. "Those are the dorms for the Olympic Training Center."

Smooth stretches of emerald lawn reached back from the building toward a red-rubber track and several playing fields enclosed by chain link fences. Tall brown bleachers towered over them at seemingly random intervals. The dorms reflected the boxy style of the sixties with square windows lining each of the three levels.

"I don't see anything."

"Give it a minute," he said, trying to brush back the dripping bangs that had fallen down on his forehead through the torn gown.

After a moment, the front door opened at the top of a short concrete staircase at the front of the building. Not all the way. Just wide enough to show a sliver of black.

"He doesn't have a chance," Avery said. "The first four didn't even make it to the bleachers."

The door opened just a fraction wider so they could see the glimpse of a face. In one swift motion, the door was thrown back and a man in a navy blue sweat suit sprinted out onto the landing and leapt from the steps, hitting the grass at a sprint. He had taken no more than three enormous strides when someone stepped out from behind the trunk of a towering elm. Two more people crawled out from beneath the lower rows of bleachers, throwing themselves forward and into a dash like sprinters exploding from the blocks.

The Infected

The man in blue hesitated, looking first at the person running at him from the left and then at the two coming straight at him. He stopped and turned on a dime, sprinting back in the direction from which he had come, but a man and a woman rounded the corner from the other side of the building, effectively cutting off his path back to the front door.

There were cries of warning from the windows of the dorm, where other heads had appeared to shout through the screen.

He glanced up at them only briefly before veering to his right. It looked as though he found another gear, widening the distance between him and his pursuit more and more with each stride. Giving wide berth to the row of elms at the edge of the property, he headed directly for the parking lot. There were only a dozen cars in there belonging to the training staff, but beyond lay the deserted street, across which was a Taco Bell with the windows smashed out and a Dodge Neon burning in the parking lot.

Weaving through the cars, he reached the curb, now a good twenty yards ahead of his closest pursuer, a raven-haired woman in a hospital gown. He feinted to the left and then ran to the right, gaining momentum on the slight decline.

"He's going to try to get here," Angelica gasped.

"No!" Avery shouted, waving his arms. "Go away!"

The man never looked up.

Angelica turned and started to run for the door leading back into the building, but Avery grabbed her by the arm.

"Let me go! If we don't get down there—"

"There's nothing we can do," Avery shouted into her face.

"We can't just let him die."

"Even if he makes it here, they'll smell him immediately."

"His death won't be on my conscience," Angelica snapped, wrenching her arm out of Avery's grasp and running for the door.

Avery looked back over the railing in time to see the man leap up onto the curb and cut across the lawn toward the emergency entrance. He only made it another five yards before a shadow lunged out from beneath a juniper shrub and clipped his ankles, sending him sprawling face-first onto the grass. Before his momentum stopped, several others raced out from where they'd been hiding, appearing as though materializing from the ether.

The runner rocked his head back and let out a single scream cut short by the teeth that tore out his windpipe.

Angelica stopped where she was, her hands still grappling with the bench she was trying to pry from atop the planter. Slowly, she turned to face Avery.

He shook his head.

Letting the iron rails clatter back into place, she headed back up the incline and over beside him.

"There wasn't a thing you could have done," he said, wrapping his arm over her shoulder and drawing her to him.

She sniffed and looked up at him.

"I could have *tried*," she said, leaning her head back into him and looking into the ash-clogged sky, careful not to get too close to the edge for fear she might be able to look down and see what had become of the man she'd hoped to save.

*   *   *

Marcy stood apart from the others, leaning against the rail on the east side of the building, looking down at the street below. She heard the others talking, but couldn't bring herself to break away from her post. Closing her eyes, she felt the wind on her face and imagined that she was a butterfly, gliding on the swirling currents, hovering above a glimmering green park where there were no monsters waiting to tear out her jugular. Where her red wings shimmered with golden dust, rather than a coating of dried blood soaking deeper within along with her sweat, nearly to her skin.

All she would have to do is climb up on the rail, raise her wings out beside her, and drift off into the clouds. In that moment she would be the butterfly, and then she would be no more.

As a trauma nurse, she'd seen more than her share of death. It was a rare night when someone didn't code on one of her beds. But life surrounded a person, even in death. There was something spiritual about the passing as a loved one knelt beside the bed with his wife's hand in his, crying onto the back of her wrist; the chaplain giving a hurried blessing or hearing a last minute confession from the corner of the room while surgeons prepared to crack the patient's chest. A woman simply closing her eyes at the end of a long journey with the morning sunlight slanting into the room through the blinds above the head of her bed. There was beauty in death like there was beauty in life; there was a divine grace in the ascension of the spirit.

But this...this was different.

There was no beauty in being butchered. There was nothing spiritual about being run down like an animal and savagely torn apart with teeth and clawed fingers.

There was now only death.

Only pain.

Only suffering.

There was no reward to be found beyond the pearly

gates, no warmth in consumption by the light. All that was in store after a brutal and shocking death was the prospect of being reborn without that which makes us human. Without laughter. Without love. Without compassion. Without mercy.

Without a soul.

She raised her face to the sky and felt the warmth of the sun through her mask, though today the heavens tasted of ash. God was still up there somewhere, wasn't He?

Lowering her chin, she opened her eyes and stepped away from the wall at last. Perhaps there would be beauty in exiting this mortal plain as a butterfly, but there would be none being peeled from the road beneath by greedy hands and shoveled into starving mouths full of broken teeth. If there was no longer any other beauty in the world, then she would cling desperately to the flower of life she held in her heart and would nurture it for as long as she was able.

She could fly anytime.

Any time at—

She whirled and looked back over her shoulder at the sound that had roused her from her trance.

Had it been thunder?

No. She could still hear it.

Easing closer to the railing, she tried to divine the origin of the sound, only it seemed to be coming from all across the eastern horizon at the same time.

"Do you guys hear that?" she asked softly for fear of drowning out the low thrumming sound with her own voice. She knew they couldn't have heard her, but she didn't want to avert her eyes for even a second for fear she might miss it.

A helicopter appeared over the horizon, what little sun permeated the smoke glinting from its windshield. It moved slowly, appearing to linger over the neighborhoods gushing black smoke up into the sky, circling them, before moving on to another area.

"There's a helicopter!" she screamed to the others, who were already shielding their eyes and looking to the east.

Marcy ran over to them, a huge smile hidden beneath her mask.

"We need to get their attention," Avery said, spinning to look for anything he could use to signal to them.

"Hey!" Angelica shouted, jumping and waving her arms above her head.

Marcy did the same, running right to the center of the helipad.

Avery dashed along the western half-wall to the area where the pot and bench had been, but there was nothing else over there besides the scarred roof where they'd been. Looking down the ramp to the barricaded door, he momentarily entertained the notion of going back into the building, but the thought was more than he could bear. Heading toward the eastern side, he looked at all of the ductwork and pipes rising out of the tarred surface. Aluminum ducts large enough to crawl through breached the ceiling beneath before slanting at angles into the various grated units that had to have been filters or fans or something of that nature. His HVAC knowledge was limited to the movies and commercials.

It didn't look like there was anything potentially useful over there either, and from where he stood, he could clearly see that the rest of the roof was bare.

"They can't see us!" Marcy screamed, jumping and flailing more urgently.

"We just have to get their attention," Angelica said, panting. She was dripping with sweat now. "They'll have to see us eventually."

Avery looked up at the chopper, which appeared to now be banking away from them.

"No, no, no," he said, rushing back over to what appeared to be a water pipe. It came up several feet from the roof before making a U-turn and dropping six inches to plug into some sort of pressure gauge. He raised his right foot and kicked it, over and over, throwing all of his weight behind it. The rubber seal around the base of the pipe against the roof broke away first, the whole works bending violently back and forth. Lips curling back from grinding teeth, he grunted with the exertion, banging and banging until with a wrenching sound, the pipe broke away from the coupling just beneath the surface.

Avery stumbled backwards as a spire of water fired a hundred feet up from the roof like a rocket launching, seemingly hovering in the stratosphere before falling again like rain.

Droplets pelted him all over his head and shoulders as he ran toward the center of the roof where Angelica and Marcy were still flapping their arms above their heads.

The helicopter was now clear off to the right and appeared to be following the circuitous route of the highway toward downtown to the west.

"Hey!" he screamed, his parched voice cracking.

A fine mist of water filled the air around them from where they could hear the returning waterfall pounding the roof.

Marcy had to double over to cough out the stale smoke in her lungs.

The windshield of the distant helicopter winked with a stray ray of sunshine perforating the smoke, and then banked toward them.

"It's coming!" Angelica shouted, spontaneous tears streaming down her cheeks with the sweat.

The Infected

Avery whooped and Marcy fell to her knees, dropping her forehead to her clasped hands in prayer while whispering "Thank you, thank you, thank you."

CHAPTER 14

Colorado Springs Community Hospital

"You did it," Angelica said, throwing her arms around Avery and twirling him in a circle.

Marcy rose from her knees and hugged them both.

In all of their lives, none of them had ever known such an overwhelming sense of relief and elation. It was overpowering; an all-consuming euphoria.

The helicopter rose steadily as it drew closer and they were able to tell that it was white, which ruled out a Flight for Life chopper, but it didn't matter. They could clearly see two figures through the front windshield, which dimly reflected the gray sky.

"Come on," Avery said, having to raise his voice over the grumble of the helicopter blades, growing louder with each passing second. "We need to give them room to land."

He pulled Angelica and Marcy from the center of the helipad, breaking their joyous celebration. Taking each by the hand, he led them toward the western edge where they had to tuck their chins to their chests and lean into the ferocious wind being driven before the chopper, throwing sheeting water into their faces like a torrential downpour.

Angelica slapped the water from her goggles and held her hand over the ridge of her brows to try to see through all of the droplets as the helicopter hovered above the roof, turning sideways just enough for them to see the News 4 logo on the side door. The pilot came into view, wearing a white helmet with sound-damping cans over his ears, a thin black microphone reaching across his mouth, which moved around soundless words.

All they could hear was the deafening thunder of the rotor as it slowly dropped toward the helipad, alighting softly on the long white runners.

With the tempestuous gusts thrown before the blades trying to force them back, all three leaned into the wind and charged toward the helicopter, keeping their heads down as far as they could. Drops of water splashed in their faces as though thrown before waves crashing against the breakers.

The pilot's door opened and a man bounded down onto the roof. He wore khaki cargo pants and hiking boots with a navy blue windbreaker featuring the News 4 emblem on the left breast. It billowed around him like a windsock, inflating with the rush of air.

"Thank you so much!" Marcy shouted over the roar.

"What the hell are you guys wearing?" he yelled, stopping once he got close enough to see the brown blood stains covering them.

"We'll explain when we're in the air," Angelica said. "For now, just please get us out of here."

Avery looked down at his arms. The water had nearly completely washed the blood from his powdery white gloves, his arms now soaked to the point that the blood had diffused on the yellow smock to a deep manila.

"Shit," he whispered, looking quickly up to the pilot.

"We aren't taking you guys anywhere like that!" he shouted. They could see themselves in the reflective silver surface of his glasses, heads and legs powder blue and wrapped with peeling gray tape, torsos yellow and drenched, crusted with blood.

"Do they have the disease?" the man called from the copilot's seat, crawling over so that his head hung out the door. Angelica recognized his face from the side of a bus, though couldn't recall the man's name.

"I don't care," the pilot said. "Either they take off all of those clothes or they aren't getting in my chopper."

"We don't have time to argue this," Avery said.

"Please just let us on!" Marcy cried.

"You take that stuff off first or you aren't getting anywhere near this cockpit." He turned and headed back toward the open door.

With a blur of motion, a body flew past right in front of their eyes, bending the pilot in half sideways and driving him to the ground. He didn't even have time to scream before he was rolled onto his back and a woman bit down right over his mouth, tearing his lips and a good measure of his cheeks away. Skeletal teeth exposed, he rocked back and opened his mouth, but she darted back down for him again in what looked like a kiss of carnal lust, only this time when she recoiled, the bloody stump of his tongue dangled from her teeth.

"Oh my God," Angelica screamed, backing away.

Where had that woman come from?

Angelica looked to her left toward the bottom of the ramp where they'd blocked the door, but she couldn't even see the cracked cement planter or the door leaning askew from its hinges as a flood of bodies poured out of the doorway, leaping over the toppled bench.

They hadn't heard them breaking down the door over the thrum of the blades.

The Infected

"Get off of him!" Avery shouted, hurling himself at the woman to knock her off of the pilot, who merely rolled over and clasped his mouth, blood pouring through the gaps in his fingers.

The woman threw Avery from atop her as easily as a bed sheet and scrabbled after the pilot, leaping onto his back and flattening him on the roof. She buried her face in the back of his neck and started thrashing from side to side, blood splashing out from around the seal of her lips.

Marcy staggered backwards, screaming, both trembling hands covering her face.

Avery rose to his feet and headed for the helicopter. The man leaning over the seat from the other side just stared blindly at him, frozen in panic. A shape passed across the side window behind him and Avery threw up his arms to shield his face from the explosion of glass. A fist shot through, blood gushing from the fresh lacerations and grabbed onto the man's back. He screamed at the top of his lungs, spun around, and kicked at the man grasping the back of his shirt. The jagged glass rimming the shattered window sawed at the thing's arm, clipping the brachial artery, which spurted streams across the other man's slacks.

Avery lunged forward and reached for the copilot, grabbing him beneath the left arm and trying to haul him forward.

"Let go of me!" the man screamed. He shoved Avery back at the same time as he booted the creature leaning through the window.

Avery stumbled away, forcing his arms to keep from pinwheeling for fear of shoving his hands up into the lethal blades. He landed on his rear end and toppled to his back.

The man in the helicopter grabbed for the control stick in front of the pilot's seat and jerked up on it, still kicking at the arm that refused to let go of his shirt. The chopper rose a couple of feet from the ground before dropping back down and bouncing off the roof.

Avery scurried away as the twirling blades dipped toward him.

The woman who'd taken down the pilot, her face shimmering with blood, charged at the open door of the chopper, only to meet with the blades and have everything above her stomach liquefied. The two stumps of arms dropped to the ground and the body fell forward to its knees, finally toppling forward with a rush of blood and organs.

Trying to scoot closer to the controls, the man pulled back on the stick again as three more people threw themselves against the side of the cockpit beside the one still struggling to clamber through the window.

The chopper elevated another couple of feet before what looked like half a dozen bodies launched themselves against the front windshield. It began to rise again, canting away from Avery as the right rail struggled against the weight of the people standing atop it and clinging to it.

A fist smashed through the front windshield and the man threw himself back in surprise, giving the toggle a firm yank. The left side of the helicopter rose while the right side dipped, the blades carving right through the roof and sending splinters and mortar in all direction. A crimson rain filled the sky from the bodies trapped beneath, throwing chunks of flesh and disembodied parts in all directions.

Avery yanked Angelica's arm, pulling her down to the ground and rolling atop her, shielding their heads with his arms.

The entire tail of the 'copter swung to the right as the main blades bent and gouged into the building, stopping them right where they were, but transferring their inertia. The man in the pilot seat was thrown out the open door, where he met with the edge of one of the stilled blades. It hacked right into his face like the blade of an ax, tearing off the top of his head and sending his body flipping into the air. Arms flailing limply, sloppy matter poured from what little remained of the cranium as the corpse flew over the western retaining wall.

The rear end of the chopper cart-wheeled over the front and slammed down on the ramp by the door, the blades still spinning, tearing through the men and women charging through the doorway with a spray of blood that covered the rooftop. As soon as the tail hit the ground, the helicopter exploded into an enormous fireball.

Avery felt the heat wash over his back, cooking his damp clothing so quickly that it felt as though he was being scalded. Angelica screamed underneath him, but all he could see of her was a heat wave-contorted vision of her face as though in a funhouse mirror.

The grumble of the explosion faded, leaving only the crackling laughter of flames consuming the rooftop.

Avery climbed off of Angelica and winced at the pain in his back. It felt as though he'd been scorched by a hot iron from his heels to his shoulders.

"Are you okay?" he asked, kneeling over her.

"Yeah. You?"

He nodded and looked back over his right shoulder. Glass covered the entire roof like a million jewels refracting the blaze. Two of the blades jutted out of the roof at a forty-five degree angle just outside of the landing circle, the others mangled behind the smoldering black wreckage. The cockpit was smashed nearly flat, though the seats still burned amidst the crumple of electronic components. Fifteen foot flames consumed the point where the tail had entered the building through the smashed doorway, already beginning to eat through the charcoaled walls beside it. There was a blackened arm five feet away, the diminutive yellow flames gnawing through flesh split like a hotdog and seeping amber-colored pus. Beyond it was a cooking foot. Avery had to turn away before he recognized the other pieces scattered all around.

The aroma drifting from them made his mouth water.

"Where's Marcy?" Angelica asked, pushing herself to her feet. She swayed momentarily before righting her equilibrium, and then turned in a circle.

Black smoke gusted at them from the wreckage, bringing with it the gut-wrenching stench of combustible fumes.

Marcy moaned from where she was crumpled against the retaining wall, her head propped awkwardly erect, her shoulders heaped against the concrete. The left half of the gown wrapped around her face was burned back from her black skin, the edges still smoldering. The left lens of the goggles was warped from where it had begun to melt.

Angelica rushed to her side, dropping to her knees.

"Talk to me, Marcy."

"It hurts, Dr. Morgan," she whimpered.

"Your face?"

"What's wrong with my face?"

"Isn't that where you hurt?"

"No...my back. Tell me what's wrong with my face!"

"It's just a little burnt, Marcy. Purely superficial. Where does your back hurt?"

"Upper thoracic."

"Squeeze my hand," Angelica said, looking up through the swirling smoke toward the doorway to make sure that no one was coming. The fire was spreading, eating deeper into the building and sending the flames up into the sky with a tower of churning ebony smoke.

Marcy's grip tightened around Angelica's hand, though nowhere near as tightly as Angelica would have liked.

"Can you stand?"

Marcy winced when she tried to nod, but allowed Angelica to pull her gently to her feet.

The entire rooftop was awash with smoke, the crackling of the blaze growing louder and louder as the temperature rose steadily. Gray ash was already starting to cling to the masks over their mouths and noses where the fabric filtered it.

"What are we going to do now?" Angelica asked, hobbling up to Avery with her arm around Marcy's waist. While Marcy could walk under her own power, she was noticeably weak and needed help with her balance.

"I don't know," Avery said, surveying the rooftop. The flames had already eroded the roof beneath the helicopter and were beginning to burn through in random sections. It was only a matter of time before the entire roof collapsed and dropped them into the fire undoubtedly burning below where the gas drained through the ceiling. He imagined the whole works falling inward in a shower of ash and debris. But what options did they have? They could either run back into the building through the wall of fire and hope they made it back out before being engulfed by flames and risk being savaged by the people down there, or they could go over the wall where at least death would be merciful and quick.

"Since the railings are supported by the outer framework of the building, if we stay close to them, we should have a better chance of surviving if the roof collapses," Angelica said.

"And then what?" Avery asked in little more than a whisper. "It's only a matter of time before that collapses as well."

"What about using the fire to our advantage and trying to knock down a section of the roof now before the fire gets too bad. We can lower ourselves to the level under us and—"

"And what? Be under the roof when it falls down on our heads?"

"What do you propose we do then, Avery?"

He looked off to his left over the side. The cars parked along the curb below looked no bigger than the Matchbox ones he'd played with as a child. By the time they reached one of the trees below, they'd be moving at such a great speed that the branches would surely impale them rather than slowing their descent. Once in medical school he'd seen what remained of a jumper from the twelfth story of an apartment building. The man's bones had been ground to powder by the impact and his innards pulped. He was more like a sac of jelly under a skin of flesh than anything remotely human.

"You're out of your mind," she snapped. "Why would you even think it?"

He merely shook his head.

"I'm out of ideas, Angie. We're looking at not choosing how we live, but rather how we die, and I, for one, like the prospect of being burned or buried alive far less than the idea of simply closing my eyes and taking a leap."

"We aren't to that point yet," Marcy whispered, raising her head. Tears poured down her black cheek from her left eye, which appeared incapable of stalling their descent. It moved, but in labored twitches following the right eye as though in stop-motion animation.

With a loud crash, the roof gave way beneath the

weight of the chopper, crumbling away and dropping it a dozen feet into the room below with the expulsion of a mushroom cloud of fiery ash. The ground canted beneath their feet, slanting slightly toward the gaping hole in the center of the roof from which flames grew in defiance of the sky.

Avery was the first to feel the heat through the soles of his shoes, raising his right foot from the roof to inspect it. The surgical bootie was burned away and the tread on the soles of his loafers was beginning to fade as the rubber melted.

There was nothing left to do now but die.

A great wind arose from behind, blowing the swirling black smoke away from them and over the opposite side of the roof, sending them staggering forward against the ferocious gale. It sounded like a storm had crept up on them from behind, thunder rocking the ground beneath them and shivering up their legs. Shielding their eyes, they turned into what felt like a hurricane, grasping for the railing to keep from being thrown backwards into the widening maw of flames.

There was another helicopter beside the building, its side to them. With the olive green paint and the sheer enormity of it, there was no mistaking the fact that it was military. What looked like twin rocket engines were mounted to either side of the rotor, the air wavering with heat behind their exit ports while they screamed beneath the roaring blades. A man stood in the open doorway leading into the cargo area behind an enormous gun on a tripod. It looked large enough to punch a hole straight through an elephant and still topple a Jeep on the other side. The soldier was in full camouflaged fatigues with a green helmet that sat high on his head and a clear shield over his eyes.

Avery was sure his heart stopped when the man

leveled the wide circular barrel of the gun on his chest. It wasn't a single barrel as he'd initially thought, but several smaller barrels in a ring.

"Are you infected?" a voice boomed from a speaker on the side of the chopper.

"No!" Angelica screamed back.

Avery couldn't find the air to breathe, let alone speak.

The man in the open sliding doorway looked over his shoulder to the pilot and nodded, the weapon never once flinching.

Avery was prepared for the flash of muzzle flare and the whir of the spinning barrel, knowing full well that by the time he even felt the bullets tearing through his chest there would be a gaping wound the size of a basketball.

Slowly, the soldier lowered the gun and pulled his sidearm from his hip.

"We can't set down on the roof," presumably the voice of the pilot announced. "You're going to have to step across onto the runner."

His heartbeat returning in pounding waves, Avery turned to Angelica and shared a panicked look.

Another soldier stepped into view and stood beside the other. Both men lowered a foot out onto the runner and reached as far as they could across the fatal gap.

"Go," Avery said, shoving Angelica forward.

"No!" the first soldier shouted. "Send the big one across first to help us grab the others."

Avery pointed at his chest and mouthed the word me, knowing full well they wouldn't be able to see his lips through the duct tape.

"Hurry up!" the second shouted.

Avery climbed up on top of the retaining wall, slipping his toes beneath the rail. He couldn't bring himself to tear his hands from it with the wind blowing at him from the massive swirling blades. It felt like someone was shoving him back as he teetered on the edge, staring down several hundred feet to the parking lot below.

"Come on!" one of the men shouted.

Avery raised a shaking hand from the rail and reached toward the chopper, but quickly jerked it back and grasped the railing.

"Listen to me," the first soldier shouted. Avery raised his eyes to meet the man's. He couldn't have been out of his twenties, his goatee still as thin as a teenager's. "We don't have time to mess around here. That roof could collapse at any minute."

Avery looked back over his shoulder to the helipad, where the flames now had to be close to a story high.

"Look at me!" the soldier yelled, drawing Avery's eyes back to his. "All you have to do is stand up and take a single step forward. We'll grab your arms. You just focus on planting your right foot on the rail."

People congregated on the ground way down beneath him in a swirling cluster that reminded him of gators at the bottom of a pit.

"Jesus," Avery whispered.

"Keep your eyes on mine! Look up. That's right. Keep looking straight at me."

Avery rose on trembling legs, holding his arms out to either side like a tightrope walker for balance. Slowly, he brought his arms out in front of him and reached across the chasm, swaying like a palm before a hurricane. Hands clasped around his wrists and drew him out over the nothingness.

"Wait!" Avery shouted, pulling his right toes from beneath the rail and stepping across it. He did the same with his left until he felt like a diver poised on the edge of a diving board.

"Come on!" the second man yelled.

Avery drew in a deep breath and stepped forward, watching his right foot alight on the rail. Before he had a chance to expel that inhalation, the men had yanked him into the helicopter on his chest.

"Get up and help us with the others," one of them shouted without turning from the open doorway.

Avery rose and again approached the door. There were three gray seats with black harnesses to either side of him in the thin aisle, those on his left backing up against the twin seats in the cockpit. All he could see of either of the soldiers up there were the tops of their helmets and their arms reaching toward the control console. The pilot held a thick control stick that looked like it had six buttons or dials on its large rectangular head, while the copilot to his right poked at a series of touch-screen monitors.

"Send the next one across!" the man to Avery's left shouted as he worked his way between them, grabbing onto the tripod bolted to the floor beneath the large gun and reaching out to help.

"You go first," Angelica said, taking Marcy by the right arm and guiding her toward the ledge.

"I can't do this," Marcy said as she raised her right foot up onto the short wall.

"Yes, you can. Lean on me."

Marcy's grip on her shoulder was ferocious, pinching the muscles so tightly that a stinging sensation stretched up Angelica's neck behind her ear. She braced her hands on Marcy's rear and helped her to find her balance with both feet up on the wall.

"You're almost there," Angelica said through grated teeth.

"Reach for us!" Avery called across to her.

"I'm trying!" Marcy screamed.

"Just a little farther," Angelica said, "I've got your

legs, Marcy. Don't worry about falling. Just try to — "

A blur of fire streaked in front of Angelica. All she saw was a flash of light and felt heat on her face before she was thrown to the side.

Marcy screamed and grabbed onto the rail, perching up there like a stone gargoyle.

Angelica hit the ground on her left shoulder and barely kept her head from ricocheting off the molten roof.

"No!" she shouted, trying to get her elbows beneath her to push herself up.

There was a woman standing behind Marcy in Angelica's stead, both arms wrapped around Marcy's waist, jerking frantically to try to yank her down from the railing. There was nothing left of the woman's hair but the coating of charcoal on her bald pate, flames rising from her scalp like snakes on the head of a gorgon. Her eyelids had burned back to crisp curls while blood poured from her eyeballs that now appeared incapable of sight. With each heartbeat, the woman's skin grew darker and darker until the flames began to dwindle with so little flesh left to consume, flapping away from her at the urging of the wicked wind.

Marcy's yellow isolation gown lit up, catching fire as easily as if it had been coated with gasoline.

"Let her go!" Angelica screamed, jumping to her feet. She barreled toward the woman who didn't even look at her, lowering her shoulder and trying to bowl her over.

Marcy tumbled backwards from the wall as the woman wrenched her away. Angelica slammed into both of them, sending all three of them to the ground.

"Get out of the way!" one of the soldiers shouted.

Both bodies came down atop Angelica, knocking the wind out of her. She attempted to roll out from beneath them, trying to suck at the air, but she was firmly pinned. The heat of the fire raced across her chest as her own gown began to burn, the ground beneath her radiating such intense heat that it felt like she'd fallen onto an iron.

"Help me!" Marcy screamed, crawling off of the woman and dragging herself back to the rail. When she stood, the flames raced from her back all the way up over the top of her head, the blue gown charring to black.

Both of the soldiers had their pistols trained directly at her chest.

"Hurry!" Avery shouted, lowering both feet to the landing gear and stretching as far toward her as he could.

The chopper banked away momentarily when the pilot saw the fire so close, but moved quickly back into position.

"Grab my hand!" Avery called, reaching so far from the chopper that he thought for sure he was going to fall.

Marcy climbed up the wall again and this time didn't even try to find her balance. She forced herself to her feet and leaned forward, preparing to lunge.

*   *   *

"Get down!" one of the soldiers shouted from above and behind Avery a split-second before gunfire exploded right next to his ear.

The woman had found her feet again, the smoldering flames now splitting the flesh, the weeping fluids sizzling like fat on a fryer. She dove for Marcy, reaching for her with fanned fingers webbed with smoke and fire. Her left hand grabbed a handful of burning fabric and yanked as the first bullet took a meaty chomp out of her right shoulder. The second grazed the side of her neck, releasing a swell of blood.

"Marcy!" Avery shouted, grabbing for her as she started to fall forward. In that instant, Avery saw the sheer terror in her good eye, peeled almost inhumanly wide. Her fingers slapped against his and he struggled to grasp her wrist, but the woman's momentum carried them both over the side of the building. "No!"

He grabbed again, but only came up with air, helpless but to watch as Marcy fell away from him. Her head swung down toward the ground like the warhead of a missile, the flames crawling up her back as though trying to get back to the roof. The woman still held the burning clothing on Marcy's back, causing them both to flounder in midair. Marcy's face struck the side of the hospital with such force that a flap of the gown tore away and shattered fragments of teeth and goggles filled the air around her head.

A stream of blood trailed from her screaming mouth as she dropped away from Avery.

Even as they plummeted to their deaths, the woman still yanked at Marcy, snapping her jaws as though trying to steal one final bite of flesh before being smashed to oblivion.

Their bodies landed in the midst of the crowd of savages that had gathered beneath, who swelled over them like a tsunami. Arms struck at their bodies like so many serpents, tearing through cloth and skin alike and tossing it into the air around them.

Avery saw what looked like an arm flung out of the melee against the side of the building and had to turn away. Tears poured down his cheeks under the mask and he was unable to stop the undulating wail of torment that bellowed past his lips.

He looked across the four-foot gap to Angelica just as she raised her head from where she'd been leaning over the rail. She closed her eyes and raised her face to the heavens while the flames rose up over her shoulders from the front of her gown, which revealed her scrub top beneath.

People crawled through the burning doorway to the left from the hospital, flames blackening their skin, blisters bubbling and popping like boiling water on their faces. They lurched to their feet and sprinted after Angelica as though they couldn't feel a thing.

"Behind you!" one of the soldiers shouted and immediately started firing into the burning crowd. A man was jerked from his feet and thrown backwards with the top of his cranium spattering those behind him, passed by the people right on his heels before he even hit the ground.

Gunshots echoed from either side of Avery's head as he reached toward Angelica, stretching out his right arm as far as it would go.

"Don't let me fall!" she screamed as she climbed onto the wall.

"You're not going to fall!"

"Promise me, Avery!"

"You have to hurry! They're right beh—!"

Angelica lunged out across the gap before he knew she was coming. Their gloved palms slid across each other and his heart stopped. With her screams ringing in his ears, he watched her start to fall away from him.

"Please!" he wailed, grasping for her hands again, knowing that if he missed there wouldn't be a second chance. His fingers closed around her wrist and he held onto her with every ounce of his strength. Her descent jerked him forward, straining against his left arm which barely held onto the gun mount. His palm felt as though it was ripping as his fingers slipped around the metal.

"Please don't drop me," she sobbed, looking straight up into his eyes from below. Flames flickered to either side of her face, creeping up over the sides and reflecting in the small pools of tears inside her goggles.

"Help me!" he shouted, fighting against his grip on

both her wrist and the metal pole as he could feel both slipping.

The man to his left hopped down beside him on the rail and grabbed onto her opposite wrist when she reached for him.

"Rise! Rise!" the other soldier yelled into the microphone in front of his mouth, lining up the closest of the attackers down the barrel of his gun.

Avery heard what sounded like a plank being broken across the base of his skull, and then all he could hear was humming like bees buzzing around inside his head. The thunder of the blades was muted to a dull clapping, each repeated report of the weapon like footsteps thudding on stairs overhead. Groaning against the pain, he pulled until his elbow bent, if only slightly, drawing Angelica just that much closer.

The helicopter rose upward with the feeling of an elevator coming to life beneath him, seemingly increasing Angelica's weight tenfold.

Both men grappled with her wrists until they'd pulled her far enough that they could grab on to her by her upper arms, the now diminutive flames lapping at their forearms.

Fiery bodies flew through the air beneath them, flailing arms trying desperately to grab anything at all before succumbing to the will of gravity and dropping like stones toward the ground. One after another, they launched themselves at a sprint over the railing until well after the helicopter was out of reach.

The grass burned down below where the bodies landed.

Avery pulled until Angelica's knees were on the landing gear beside him, then wrapped his arms around her back. Flexing his legs, he threw himself back into the cabin, bringing Angelica down on his chest and slapping at the flames to smother them.

"Are you all right?" he asked, the latex gloves burning away from his bare palms. "Angelica, are you all right?"

"I think so," she whispered into his ear. Her goggles were smeared with soot and ash, the clothing shielding her upper body blackened, but he could see her eyes. Though tears flowed from them like water rising over a dam, he could see the fear and the relief.

They locked stares, communicating everything neither could voice with their eyes.

Angelica rolled off of Avery and they sat up, staring out past the soldiers' legs at the hospital as it fell farther away. The entire upper half of the building was shrouded in thick black smoke that rose from it like a freshly-struck match head, save for the human shapes of flames that swarmed through the haze. Neither could take their eyes from it until it was nothing more than a single tombstone rising from the eastern plains.

CHAPTER 15

Above Colorado Springs

Angelica and Avery strapped themselves into the seats backing to the pilot, watching out the side doors as the city raced past beneath them. The soldiers sat across from them, their knees almost touching across the slim walkway. They flew low enough that it looked as though they could step out onto the treetops, scanning the ground for signs of survivors.

"This is our third sortie today," the pilot shouted back over the roar of the blades overhead. "We've got about a half dozen other Hueys doing the same, but I can't imagine we've been able to scavenge more than a hundred souls between us."

A man appeared beneath them, sprinting through the front door of his white Victorian onto the front lawn. He waved both hands over his head, screaming at the top of his lungs.

"Set'er down," the first soldier they had seen said into his microphone. They were now close enough to be able to read the name stitched onto his fatigues: Madigan. The soldier beside him looked like a young

James Edward Olmos with his pock-scarred olive skin. He wrung his hands nervously in his lap, tapping his feet on the floor so fast they were a blur. His uniform identified him as Rodriguez. "We've got a live one."

Throwing their harnesses aside, they rose to their feet and took their posts at the twin GAU 17/A 7.62-mm miniguns, grasping the handles and sighting down at the ground beneath them as the chopper hovered in place.

The man on the ground whooped, pumping a triumphant fist to the sky and raced back up the front steps into the house. He emerged a moment later with a dark-haired woman holding a screaming toddler. They ducked their heads against the torrent that blasted them in the faces as the chopper lowered, snapping their wild hair around their heads.

"Are there any more of you?" the pilot's voice boomed over the speakers affixed to either side of the cockpit, facing the ground.

The man raised his face and shouted something they couldn't hear, but they were able to see him shaking his head.

"Are you infected?"

The woman screamed and ran to the spot where the helicopter was preparing to land in the middle of the street in one of the few gaps between the towering elms lining the sidewalks, the blades stripping the ancient trees of their leaves and sending them bounding down the street.

"You have to move back or we can't land," the pilot said, his voice metered by the thrumming blades like a bass beat.

"Jesus!" Madigan shouted, following the woman's stare back over her shoulder to the hedge-lined yard of the house next door. Two bodies threw themselves over the wrought iron gate from the rear of the house, hitting the ground in a crouch and launching themselves across the front lawn at a sprint.

Squeezing the triggers, he fired a barrage of bullets at what looked like two teenagers, tearing deep divots from the lawn in front of them before the whirring barrage of bullets ripped through them as though they were no more substantial than tissue paper, spreading their liquefied remains across the grass behind them and sending limbs and chunks of flesh flying off in all directions as though fired from a wood chipper.

"Yeah," Madigan shouted. "You want some more of that? Huh? Come on you stupid mother —"

He tightened his fists on the triggers again as three more people appeared from nowhere by the front of the brown Victorian next door, barreling toward the woman beneath them across the yellowed lawn riddled with elm roots like eels swimming in shallow water.

Madigan's whole body shook, his arms bouncing at the mercy of the weapon. The barrels whirled in circles so fast that they were a blur of metal, only the thin wisps of smoke rising from them betraying the fact that they were even firing rounds at all until they tossed hunks of lawn out around the feet of those below. One of them, a woman in shorts and a white halter top stained brownish-yellow stopped and threw her arms up above her head a heartbeat before a cloud of bullets pounded her in the center of her abdomen and rose up her body. Her shirt flashed red before being torn apart and scattered across the others with the mess of flesh and bone. The man behind her stopped and fell to his knees, barely beginning to raise his hands in surrender when the first of the furious bullets gouged a trench in the lawn leading up to him before splitting him in half, his head exploding like a rotting pumpkin.

"Oh God," Madigan gasped, jerking his hands away

from the minigun, the barrels falling to swing in a limp arch. "It was firing so fast I couldn't...They came out of nowhere!"

The remaining woman who had just seen her companions torn to pieces before she could even stop her momentum, turned and sprinted in the opposite direction, her ponytail flagging behind her. Dirt rising from her bare heels, she made it a dozen strides across the front lawn of the house next door before a man dashed out from behind the enormous trunk of one of the trees and threw his shoulder into her, cleaving her from the ground and slamming her onto her side. She tried to replace the air that had been pounded from her chest, but the moment she opened her mouth, the man's jaws snapped shut on her cheek.

"...out of nowhere..." Madigan was still babbling, staring down at his twitching fingers as though testing the reflexes to find out why he hadn't been able to stop in time.

Another man leapt a row of boxwood hedges from the yard beyond while a woman appeared from the far side of the house, rounding the corner from the back yard.

"Shoot them!" Avery shouted, struggling to unlatch his harness.

The helicopter was now only ten feet above the ground and throwing up a cloud of dead grass. Angry faces, contorted into snarls by rage, sprinted through the debris, oblivious to the brown blades that slashed at their exposed skin and prodded their unblinking eyes. Their blood red eyes.

The prattle of whirring gunfire exploded from Angelica's right and she screamed as a handful of people charged across the street from the opposite side, ducking out from behind parked cars and slamming through fences. Blood rained backwards from them, filling the air in a red cloud, yet still they ran at the chopper. A man with a thick black mustache had his right arm severed just below the shoulder, but didn't even seem to notice as he simply swung that stub of an appendage in the air, throwing off spurting arcs of ripe arterial blood.

"Rise! Rise!" Rodriguez shouted, his assault pounding a hole through the fourth body and launching it away as the remaining one dashed underneath his whirlwind barrage and disappeared below the helicopter. He released a final flurry of bullets that ricocheted from the asphalt with so many golden sparks and hammered a Lincoln before battering the front of the house across the street.

"We can't abandon them!" Angelica shouted, struggling against the latching mechanism of her harness. Avery finally slipped out of his and helped her do the same.

"We're no good to anyone dead, lady," the copilot called back over his shoulder.

"Just lower us a couple of feet and we can get them in," Avery said.

"Please," Angelica said, leaning between the seats in the cockpit. The pilot gave her a quick glance over his shoulder, their eyes locking. Finally, with a nod, he turned to his copilot.

"You can't be serious," the man said.

"You've only got one shot at this," the captain said.

"That's all we'll need," Angelica said, scrambling off of the seat and toward the right side door.

Madigan stood above her, merely staring out the open hatch at the world beyond.

"They weren't infected," he mumbled over and over.

Angelica grabbed onto the rail beside the door and lowered her feet to the landing gear, reaching her arm down as far as she could toward the woman, her arms shielding the child's head against her chest while the artificial wind whipped her hair around her face.

The floor shook beneath them with the pounding of fists from the man that had gotten past Rodriguez.

"Keep them back!" Avery shouted into Madigan's face, taking the man by his shoulders and shaking him until some semblance of sentience flashed in his eyes. "We're all dead if you don't!"

With a curt nod, Madigan straddled the pole, widening his stance and gripping the triggers. His body bucked convulsively with the first spray of fiery lead, the bullets dancing off the street and ricocheting from the curb as he swept the barrels from side to side like a firefighter battling an untamable blaze.

Avery climbed down on the other side of him, watching the ground rising beneath them until he was looking directly into the man's frightened eyes.

The banging of fists beneath intensified, growing faster and faster until the whole chopper shuddered against the resistance, tilting slightly to the right before alighting on the ground. A pool of blood crept out from beneath the runner under their feet.

"Take my baby!" the woman screamed, passing her child toward Angelica, who brought the small boy to her chest and ducked back into the cabin.

Avery extended his right hand toward the man, his features thick with dirt and mud, crusted in his beard and closely-cropped hair.

"Take my wife first!" the man shouted, grabbing the woman's hand and jerking her toward him. Once she was in front of him, he shoved her toward the chopper from behind.

"Not without you!" she wailed.

"I'm right behind you," he said, casting a nervous

look over his shoulder at the woman coming directly for them, leaping off the curb and streaking into the road.

Cradling the child to her hip, Angelica offered her left hand to the woman while Avery grabbed for her other arm and they hauled her up, ushering her past Madigan and to the seats. She pried her sobbing child from Angelica and screamed for her husband.

With a purring sound like a Saber-toothed cat, the soldier fired a volley of steel at the woman, taking a meaty bite out of the left side of her abdomen and spattering the ground with visceral spew, yet still she continued forward.

"Eric!" the woman screamed.

"Come on, come on!" Avery called, waving the man toward him.

The chopper rose a couple feet from the ground before bouncing back down. Rodriguez shouted something in Spanish and began firing again as people started rounding the corners from the streets beyond and slipping through the back yards.

Avery grabbed the man's arm and wrenched him forward. He struggled to balance his feet on the runner, but managed to perch there long enough for Angelica to grab his other arm.

"We've got him!" she screamed. "Get us out of here!"

The helicopter leapt up from the ground with a roar of the blades as Rodriguez continued bellowing and strafing the opposite side of the street with bullets.

"Sit down, lady," Madigan said, pushing the woman and her child toward the bank of bucket seats.

"Not without my husband!"

"Sit down!"

"Eric!"

"Climb in," Avery said, groaning against the man's weight, which felt as though it was fighting him in the opposite direction.

The man looked his wife in her eyes, tears streaming through the grunge on his cheeks, and raised his right foot to step up into the cabin right as a hand closed around his left ankle and yanked.

The woman's screams drowned out even the thunder of the blades and the prattle of gunfire.

Avery felt the man's left hand slip right out of his grip, leaving him to snatch at thin air. He looked down to the ground as they rose. The woman had managed to leap up and grab the landing gear before they had taken off and was tugging at the man's leg. She wrapped both arms around his foot and pulled him closer, tearing a mouthful of flesh and tendon from the back of his heel.

The man's eyes grew wide as he flailed his arms, trying desperately to grasp either of them before being ripped away by the wind of their passage.

Avery could only watch, with the woman's screams piercing his eardrums, as the man fell away from him, the bloodthirsty woman wrapped around his legs and gnawing on his lower calf like a drumstick. It felt as though it took an eternity for them to reach the ground, twisting and writhing atop one another in the air, watching the fear in the man's eyes before he was slammed to the ground fifteen feet lower, the back of his head smashing against the asphalt. Before the first rivulets of blood could rush from his nose, the others were upon him. Half a dozen bodies swarmed over him like jackals, tearing into his carcass. Tatters of flesh flew in all directions, the air around him filled with a cloud of blood.

"NO!" the woman railed, throwing herself toward the open doorway. It was all Avery could do to get his body between hers and the nothingness beyond, propping her up just long enough for Angelica and

Madigan to help drag her back to one of the seats and strap her in. She clawed at them and cried, tears pouring from bruised-looking eyes until Angelica managed to force the woman's child into her lap. Tightening her arms around the small boy, she buried her face in his shaggy blonde hair and sobbed uncontrollably while he cried back into her chest, curling his little fingers into the fabric of her blouse.

"Finish them," the pilot said through the loud-speaker, hovering fifty feet up, just above the treetops.

Rodriguez resumed firing, and with a curt nod, Madigan stepped up to his mount and let loose a lethal stream of steel.

Angelica looked past the Madigan, his body quaking against the kick of the weapon, and down to the street. Bullets tore through the mob of people fighting over the man's remains, oblivious to the fact that they were being shredded to ribbons in their feeding frenzy. The man's exposed ribcage and hollowed abdomen were the only testimony to his former life, while around him were spread the remains of the scavengers. Six feet away was the man who'd been crushed beneath the body of the chopper, his flesh still whole and unconsumed.

"There's nothing more to see," Madigan said, turning to face her. She'd seen the expression on his face a million times before. He was bordering on shock. "Why don't you go ahead and grab a seat?"

Angelica could only look at the man and nod, his eyes glassy, pupils fixed and dilated, and head back to the line of chairs abutting the cockpit.

"Here," Avery said, sitting down beside her. He raised his hands to her face and removed her goggles, dropping them to the floor and kicking them out the open door. Carefully, he peeled back a corner of the duct tape and began to unravel it from her nose all the way down to her neck, twisting the sticky remains in circles around her until his right hand was bound in an enormous knot of gray tape, the dried blood flaking from it like week-old mud from the bottom of a shoe. With his left, he pulled the gown off of her head like a caul and exposed her face. Sweat dotted her features, her startlingly blue eyes dulled and sunken into dark rings. Her hair was knotted and tangled, crumpled up against the back of her head and positively dripping with sweat.

He stared at her a moment, through weary eyes set behind goggles smeared with blood, his vision constricted by the slashes of fabric behind. Their eyes locked as she in turn brought her hands to his cheeks and removed his goggles, dropping them to the floor. The tape around his mouth was already peeling away, making it easy to grab hold of it and rip it back, unwinding it around his face and then his neck. The gray wad clung to her hand until she shook it loose and grabbed a handful of the crusted gown atop his head and drew it off.

Avery lowered his head to help her, feeling the wondrous rush of cool air flooding across his face and slithering through his hair like divine fingers. When he raised his eyes again, they were filled with tears.

"We're safe," she said over the clamor of chopping blades.

He could only nod, the flood of emotions he'd been holding at bay finally breaking through his defenses. Exhaustion gripped him and squeezed every last ounce of energy from him, chasing away the already spent reserves of adrenaline.

"Yeah," he said, again looking deeply into her eyes. "We made it."

Angelica peeled the tape from around her right wrist and cast it to the floor, tugging off both pairs of gloves at once and throwing them down with a wet slap. She brought her damp hand, her fingers pruned with sweat, to his cheek and grazed the stubbly skin. He closed his eyes against the electricity from her touch, the simple pleasure of her skin on his the most amazing sensation he'd ever experienced. Closing his eyes, he leaned into her hand like a purring kitten, reveling in the moment until he felt her warm breath against his lips, the softness of her lips pressing against his.

When she withdrew, he opened his eyes and stared deep into her fathomless blue irises, time standing still with the wind racing through the open doorways to either side, smoke obscuring the sky from the untamable blazes that burned all around the city.

"Thank you," he whispered, knowing that there was no way she could have heard him.

"Thank you," she whispered back, his eyes prying the words from her lips.

He leaned closer again and gently pressed his lips to hers, closing his eyes and for that one precious moment chasing away the rest of the world.

Until it came crashing back in with a vengeance and he quickly pulled away.

"What is it?" she asked, her eyes widening as she registered the fear on his face.

"Nothing," he said, scratching at his left forearm, where he could now see the black amoeba of blood leeching through the gown to the surface from the stinging ulcer beneath.

CHAPTER 16

Above Colorado Springs

"Why were you guys wearing that crap anyway?" Rodriguez asked.

Avery finally finished unwinding the tape from around Angelica's waist and down her legs, peeling off the tattered remains of the yellow isolation gown over her chest and the wrapping of torn gowns covering her legs down to the charred remnants of the surgical booties. All the while he scrutinized every inch of exposed flesh for any signs that the contagion had taken hold and she'd become infected, but as he could only see her arms and a small stretch of skin above her socks, it was little more than a cursory inspection.

"They can smell the infection," Avery said, peeling his own tape away. "I think that's why they don't attack each other."

"Are you saying that's blood you guys had all over your clothes?" His eyes grew wide, his chest heaving as his breaths came faster. "You willingly exposed all of us to whatever the hell this disease is? Jesus Christ! We saved you guys on top of that burning roof, and this is the thanks we get?"

"I don't think that—"

"I should throw you out over the city right now!"

"Please," Avery said. Angelica shrunk into him and away from the enraged soldier. Rodriguez's face burned deep red. "There has to be direct physical contact with the live virus. I'm sure that once it's out of the body for an extended period of time and exposed to direct oxygen rather than a permeable membrane it can't survive."

"How would you know that?"

"I don't...not for sure anyway."

The child's cries tapered off as he finally fell asleep in his mother's arms. She no longer wailed, but cried silently into his hair, pinching her eyes tightly closed.

"Let it go, Rod," Madigan said. He sat on the other side of the woman and her little boy from the other soldier. "For all we know, the virus could be airborne and we're all dead men walking."

Rodriguez opened his mouth to say something, but looked like he changed his mind at the last second, simply allowing his mouth to hang open for a moment.

Avery peeled the last of the duct tape from his legs and finally slipped out of the sweat-dampened mess of cloth covering his legs. The last piece of the ensemble to go was the formerly yellow smock, which he tossed down to the ground atop the rest of the pile, kicking it toward the open doorway to be ripped out and scattered in the air.

He held his right hand over the painful sore on his left forearm, trying to look casual so that no one would see. They were already eating through the flesh beneath his clothing like acid. He could feel them, on his chest, his back, his legs, the skin melting away in itchy blotches that he had to fight not to scratch for fear of being seen. Turning to his right, he looked at Angelica, whose eyes had fallen to his right hand. When she finally raised her stare, he could see the fear in her eyes.

She leaned closer and rested her head on his shoulder.

"How long?" she whispered beside his ear, just loud enough for him to hear.

He shook his head.

She slid her hand across his stomach, noting the visible flinch when she passed over the skin, and carefully lifted his hand just enough to see the weeping wound beneath. A tear rolled from her eye as she placed his hand carefully back into place.

They both knew it was only a matter of time before the sores started appearing on his face and neck, or some other place where they would be easily seen. And then what? Avery couldn't tolerate the prospect of turning into whatever everyone else had become. He'd sooner take a dive out the side of the chopper. He looked across the aisle at Madigan. The butt of the soldier's side arm hung out from the holster strapped across his chest.

At least Avery now knew he had options.

"I have a visual," the copilot said, summoning their attention.

"Where?" the pilot asked.

"Ten o'clock. About two thousand yards."

"I don't see…There. Call it in." The helicopter veered to the left, tilting just slightly. "You boys locked and loaded?"

"Yes, sir," Rodriguez shouted, unlatching his restraining belt and staggering through the wind toward his mount.

Madigan hesitated, his lower lip slipping between his teeth. He closed his eyes, took a deep breath, and then jumped to his feet and strode to his minigun, readjusting his grip on the triggers over and over before wiping his palms on his pants and repeating the process.

Clear off to the left they could see the charred remains of the airport, wreckage strewn all across the runways, the fields still burning away from it, gushing black smoke into the sky. The roadways leading up to it looked like parking lots. Cars bumper to bumper. None of them moving. The shoulders charcoaled from the fires that had already burned past them. The city sprawling toward it to the east was lifeless. There were no flashes of what precious little sun permeated the cloud of smoke on the roofs of moving cars, no joggers on the sidewalks or children playing in the parks. The entire city below was either dead or barricaded in basements, except for the sporadic movement that was never quite visible, always lurking in their peripheral vision, yet never clearly enough to be recognizable.

"Saddle up!" Rodriguez shouted as the chopper started to descend. The thunder of the blades intensified as they slowed, the tail swinging around to the left so that they were moving sideways. A Holiday Inn came into view, a three-story rectangular construct with the traditional green sign. Three people rushed to the edge of the roof, two holding shotguns while a third waved her arms above her head.

"Drop your weapons," the pilot's voice echoed from the speakers.

The helicopter finally halted its advance about ten feet from the western edge of the roof, hovering just out of reach.

The two men, both of them nearly completely brown with dried blood, still trained their shotguns on Rodriguez, who stood his ground, lining the barrels up on the man to the left and preparing to jerk it to the right to annihilate the second man before he could get off a shot.

"This is the United States Air Force," the pilot's voice boomed. "Lay down your weapons or we will fire on you."

The men looked at each other, then finally at the woman between them.

"Drop your guns and we'll allow you to board this chopper. If you even think about firing on us, we'll blow you to hell before you can squeeze the trigger."

Madigan constantly looked back over his shoulder, uncomfortable with all of the action transpiring behind him, and then back to the ground where people were swarming out of the front doors of the hotel into the half-circle drive, trampling the bed of flowers in the middle to get a better view of what was going on above their heads. From three stories up, they looked like those on the roof. He couldn't tell if they were infected, and after strafing two people who obviously weren't, the prospect of turning his gun on a crowd made his stomach roil.

"We're not dropping our guns!" the man to the left yelled from across the roof in a thick Texas drawl. "They're the only reason we're still alive."

"Then you can stay on this roof," the pilot said, raising the chopper and turning slightly to the right.

"Wait! Wait!" the second man yelled, then turned and shouted something to the other man that they couldn't hear. He turned back to the helicopter and raised the shotgun over his head in both hands, making a deliberate show of lowering it to the tarred rooftop in front of him and again standing slowly, leaving his arms up over his head.

The other man still had his weapon pointed at Rodriguez.

"Drop you gun!" Rodriguez yelled.

The man looked to his companions, the other three now joining them from the far side of the roof where they'd been trying to signal for help, nervously reaching the edge of the roof, but staying as far from the man with his shotgun raised as possible.

One of the women ran over to him and grabbed the gun, wrestling with the barrel until it pointed down. The man raised a fist to knock her away, but the momentum of his backswing toppled him in reverse onto the roof, the shotgun clattering from his hands. The woman scurried around him and grabbed the gun, running back to the others.

The man's chest started bucking and he spouted a geyser of blood past his lips before falling still.

"He's infected," Angelica said, and then leaned between the front seats. "He's infected. Hurry and get the others off the roof!"

The chopper swung to the left, causing the five on the roof to duck for fear of having their heads taken off. Swinging the tail around so that Rodriguez had a clear line of sight should he need it, the helicopter set down in the middle of the roof, the landing gear bouncing roughly.

"Hurry up and climb on board," the pilot said through the speaker.

A woman shoved her teenaged daughter forward, the blades blowing her long blonde hair in her face. She swiped at it with her hands, her long legs trailing from Daisy Duke's smeared with blood, and clambered up past Rodriguez. Madigan ushered her past Avery and Angelica and around the corner toward the back where there were more seats. Her mother was right behind her, her graying bangs swirling in front of her, loose strands wrenched from the bun atop her head splayed like tentacles. Stumbling into the cabin, she nearly collapsed forward, her features so stark white that purple veins marbled her cheeks, her eyes recessed into darkness.

Avery unbuckled and helped her around to the back beside her daughter, leading her by her wrist so that he could feel her weak pulse. She almost made it to the seat before collapsing to her knees. Avery barely grabbed her in time to keep her head from hammering the floor.

"Help me get her into her seat," he commanded the younger girl, whose wide eyes were so terror-riddled that she looked like a meth junkie. She grabbed her mother with hands that trembled uncontrollably, but held on to the woman's sweater long enough to drag her into a seated position and help Avery buckle her in.

"Eleanor! Is she all right?" a man shouted from behind him.

"She's in shock," Avery said without turning to face the man he assumed to be her husband. "I want you to sit right next to her and help strap her into the harness. Keep talking to her and make sure she stays conscious. Can you do that?"

The man didn't immediately answer so Avery whirled to face him. The man's bald head was spotted with swelling globules of sweat, dragging the blood down from the crown of his skull and through the dried mess on his face.

"Can you do that?"

"Yes…yes," the man said, sliding into the chair right behind Avery so he could slip Eleanor's left arm through the strap.

"Keep her talking."

"Come on, Eleanor," the man was saying as Avery hurried back around the row of seats. "We're almost out of here, talk to me. Where should we go from here? Do you remember…?"

Avery nearly slammed into a larger woman rounding the middle row of seats toward the rear. Her short gray hair was streaked back with blood and bobby-pinned into place, whatever wig she'd been wearing long since gone. There was so much makeup on her face that she appeared painted, the blood and tears running through it revealing pasty blotches of pallor. Only one eye still had the long false lashes, while the other appeared battered, the green iris drifting lazily to the right. Her suede top was splotched with black blood, several handfuls of the tassels dangling from her chest torn away. She had the terrified, open-mouthed look of a rabbit cornered deep in its burrow by a rattler and she positively shook, but she managed to stammer something as she shoved past him toward the available seats at the rear of the chopper.

A younger man trailed at her heels. He looked to be in his mid-twenties, though with the swelling covering his mouth and nose it was nearly impossible to tell. When he breathed, crimson spittle flew from his tattered lips, behind which were rows of fractured and sharpened teeth. His panicked brown eyes flashed at Avery's before being wrenched away and back to the floor where only his left foot was still inside a shoe. The right was bare and appeared to be missing the two smallest toes on the outside, the skin surrounding the wound taut and black as though they'd tried to cauterize it with a burning stick. He mumbled something, blood dribbling through a tear from his lower lip to his chin, but Avery was already positioning himself behind the man to shove him toward the rear.

Angelica brushed past him toward the back to help tend to the injured.

"They're covered in blood, don't get it on you," Avery called back after her.

He reached the main aisle and looked to both sides. Madigan now had his back to the open doorway behind him, through which there was nothing but the churning black clouds of smoke that were now simply hanging above the city. Twirls wafting past were sucked in by the blades. Madigan pulled his undershirt over his nose and mouth, biting it to hold it in place to keep from inhaling the smoke.

"Is that all of them?" Avery shouted, but Madigan only shrugged.

Avery hurried behind Rodriguez as the chopper again rose from the rooftop. He could see the black-tarred roof falling away, the backdrop of the burning city coming into view over the far lip of the roof.

"Did we get them all?" he yelled.

Rodriguez turned to face him. "All but the infected one." He leaned toward the cockpit. "That's a full load, Bass."

"We can stuff a few more," the pilot called back.

"Only if they're on our way back to the base. The last thing I want is for this bird to fall from the—"

Rodriguez looked directly into Avery's eyes. In that fleeting moment, Avery watched the soldier's eyes grow insanely wide and his mouth open in astonishment. His legs were ripped out from beneath him and he fell flat on his face, reaching out across the floor toward him. Falling to his knees, Avery could only watch those hands race away from him toward the open doorway. Rodriguez's legs flew over the edge, his curled fingers clawing for traction on the metal. He let out a scream as he slid away, grabbing onto the tripod at the last moment.

Avery dove toward him, grabbing for the soldier's wrist.

A wild head of bloody hair arose over Rodriguez's back like a fiery sun as Avery clasped onto his wrists. A pair of bloody eyes, issuing rivulets of blood over the dams of his lashes, followed the soggy hairline and locked directly on Avery's.

"Don't let go!" Rodriguez screamed, the surprise

loosening the pressure of the hands on his wrists. "Please don't let go!"

Avery struggled to maintain his grip, helplessly watching as bloody hands climbed up Rodriguez's back, lancing into the flesh like a climber's ice picks. The full face leered over the soldier's shoulders, blood-drenched teeth bared from torn lips.

"God, no!" Rodriguez shrieked.

The man who had refused to relinquish his shotgun opened his mouth as wide as the hinges would allow and snapped his jaws closed on the back of the soldier's neck. Blood rushed out around the seal of the man's mouth, but it wasn't until he tore out the bite that the fluid sprayed. Avery only had time to turn his face, the warmth spattering him on the cheek.

Rodriguez let out the most piteous and pain-laden scream Avery had ever heard, and then he was jerked away. Clinging to the soldier's wrists, Avery slid forward until his right shoulder pounded the metal post of the weapon mount, the pain racing down his arm. He could only grit his teeth and try to hold on as he watched Rodriguez's left hand slip out of his right. Tears spurting from his eyes, the wind from the blades throwing droplets of blood back into the cabin, Rodriguez's right hand was wrenched out of Avery's grip. In a blur of motion, Rodriguez flew backwards out of the cabin as the man on his back lunged forward, using Rodriguez as a launching pad to dive onto Avery.

Avery's breath was pounded past his lips as the weight came down upon him. He could feel the warmth of the fresh blood soaking into the back of his shirt.

There was a loud crack like a hammer and chisel driven into a spine.

Avery rolled to his left, grabbing onto the metal leg of one of the chairs where it was bolted to the floor. Tugging himself out from beneath the man's weight, he looked back in time to see Madigan lower his bloody right boot to the floor, crunching on the teeth he'd knocked from the thing's mouth. He reached down and grabbed the man by the hair, yanking his head up and back to expose his wet throat. In one swift motion, Madigan grabbed his sidearm from the holster and jammed the barrel into the hollow of the man's mandible from beneath. A spray of blood preceded chunks of cranial matter out the open doorway where they were swept along the side of the 'copter and over the city, now hundreds of feet below.

"Jesus," Avery gasped, scuttling as far under the line of chairs as his body would permit.

Madigan stood over him, still holding a fistful of hair torn from the top of the man's head, though his face had fallen to the floor with a pool of blood expanding around it like a backed-up sewer drain. There was a hole in the back of his head large enough to wiggle a fist through, pouring out blood so fast that it covered the ground around the soldier's feet. Avery scrambled away from its advance, finally reaching the seat closest to the open door and crawling out from beneath it. The woman beside him clutched her child to her chest, the boy's head smashed into her bosom, both legs tucked up to her chest. She was freckled with an obscene amount of blood, but it hadn't seemed to register yet as she simply stared straight ahead, her shoulders heaving as she began to hyperventilate. It wasn't until a trickle of crimson rolled down her forehead from her hairline that she started to scream.

Madigan nudged the man's body toward the side of the cabin, the ferocious wind flagging his clothing. He grabbed onto the tripod for support, slipped his right foot underneath the man's chest, and rolled him onto his back. It only took a small shove from his boot to send the man tumbling over the edge and out of sight.

The Infected

There was a thud as he bounded along the outer shell of the helicopter, and then nothing.

"Is everything under control back there?" the copilot shouted. He was climbing between the two front seats, trying to get over the row of chairs behind with his service pistol drawn.

"Yeah," Madigan said, finally tearing his gaze from the open doorway.

The copilot gasped when he saw the sheer volume of blood on Madigan's face, his eyes lifeless and unblinking, though blood overflowed his lashes and dripped to his cheeks from his brows.

"Good God, Mad. Are you all right?"

"Better than Rodriguez," was all he said as he dropped his gun to the floor with a clatter and plopped into the nearest seat. He sat there staring at the blood on his hands and pulling the thin strands of hair from where they were stuck between his fingers.

CHAPTER 17

Above Colorado Springs

Angelica sat in the seat beside Avery, staring out past the unmanned turret as the city blew by beneath. A westerly wind had arisen to chase all of the smoke from the burning eastern half of the town up against the foothills where it accumulated as thick as night, billowing around the chopper as the twirling blades stirred it. It was like trying to breathe while sitting right at the edge of a campfire, the air heavy, parching, burning in her lungs. Every so often the smoke would clear just enough to allow her a glimpse of the ground. Vacant streets filled with abandoned cars passed, the unoccupied houses standing sentry like tombstones marking what should have been the graves where the owners had fallen. There was no life down there, nothing but the charred remains of lives, the burning, and those waiting to burn. Tears streamed down her cheeks, but she had to fight the urge to swipe them away as her bare palms were thick with crusted blood.

"I'm so sorry," Avery said into her ear only loud enough for her to hear. He'd noticed her chipping the crusted blood from her cuticles and nails, unconsciously scrubbing her hands on her pants. "I should have been the one treating them. I'm already infected."

It was the first time he'd even admitted as much to himself. He'd known for quite some time, but vocalizing the thought truly brought home the ramifications.

He was going to die.

And worse, he was going to become like the others: an unthinking killing machine, a creature at the mercy of his baser instincts.

The living dead.

"I'm a big girl, Avery. I made the choice for myself, knowing full well what the consequences might be."

"Is it possible that the blood was dry? I mean, if it wasn't still wet then maybe — "

"Shh," she whispered, placing her finger along the side of his jaw, running it gently down to his chin. An ulcer was beginning to form beneath his right cheekbone, that tiny mouth only now beginning to open. "We make our decisions in the moment."

She leaned closer and kissed him right beneath the line of his jaw.

"Please," he whispered, turning his head away. "I can't let you do this."

She held out her left hand to him, the entire palm coated with an almost brown layer of blood flaking like rust from a trailer hitch. The woman in back had an obvious concussion and Angelica had been forced to take her by either side of the bloody face to steady her head while she pulled down her lower lids to check her ocular reflexes. Her husband's right arm had been sliced right across the biceps and she'd bandaged it with a strap of cloth torn from his sleeve. She'd also had no choice but to tie a makeshift tourniquet around the younger man's foot to stop the blood from flowing freely from the infected wound where his toes had been bitten off. There had been a moment when she could have turned back and buckled herself into her chair. None of them knew that she was a doctor. She could have just easily left them to their own devices until they arrived wherever it was they were headed, but that just wasn't how she worked. Granted, maybe it would have guaranteed that she would live, but she would still have to live with herself.

"It's okay," she said, finally lowering the back of her hand onto his thigh.

He looked deeply into her eyes and she could see his trepidation, but more than that, she could see the fear, not just the fear for his life, but the fear of hurting her. The day before he'd been a smug resident with a God complex wielding an ego the size of a club, but beneath all that he was just a scared little boy, afraid of being hurt and even more afraid of hurting her.

Looking down at her palm, he placed his hand atop hers, lacing their fingers together.

There was nothing more to be said. Only the moment mattered now as there was no promise of the next. Angelica leaned her head against his shoulder, her hair tickling his chin, the warmth of her body in stark contrast to the rapidly cooling blood on his clothes. He kissed the top of her head and leaned into her, watching a different world race by out the open doorway through the loose strands of her hair snapping on the wind. In that one fleeting instant, everything was all right with the world.

*   *   *

The city proper fell behind them as they climbed up into the foothills, cresting rising and falling hills and valleys filled with the rich green of pine trees and the silver of spruces. Emerald-leafed aspen shimmered beneath like a reflection of the sun on a choppy lake. The large Victorian houses had given way to the boxy tract homes, only to be replaced by houses becoming increasingly larger as they ascended. Short driveways metamorphosed into long and winding asphalt drives, the dwellings growing farther apart, the fences taller. These houses had been built to lord over the land, so the owners could look down on the rest of the city, whether with contempt or admiration, and enjoy all of the trappings of wealth and status.

Avery wondered if from that vantage they'd been able to see the end coming in time to escape or if even the state-of-the-art security systems had been unable to halt the marauding packs of the infected.

The streets wound tighter and tighter as they slithered up the mountainsides, doubling back upon themselves and becoming thinner as the forest advanced from either side. At the top of a steep incline with houses perched amidst the ageless pines, the crest of the slope had been leveled off and widened.

The northern edge of the zoo passed beneath them, and while Avery's first instinct was to rouse Angelica so that she could see what was happening, he figured that it would only be fair to spare her this one nightmare. Besides, he didn't want to risk doing anything that would cause her to move away from him. The point where their shoulders touched, where her cheek rested on his shoulder and drool dripped from the corner of her mouth was the most wonderful thing he'd experienced in days. Feeling her chest rising and falling against him as she breathed, becoming more rhythmic as finally sleep washed over her. Let her rest while she could.

With a gasp, the woman across the aisle from him began to sob anew as they passed over the giraffe pen, her sleeping child still drawn to her chest, the seat to her left by the door conspicuously vacant in Rodriguez's absence. Avery could remember seeing the giraffes as a child, but he could never recall ever seeing them run. Those giant spotted animals sprinted around their outdoor enclosure faster than he would ever have imagined possible, front haunches rising and falling in an awkward gallop, neck straight and bending up and down like a car jack. There were four of them, three enormous males judging by the knobs atop their crowns, purple tongues lolling out with the exertion. A dozen men raced after them, clawing wicked stripes of blood through the golden fur, but appearing unable to gain leverage, leaping over the fallen bodies sprawled out on the dirt, the red flesh ripped away from the exposed ribcages, chunks torn out of tattered necks. There was a smaller giraffe in the far rear corner, the tiny legs ripped right out of their sockets, the lighter, buff-colored fur peeled back. A long neck stretched out through the tall rectangular doorway leading into the tan brick building, the head lying on its side several feet away.

One of the men stopped and looked up at the thunder of the chopper blades, his crimson face glimmering with wet blood in that second before one of the bull giraffes charged him, its strong chest hitting him squarely in the face and knocking him to his back before trampling him beneath massive hooves. The animal reared up and slammed both front legs down on his chest, powdering bone and mashing organs.

More people dashed along the path leading from the front gates up the side of the mountain toward the rest of the zoo. A cluster congregated around what appeared to be the remains of an ape, its black hide cast aside with the long hair shifting on the wind. None of them even looked up. One woman ran down a peacock, tearing out a fistful of the gorgeous tail feathers before biting right through

The Infected

its thin neck. There was a stroller on its side along the rail in the middle of a large black puddle.

More cages passed beneath as they followed the face of Cheyenne Mountain to the south. A lone impala cowered at the back of the dirt cage by the small concrete shack, one of its candy cane-twirled horns snapped off midway up, its brethren scattered across the blood-induced mud in a macabre display of carnage. An orange-furred orangutan had managed to escape its cage and was now atop the wire mesh roof, cringing away from a pair of people who'd managed to scale the side of the enclosure, but couldn't quite reach it. Several of the larger predatory birds circled over the cages that had once housed them, the walkways beside them covered with feathers like fluffy snowflakes. A pair of water buffalo lowered their heads as they were backed into a corner, preparing to charge. Only the pair of rhinos appeared remotely unharmed, though one of them had a long bloody streak down its side. Their cage showcased indistinguishable, only-vaguely human shapes smashed flat and pounded into the dirt. From above they looked like red and white bird droppings. The largest rhino was trying to drag its face on the ground to extricate a human torso from its horn.

The helicopter passed over the visitor center and finally the front gates. The parking lot was still half-full of cars, the asphalt covered with shattered glass from the demolished windshields and side windows, spattered with blood from where motorists had been pulled from their vehicles and slaughtered, their rotting corpses strewn about like so much garbage. The parking lot bled into another before tapering to a small road again that wound up the slope toward what had once been the Broadmoor ski area, now the wavering grasses of the slopes marred only by the cement trenches of the alpine slides paralleling the wires strung between the towers of the ski lift, the empty chairs rocking gently from side to side as they passed overhead. The tower of the Will Rogers shrine stood from the mountainside to the right like a middle finger raised to the heavens, appearing only briefly before becoming shrouded by the forest surrounding it. Dense woodlands raced by under them, interrupted only briefly by thin gravel roads and paths cut by foraging deer. Occasionally there would be a flash of color as what looked like a human would dart out from beneath the lush lower canopy, only to disappear under the next tree.

Their gradual ascent brought them around the face of Cheyenne Mountain. The city was now far off to the northeast, swaddled in a cloud of its own fiery consumption. The flames glowed like the setting sun at twilight.

The chopper slowed and the trees fell away beneath, revealing a paved road leading up to a tall, secured chain link fence topped with coiled concertine wire. A line of guards stood sentry along the inside of the fence. Behind them was a wide stretch of asphalt with a circular helipad painted in yellow with flashing red beacons surrounding it. Two military transport vehicles were parked beside it, fumes pouring from their tail pipes as they idled in wait. The drivers stood outside the doors, their rifles pointed back toward the gate, where a wall of humanity surged against it as though laying siege to a fortified castle. Men and women thrashed against the chain link, bowing it inwards, but only so far before it simply withstood their assault, their faces and bodies pressed so hard against the wires that their skin tore. Occasionally one managed to clamber up atop the others, reaching up and slipping fingers through the mesh. Before he could raise his arm to drag himself higher toward the curls of razor wire, several of the guards fired their automatic weapons and tore him to shreds. It wasn't until Avery witnessed one such occurrence that he noticed the mass of corpses accumulated under the feet of the mob, the black, necrotic flesh, the blood and liquefied tissue seeping under the gate.

"Home sweet home," the copilot called back over his shoulder.

They hovered about twenty feet above the ground for a moment, waiting for the armed soldiers from the convoys to leave their posts and charge through the ferocious wind to the edges of the helipad. The men turned their backs to the 'copter as it descended, training their weapons past their comrades toward the teeming mass of humanity.

"God," Madigan said, staring out the side door toward the gate as they set down on the ground with a gentle bounce. "There were only half that many when we left."

His face was ashen and freckled with blood like a redhead who hadn't seen the sun in ages. He reflected his true age, looking much smaller, like a scared child.

"Buckles off!" one of the soldiers on the ground shouted as he turned and charged toward them. He wore full fatigues and a hard helmet that obscured his eyes, the strap so tight across his chin that it creased his cheeks. Avery caught a glimpse of the name embroidered above his pocket. Porter.

"Where are—?" Angelica started, raising her head from Avery's shoulder, but the soldier had already leapt up beside her and was unlatching her buckle. He tugged her out the doorway by her right arm, nearly hurling her to the ground before she managed to gain her balance and stagger forward toward the next soldier, who was simply a blur of olive green as he rushed her to the back of what appeared to be an extraordinarily large Jeep with canvas drawn over some sort of framework to make it look almost like a camouflaged moving truck. The soldier threw back the canvas sash and urged her up onto the tailgate, where she scurried back out of sight into the darkness.

"Come on, come on!" the soldier outside the chopper yelled to Avery, who'd barely managed to get out of his harness before Porter was shoving him from behind. He was hardly able to slow his momentum enough to clamber down from the cabin without having to leap through the air. "Hurry!"

Though the spinning blades were still several feet over his head, Avery ducked and ran toward the soldier, casting a quick glance over his shoulder at the front gate to the left. All he could see were bloody, snarling faces fighting for position against the fence, trying to shove through each other, their mass growing taller as they trampled the ones up front beneath their advancing tread, using their fallen ranks to raise them toward the top of the fence.

"Get a move on!" the soldier shouted into his face, spraying him with spittle as he shoved him toward the open gate of the truck.

Angelica reached out toward him, helping him to his feet and pulling him to her.

"Where are we?" she nearly screamed.

"NORAD...I think."

She tore herself from him as the tailgate bounced again. The woman with the child was trying to slide her rear end up so she wouldn't have to relinquish her hold on her child.

"Pass him to me," Angelica said, reaching down to the woman's chest and sliding her hands under the wailing boy's armpits.

"No!" the woman screamed, clinging to her child and

nearly losing her balance.

"There's no time for this!" Angelica said, grunting as she wrenched the child, kicking and flailing, out of his mother's arms.

She screamed hysterically, flopping onto her stomach and jumping to her feet. Charging Angelica, she appeared prepared to tear her apart, but slowed as Angelica handed her the boy and passed her toward the rear of the cab, where Avery was already helping the younger man into the back of the bed. The man tried to step up onto what remained of his bloody foot, only to fall forward and have to try again.

"What's your name?" Angelica asked the woman, who had wedged herself into the corner of the cargo area so that Angelica wouldn't be able to reach through her to get at the child.

The woman only flinched in response as if she'd been struck.

"My name's Angelica. I'm a doctor at Community."

The woman looked back over her shoulder and studied Angelica, barely able to decipher more than her outline against the open back door where others were clambering in.

"Lisa," she finally said. "Lisa Anderson."

"And who's this?" Angelica asked, trying to use her best child-friendly voice, though under the circumstances she imagined it must have sounded more like a screech.

"This is Nick...my son."

"Hi, Nick. Are you hurt anywhere?"

His screams only intensified.

"I think he's okay," Lisa said, finally turning enough for Angelica to survey the child. In the wan light, she could only make out the fact that he had all four appendages. Palpation confirmed that his belly was soft and pliable, his pulse, while understandably fast, was within the normal range. His breathing was quick, but not labored.

"How about you?" Angelica asked.

"My hus...my husband, he..." the woman said, the words triggering her to begin to hyperventilate.

"Focus on your breathing."

"My husband..."

"Tell me how you feel physically. Are you in any pain?"

"Only my...my ankle," she said. "Where Jack bit me."

"Who's Jack?"

"Jack was our neighbor...Frank...Frank shot him in the face...Oh god, Frank!" Lisa was overwhelmed by the emotions her dead husband's name summoned. Sobbing, she slid down the side until she was on her rear end, cradling Nick to her chest.

Angelica whirled away from her and nearly ran headlong into the man with the gnarled foot limping toward her.

"Is it still bleeding?" she asked.

"I don't think so, but it still hurts like a mother."

"You should start to feel pins and needles any time now. After that, it should start to go numb."

"Thanks," he said.

She started to brush past him to see to the next person climbing up on the tailgate when he grabbed her by the arm.

"Wait! Am I...Am I going to lose my foot?"

"What's your name?"

"Ben. Ben Litton."

Angelica tried to temper her tone as she pried at his fingers. Noting her discomfort, he released his grip and took a small step back.

"Listen, Ben. I had to tie a tourniquet around the

middle of your foot to stop the flow of blood. There were two options. You could either have lost the end of your foot and your toes — of which there were only three left — or you could have bled out through that sloppily cauterized wound. I made the choice to save your life."

She paused for a response, but as none immediately followed, she turned and headed again toward the older woman.

"Thanks," he called after her, shuffling toward the front of the bed.

"Are you all right, Amelie?" Angelica asked the older woman, whom she recognized by the shadow of her head with her balding hair pinned back across her head.

"My stomach hurts."

"Focus on your breathing. Deep breaths. In...then out."

"I think I might vomit."

"Move to the front with the others and focus on your breathing."

"But what if I have the sickness?" Amelie shrieked.

"Just try to stay calm. Go up there. Sit down, and we'll take a closer look at you when we get to wherever we're going," Angelica shouted, already taking the young girl by the arm and ushering her toward the front of the vehicle. "What's your name, sweetheart?"

"Dee," she said, her voice tremulous.

"Are you in pain?"

"No, but my mom —"

"Keep heading up with the others. We'll take care of your mom."

"But she's —"

"I promise we'll take care of her as soon as we can."

"You don't understand, she's —"

"Just move back up with the others."

Angelica watched Avery hop down off of the fender

and hurried away from the young girl to see what was transpiring.

Holding back the canvas to get a better view, she saw the man holding his wife in his arms, her legs hanging limply over his right forearm, her arms simply dangling. Her neck was flopped back over his left forearm, her mouth wide open, hair tangling with the gusting breeze. Angelica watched the woman's chest as she jumped down, but didn't see it move in the slightest.

"I'm not going to say this again," the soldier shouted. "You can't bring that body on this vehicle."

"She's my wife!" the man shouted, his eyes wild and unblinking.

"Look buddy, I know how hard this must be, but we can't risk bringing a corpse into the base."

"I won't leave her here!" he screamed, spittle flying from his mouth. Several long strands of hair stood erect in the wind from the comb-over on his bald head.

"Look. Either you drop her right now or—"

"Hold on!" Avery yelled, getting between the two men. "Let me try."

"You all are risking your lives for every minute—"

"Just give me a shot," Avery interrupted.

He turned to his right and waved off a pair of men in full Hazmat gear. He couldn't see their faces behind the plastic shields due to the reflection, but both men stopped where they were.

"Listen to me!" Avery shouted right into the man's face. "That girl we just put on the truck…She's your daughter, isn't she?"

The man gave several short nods.

"Right now she's scared to death and really needs her dad."

"But I can't—"

"There's nothing more we can do for your wife."

The Infected

"But she's—"

"Going to turn into one of them," Avery said.

The man opened his mouth, but said nothing, his eyes slowly falling to look at his wife's pasty face. Her blue eyes had rolled upward, the lower crescents barely visible from beneath her upper lids. The blood on her face was already drying to a scabby black.

"I can't," the man sobbed, finally blinking and releasing a stream of tears down his cheeks. "I love her so much…"

"Do you love your daughter?"

The man's eyes shot toward Avery, this time reflecting only thinly-veiled anger.

"Of course, I do!" he growled, his lips writhing over his bared teeth.

"Then you need to get on that truck," Avery said, softening his tone just enough to be heard over the rising thunder of the helicopter as it again lifted off. Porter had boarded it to man the weaponry, leaving Madigan standing there watching the Huey rise like a forlorn dog tethered to a stake. "She needs you now. She's just lost her mother and she's scared. Right now, what she needs more than anything is her father."

The man's eyebrows rose and his features softened slightly, his quivering lips curling downward.

The two men in Hazmat suits began slowly advancing on the man.

"You're out of time," the soldier bellowed, pounding the side of the bed. The engine growled and gushed out more black smoke. There was the wrenching sound of a gear being slammed into place.

"Give her body to these men," Avery said, nodding in the general direction of the encroaching pair who looked like they'd just stepped off a space shuttle.

"What are they going to do with her?" he sobbed.

"They're going to make sure that she doesn't turn into one of them," Avery said, locking his eyes on the man's.

He glanced back over his shoulder at the wave of humanity threatening to crash through the gate. The bratta-tat-tat of machine gun fire tore through the crowd, throwing blood in the air like a cloud of pain as the guards sensed they needed to try to stall the flood.

The first of the isolation-garbed soldiers reached the man's side, gently placing his right hand beneath the woman's head.

"What's your name?" Avery asked the widower.

"Don," he said, cringing away from the man beside him.

"Don...Let this man take your wife. She can't suffer anymore. Let him do what he has to do to make sure that she doesn't come back to life. If she does, you know what they're going to have to do to her, don't you?"

Angelica stepped past Avery and quietly said something to the impatient soldier, who looked toward the mirror on the passenger side of the truck and signaled the driver with a reluctant nod. The growling engine became a muted purr.

"Come on, Don," Avery said.

Don's head rocked back and he let out a horrible moan as the two men lifted the woman out of his arms and carried her away. He held his hands out in front of him as though he were still holding her for a moment, before finally letting them drop to his sides with a slap.

"Let's get you on the truck," Avery said, taking the man by the shoulder and guiding him toward the open sash where his daughter stood with both hands clasped over her mouth, her red face soaked with tears. "Let's get you to your daughter."

"Thank you," Avery turned and said to the soldier,

who averted his eyes and acknowledged him with a nod.

Avery helped Angelica up into the truck behind the man and climbed in himself. He was just about to head deeper into the transport vehicle when Madigan ran up to the tailgate and hopped on. The soldier sat on the very edge, dangling his legs over the road as the truck began to roll forward.

Avery hesitated, watching Angelica head deeper into the darkness, throwing her arms out to her sides to maintain her balance, then finally sat down beside Madigan.

"You okay?" Avery asked.

The soldier merely nodded, looking off to the right toward the brick guard shack built right up against the carved granite face of the hillside.

Avery followed his gaze and saw the two men who had taken the woman away set her down atop a large steel table on wheels. It reminded him of the surgical tables back at the hospital, which now seemed like a different lifetime entirely.

One of the men knelt and hefted something large and metallic from the ground. A long hose stretched away from it, terminating in a brass coupling against the side of the building. There was a bright red placard above it, but Avery couldn't read it from so far away. The second man cranked a handle to the side where the three-inch hose met the bricks, then walked back over to the other, who held some sort of small mechanical device in his left hand, the nozzle of the hose in his right.

The shadow of the mountain fell over them from behind, bringing with it a chill that sent their hackles rising.

The man held the device in front of the nozzle and a stream of flame erupted, firing a good twenty feet in a straight line. Shoving the lighter back into one of the exterior pockets of his Hazmat suit, he directed the high-velocity fire at the woman's body, which immediately turned black and ignited.

Avery glanced back over his shoulder to ensure that the woman's husband wasn't standing right behind him.

Shaking his head, he turned again to face the outside world for the last time as it constricted through the mouth of a tunnel leading into the hillside, falling away behind them as though through a telescope.

The man turned the spray of liquid fire from the woman, whose smoldering corpse looked like little more than charcoal, and hosed down the gathering of people outside the gate, setting them ablaze.

Rounding a slight bend in the tunnel, the sunlight was replaced by artificial in parallel lines of fluorescence overhead, the natural, though smoke-laden air by artificial circulation.

"We're never leaving here," Madigan said over the squeal of the wheels on the concrete floor. He looked Avery dead in the eyes. "Ever."

CHAPTER 18

Inside Cheyenne Mountain

Avery rolled over and crawled into the cargo hold. He could hear Angelica talking, but could barely make out her silhouette in the darkness.

"You'll need to keep pressure on it right here," she said, taking Lisa's hand and bringing it to her left ankle where she pressed it down atop the wad of fabric she'd torn from her own sleeve.

"Like this?"

"Exactly."

"Angelica?" he said.

"Hmm?"

He took her by the arm and guided her back toward where Madigan sat, stopping halfway between. Bringing his lips to her ears, he whispered so that no one else would overhear.

"Let me see your hands."

"Why?" she whispered, though she held her hands out in front of her.

He gripped her by the wrists and turned her palms up, tilting them from side to side to inspect the dried blood.

"What are you—?"

He spat on her hands, gummed around to gather what little saliva he could produce, then spat again.

She tried to jerk them away, but he held on tight.

"Rub them together," he said, sliding the palms against each other. "Now you."

He let go of her wrists and she yanked her hands out of his reach.

"What in the name of God are you doing?" she gasped.

"Shh!" he hissed, looking back over his shoulder to make sure that Madigan was still staring out the back of the truck and they hadn't drawn his attention. He scooted closer, eyeing the others over her shoulder. When she tried to wipe her palms on her pants, he took her by the wrists again and wiped them instead on his pants. "Something's not right."

"What do you mean?"

"I don't know for sure. It just doesn't…*feel* right."

"Avery, we're safe now. We don't have to worry about—"

"The dead woman. That man's wife. They incinerated her."

"What else would you expect? She was infected."

"It's not just that. Don't you think it's strange that there weren't medical personnel waiting to triage us when the chopper set down?"

"Surely that's where we're heading now."

"That soldier," he said, nodding his head toward Madigan. "He said we'd never be leaving here again. Ever."

"Once they figure out how to treat this infection— and you and I both know it's only a matter of time—we'll be able to go back to our normal lives."

"Do you believe that?"

"Of course I do."

Avery paused, welling his saliva on his tongue. He spat onto his own hands this time, rubbing them together and then rubbing them on hers. When the saliva was nearly dry, he wiped her palms and the backs of her hands on his pants again.

"Why do you keep doing that?" she asked, holding her hands away from her body, thoroughly repulsed.

"I don't want it to appear as though you've been exposed to any blood."

"What about you?"

He smiled. "I think it's pretty obvious that I've been exposed."

"What are you suggesting?"

"Do you think they have a cure yet?"

"Probably not."

"Then what do you think they'll do with those of us who have been exposed?"

"You're being paranoid, Avery."

"I hope so," he said, whirling to face the back of the truck as the screech of brakes became deafening.

"End of the line," a loud voice called from outside when the truck finally stopped, abandoning them in the silence.

"Don't let them know," Avery said, grabbing her by the shoulders and bringing her to him. Surprised, she opened her mouth as he kissed it, his right hand rising to the base of her skull, his left around her lower back to hold her to him. She melted into him, wrapping her arms around his back, until at the sound of the tarp being drawn back, he pushed away from her and hurried toward the doorway.

Three soldiers stood just beyond the tailgate, two of them directing automatic rifles into the truck, flashlights mounted on top to direct staggeringly bright beams into the darkness. Avery threw his hands in front of his face as the first beam nearly blinded him.

"Stay where you are!" the man shouted at him.

Avery halted, pinching his eyes shut and slowly raising his hands over his head.

"I'm a doctor," he called. "These people need medical attention."

"We'll see to that," the man said. He moved the beam out of Avery's face and searched the bed of the truck, that circular beacon playing off the faces of those huddled at the front.

Avery opened his eyes again, the residual glare marring his vision in red splotches.

"Everyone off the truck," the man without the weapon said, his tinny voice echoing in the long, dimly-lit corridor. "You first, Madigan."

Nodding silently to himself, Madigan hopped down from the tailgate, the clamor of his boots hitting the concrete echoing like gunfire.

The armed soldiers trained their weapons on him.

Avery looked back over his shoulder at Angelica, the vague outline of her features betraying her confusion.

"Now you," the unarmed guard said. The patch sewn above his breast pocket read Vincent. Avery turned to face him and their eyes met. There was no emotion within, as though the man's irises were cast of steel.

Avery moved slowly toward the edge of the bed, looking from one armed guard to the next. Both men's lights were affixed to him, moving alternately from his hands to his feet and his face. He couldn't see their eyes beneath their lowered helmets, and he hadn't noticed until that moment that both wore protective masks over their mouth and nose. It betrayed the fact that either they hadn't officially isolated the mode of transmission, or they hadn't disseminated that information to the troops. Either way, it was unsettling.

"I'm a doctor," Avery said again.

"You'll go in with all the others," Vincent said. "You won't find any red carpets here."

"No, no. All I'm saying is that I believe I understand this infection. It's a strain of leishmaniasis that—"

One of the armed soldiers reached out a gloved hand and yanked him down out of the truck. Avery staggered forward, trying to keep his feet underneath him, but eventually fell, the soldier holding him by the arm yanking him back to his feet. He barely found his equilibrium before he was shoved forward again. In the pale yellow light he could see precious little. Smooth cement walls rounded away from the passage, leading toward a dead end. There was a steel door to the left, a thick rectangle of glass set into it at eye level, crisscrossed with veins of metal, and what looked like an elevator to the right: a flat slab of polished steel recessed just slightly into a wide rectangular frame.

"Wait beside the door to the left," a voice shouted from behind him.

Avery looked back over his shoulder as he approached the door, watching as Angelica received the same less-than-hospitable treatment. The soldier tugged her off the tailgate, turned her to face Avery, and gave her a firm shove in the back that caused her to wince.

She jogged over to him and stopped right beside him, standing so that she was between Avery and the soldiers as they shouted orders at the others, hauling them down.

"Don't," he whispered, pulling his hand away from hers before she could take it. "We can't let them see you come into contact with any of us. Don't touch me. Don't touch any of us. Whatever you do, don't tell them you're a doctor."

"I don't understand why—"

"Angelica, listen. Don't tell them you're a doctor. Do you hear me?"

"Yes, Avery, but—"

"Promise me, Angelica."

"Avery…"

"Promise me you won't say a word."

She looked him in the eyes. The fear within chilled her to the marrow.

"Yeah…" she whispered. "I promise."

Avery nodded and looked past her as Lisa walked toward them, cradling Nick to her chest, his arms so tight around her neck that she had to breathe with her mouth open. The child was no longer screaming. He appeared resigned to the situation to some degree, his head lying on her shoulder, his fixed eyes staring at nothing in particular.

Madigan was still standing with the rest of the soldiers, though he'd pulled Vincent off to the side where they were conversing in inaudible tones. The more the soldier gestured with his hands as he talked, the further Madigan's shoulders appeared to sink until he finally acquiesced to the other man, lowering his eyes to the ground and walking toward the door in the mountainside with the others.

Amelie and Ben were right on his heels, the older woman serving as a crutch for the younger man, whose limp had grown significantly more pronounced. He hardly appeared able to bear any weight on it at all, whimpering each time he set the bloody stump down, the distal end obviously swollen, even in the wan light.

"You're my meal ticket," Madigan whispered to Avery, sidling up beside him. "Stay with me when we go in."

"What do you mean?"

The Infected

"You said you knew what was going on, right?"

"I think so. I'm not completely sure—"

"Whatever you say, say it with authority. Don't let them think for a second that you aren't one hundred percent sure of yourself. Do that and we'll live through this."

The words *live through this* resounded in Avery's head, solidifying his paranoia.

"I hope," Madigan whispered. He turned away and looked back at the other soldiers as they brought Don and his daughter along from the rear, herding them together. *Like cattle to the slaughter,* Avery thought, but quickly chased away that ghastly image.

"All right," Vincent said, the tone of his voice conveying a coldness that was almost palpable. "Everyone in a single file line."

There was the scuffing sound of shoes on cement as they shuffled themselves together like a deck of cards.

The soldier turned and said something they couldn't hear to one of the armed men, who gave a brisk nod and ran past them to the door, opening it and stepping inside into a red-tinged darkness that made Angelica gasp. It looked so much like the hospital had after the emergency generators had kicked on and stained every room and hallway with crimson like blood on the walls. Still training his gun on them, he backed away until he reached a cement staircase leading down out of sight.

"You all need to follow this man down the stairs until we reach our destination and he opens the door for you. Stay in that single file line. Step out of line and he will be forced to shoot you."

Shoot you? Angelica thought. She looked at the back of Avery's head in front of her, pressing forward just enough to feel the warmth of his body heat, grazing her finger along the back of his pants for no other reason than to feel that he was for sure near.

"A state of martial law has been declared throughout the country. Until we are able to control the situation, you civilians will do exactly what we say, when we tell you to do it. There is no room for argument or negotiation. You will be safely under our protection while you are here, but we will not tolerate insubordination."

"Are we under arrest?" Ben asked.

Vincent walked to the middle of the line, towering over Ben as he tried to bear most of his weight on his left foot, puffing up his chest and jutting forth his jaw.

"This is the United States Air Force Command at NORAD," the soldier said firmly. "We will do everything within the power of the mightiest force this planet has ever witnessed to insure your safety. Think of us as angels commanded by God. When the word comes down, we will obey it without question."

"So we could leave if we wanted to?"

"Once you pass through that doorway, you will stay until we have been given the proper clearance. However, you are free to leave now if you want. I understand there are about two hundred diseased men and women just outside of the gates who would welcome you with open arms."

Ben lowered his eyes from the soldier's intense stare.

"Now. If we're through with the questions, start moving. Follow this man as though your life depends upon it. Step out of line and he will drill a hole through your head so quickly you'll never even hear the report. Are we clear?" He didn't even wait for them to reply before heading to the elevator. He pressed his thumb to the wall, where there was a small scanner hidden in the shadows. A horizontal red line appeared above his thumbnail, moving downward until it reached the bottom, then rose back up and vanished. The steel door slid back into the wall with a shucking sound that reminded Avery of pressing a scalpel through the back of a patient's neck until the dura mater shielding the spinal cord popped.

Vincent turned to face them again, the door sliding shut in front of him so fast it was as though it had never opened at all.

"You heard him," the soldier called from the top of the staircase. "Start marching."

The other soldier had fallen in at the back of the line and shoved Don forward with his rifle like a hockey player giving a cross-check, slamming the man forward into his daughter.

Avery followed Madigan across the threshold into the stairwell, the scent rising from beneath reminding him of walking into a surgical suite, the smell of disinfectants and ammonia swelling all around them. It rose straight through his nose and into his sinuses, where it felt as though it was igniting, causing tears to well in the corners of his eyes. He turned and looked at Angelica, noting that her eyes were already beginning to water as well. The smell seemed oddly out of place with the drab gray walls and the red-painted pipes running along them. At the top and bottom of each set of stairs was a pair of red lights pointing at the floor ninety degrees apart.

The soldier stayed half a staircase ahead of them, looking back at them every time he reached one of the landings, and then again as he prepared to descend the next set of stairs. They'd gone down four, no…five sets of stairs and had yet to encounter a single doorway. Avery was beginning to wonder if they ever would when the soldier finally stopped at the bottom of the tenth flight, where he pressed a button that activated some sort of bell or alarm on the other side of the thick concrete wall.

There was an almost imperceptible whir as a camera zoomed in on them from the far wall to the left at the top of the stairs, which apparently continued deeper downward into the earth.

"Stay in your line," the soldier shouted, his voice like an explosion in the close confines.

A series of bolts disengaged in the door with loud thuds, followed by a hiss of air escaping through the seal as the door opened outward. The soldier grabbed it and pulled it outward onto the landing. It had to be close to a foot thick and made of solid, gleaming steel. There were large rings running up the side, nearly the size of softballs, where presumably the disengaged bolts had slid back within. A swell of air blew out into their faces, bringing with it the scent of hospital-grade cleaners; more intense than before, if that was even possible. A mist blew from above, below, and to either side of the doorway, just inside, making it impossible to see through as if the room beyond were on fire.

Ben stumbled into Angelica from behind. She whirled to help stabilize him, but realized that the entire line was being shoved forward from the rear, so she descended, inconspicuously slipping her fingers between Avery's and giving his hand a squeeze. He returned the gesture in kind and released her hand, stepping from the bottom stair onto the landing as the soldier ushered Madigan past and through the high-pressure flumes of mist.

Avery took a deep breath, the stench of cleaning agents stabbing him in the lungs, but the last thing he wanted was to take in a deep breath of the concentrate blowing at him at such high velocity. He imagined it would be toxic enough to tear a hole right through his lungs. Closing his eyes, the wind assaulted him from all sides as he walked through, feeling as though it were trying to compress his vertebrae. The mist was staggeringly hot and the moment it touched his skin felt like acid melting right through. He had to fight the urge to scream, clenching his jaws against the nearly undeniable reflex, finally stepping out of what felt like a curtain of sheer agony, peeling off his skin as though lancing beneath it with so many dull blades.

He raised his forearm and wiped the condensation from his forehead, struggling to open his eyes. The rims of his lids felt like they were scalded, the room obscured as though he were looking at it from underwater. When his vision finally cleared enough to decipher his surroundings, Angelica stepped into the room behind him, coughing so violently that he thought for sure she might vomit. It had that harsh, barking whoop that must have burned as it tore from her trachea.

"Are you all right?" he asked, reaching down to help her up, but stopping before he came into contact and bringing his arms back to his sides. It looked as though they'd walked through a car wash from this side. There was a square tunnel leading to the doorway that had to have been five or six feet long, the entirety of it filled with high-pressure jets firing whatever sort of sanitizing solution they were using onto them from all sides.

He slapped his hand to his cheek as it felt like something stung him, only to realize that it was the cleansing agent burning into the open sore where the infection was taking hold.

He turned around and stared off into a room the size of a high school gymnasium. The walls to either side were bare and stark white, clinical, covered with some sort of glistening coating that must have been made for ease of cleaning should they need to sanitize the entire room in one fell swoop. Intense sodium halide lights burned down on them from monstrous silver domes recessed into the concrete ceiling, each one appearing as bright as the sun. There were three lanes in front of him, each one separated not by velvet ropes, but by metal rails that looked like split-rail fences. It reminded him of some sort of futuristic airport, though instead of having small x-ray machines at the end of each lane, there was a large clear plastic enclosure that glowed with a purple-black light that could only have been in the ultraviolet spectrum. There was a guard in full Hazmat gear posted beside each of the acrylic cages.

"Each of you come through one of the lines," a voice blasted from the speakers above. Until that precise moment, Avery hadn't noticed the giant mirror halfway up the twelve-foot wall to the right, surely two-way glass that allowed them to be safely observed from the other side.

Madigan went first, walking along the first lane to the left, his sopping clothes draining onto the floor, the ribbons of fluid trailing along the slanted lane toward a recessed drain.

Angelica stayed at Avery's side as they both walked toward the one in the middle.

"You two. Separate," the overhead voice said. "One of you use the lane to the right."

Avery cast Angelica an uncomfortable glance, then headed for the lane beside hers.

*   *   *

She walked down the aisle, panic growing with each step. *What in the name of God was going on?* The guard waited for her with his right hand resting on an automatic rifle slung over his shoulder.

"Keep on coming," he said.

Angelica glanced to her left as the guard in the first line opened the Plexiglas cage. Madigan stepped inside, rich purple light draping over him like velvet. Immediately several pinkish-purple spots appeared on his face, glowing like beacons.

"Oh, God," Angelica whispered.

She turned back to the guard in front of her, all of the color draining from her face. There must have been some sort of dye in the jets of steam that somehow bonded with the infection to make it clearly visible in the ultraviolet spectrum.

"Move along," the soldier said, wrapping his fist around the butt of his service pistol. He licked his lips, his eyes unblinking.

Angelica nodded, slowly making her way to the clear enclosure.

She glanced to her left in time to see the guard beside Madigan's cage nod once, then open the back door. Madigan stepped out, discretely looking at the large mirror high up on the wall.

"Into the box, ma'am," the soldier said.

"What is it?" she asked.

"Ultraviolet radiation."

"What if I...?" she started, but let the words fall as the soldier's finger slid toward the trigger guard. "Never mind."

He swung the door open like a shower stall and she stepped in, pressing her arms to her sides and her palms to her thighs.

"Turn in a circle," the soldier said, his voice muffled.

Her heart rose up into her throat, beating faster than it ever had. She couldn't bring herself to breathe, the air growing stale in her chest. She twirled slowly, unable to look at the soldier when she passed by, stopping so that she faced the exit door on the other side, her arms unmoving.

The soldier opened the door for her and she walked

straight out, her arms not budging a millimeter.

"Continue ahead," the soldier said. She couldn't bring herself to turn until she heard the clomping of his boots heading in the opposite direction. She looked to her right, where Avery was standing in the middle of his purple enclosure.

"No," she gasped when he turned to face her, half of his face turning nearly fluorescent pink. His sad eyes met hers, lingering long enough for him to try to force a smile, but failing miserably.

His pink lips mouthed something that looked like *I love you*, even his gums glowing pink around his purple teeth.

"I love you too," she whispered, tears streaming down her face, burning her already abraded cheeks.

CHAPTER 19

Inside Cheyenne Mountain

"Through the first door on the right," a guard said, appearing behind Angelica.

She nearly jumped at the sound of his voice, whirling to face him. He wore Hazmat gear as well.

"Move along," he said, nudging her forward.

She cast a glance back over her shoulder at Avery as he emerged from the Plexiglas chamber, their eyes locking only briefly before she was shoved forward toward another steel door. Her stomach roiled; a sense of panic gripping her and squeezing until it felt like she couldn't even draw breath.

The pristine steel door slid back into the wall.

"Through there," the guard said, watching her only long enough to ensure that she walked across the threshold and heard the hiss of the door sliding back into place behind her.

Angelica stood in the bottleneck of a room that expanded outward from the doorway into a larger chamber, which appeared to have half a dozen stalls to either side like walking into an enormous locker room.

Two-inch square tiles covered the floor, the same shade of off-white, mere degrees away from the pristine white of the religiously scrubbed grout between.

"First stall on the left," a voice announced.

Angelica turned to the origin of the voice, a black speaker box built into the wall above another two-way mirror. For the first time in what felt like ages, she could clearly see herself. It looked as though she'd aged a decade in the last twenty-four hours. Her face was pallid, her eyes recessed into darkness. Tiny wrinkles she'd never noticed before lined her face, her wild bangs hung down over her eyes, the rest sloppily tied back in a ponytail that appeared to come out of the left side of her head, the loosened strands on the right draped over her shoulder. Her clothes were thick with filth and grayed by smoke.

"Remove your clothes and step into the stall. Feel free to take your time cleaning. The soap is fairly abrasive to help remove the outer layer of dead skin, but you'll feel better when you're through. When you're done, walk past the remaining stalls into the next room. There will be a new set of clothes waiting for you on the cart." For the first time since she'd arrived, Angelica detected a note of sincerity in the voice. "You should be proud of yourself, ma'am. Lord only knows how hard it must have been to survive out there, especially without becoming infected."

She nodded to her reflection, tears still rolling down her face, and walked past the mirror to the first stall. There was no door, only two gray walls supported by steel posts: starting a foot above the tiled floor and rising above her shoulders. The floor sloped gently toward a simple circular drain toward the rear wall beneath a single showerhead. A steel box was affixed to the left side of the rear wall.

Angelica pulled out the hair tie, yanking what felt

like half of the hair out of her head in the process, and cast it to the floor. Her shirt and pants followed until she was standing there completely naked. She supposed she should have felt self-conscious, but the prospect of a hot shower was nearly euphoric. Stepping forward, a red light appeared in an oblong black strip on the faceplate in the wall, triggering the water to shoot from the shower. It was far hotter than she would have liked, but she forced herself to step forward in increments until she was immersed in the high-pressure spray. Her skin reddened as the heat consumed her, melting through her and soothing her aching muscles. The propulsion was so hard it felt like it was bruising her and the stream was so hot she feared she might boil, but it was still the most incredible sensation she'd ever felt in her life.

She waved her hand beneath the spout on the box on the wall and a spray of soap slapped into her palm. Rubbing the syrupy ooze between her hands, she lathered it all over her body. It felt as though there were grains of sand within, scratching her with each and every stroke, but the bubbles made her skin tingle until she washed it away.

Finally satisfied and bordering on heat exhaustion, her head swimming, she stepped out of the stream of water and into a cloud of steam. Her dirty clothes were already gone, replaced by a fuzzy white towel that hung from a hook outside the stall. Wrapping it around her chest, it barely reached to the middle of her thighs, but it was so soft it was like being swaddled in pillows.

The cold air settled in around her, prickling the goosebumps on her skin, turning the water running down her back from her wet hair into fingers of ice. Even that feeling was welcomed. Anything was better than sweating furiously beneath saturated clothes covered in a crust of blood. The cold tile against the soles of her feet felt like icicles lancing through the tough skin, but right now she wouldn't have traded it for anything in the world.

She passed through the doorway at the end of the room and into a smaller, more dimly-lit room. There was a lone bench in the middle, encircled by rows of lockers, a single door directly across. Beside the doorway was a cart covered by a drape, which she brushed aside to reveal rows of bundled clothes sealed inside plastic bags. She pulled one out and tore open the coating, dropping the contents onto the bench. There were powder-blue scrub pants and the matching top, a long-sleeved white undershirt, a pair of elastic-rimmed slippers that appeared to be designed as one-size-fits-all, and a wide-toothed comb. After dressing, she ran the comb through her hair to remove the tangles.

"Please follow me," a voice said.

She hadn't even heard the sound of footsteps.

Angelica turned and matched gazes with another woman, her blonde hair cropped closely to her skull, full, sensuous lips framing brilliant white teeth. Her attire matched Angelica's, though it appeared tailored to fit her. Instead of the baggy top and the pants she had to cinch way down to hold up, the woman appeared very professional, like a surgeon in many ways.

"My name is Dr. Samantha Roberts," the woman said, smiling. She opened one of the lockers and pulled out a box, setting it on the table and removing a pair of stethoscopes and a sphygmomanometer. "I'm an Air Force physician. It's my job to give you a thorough physical and welcome you to NORAD. On the other side of this wall is Isolation Room Alpha, or what we like to call Heaven."

"Why do you call it Heaven?"

"You'll see when we get there, but the simple answer

is because everything's white."

Dr. Roberts smiled again.

"Now," she said, pressing the stethoscope nubs into her ears. "Pick an arm, any arm, and roll back the sleeve."

*   *   *

"Through the door to the left," the man in Hazmat gear said, standing deliberately between Avery and the door to the right.

Avery tried to meet the man's eyes beneath the plastic shield, but they were elusive and twitched away. Nodding, he stood before the door to the left, the steel plate sliding back into the wall with a whoosh. He glanced back over his shoulder at the sound of crying to where one of the soldiers was prying Nick out of Lisa's arms.

"Step through," the man said from beside Avery, patting the automatic rifle slung over his shoulder.

Turning back to the room, Avery took a single step forward and the door slid shut behind him. There was a soft hiss of the air adjusting inside the room.

Madigan was ahead of him, walking naked into what appeared to be a shower stall. It was obvious where his clothes had been as there was a ring of dried blood around his neck where it had collected against his collar, his hair black with it. It almost looked as though he was wearing dirty brown gloves. He was thin, yet muscular, his skin a pasty white.

"Take off your clothes," a voice said through a speaker above a mirror to his right. He could only imagine the men on the other side of that two-way glass watching with clinically detached interest. The rage within him bubbled up and he wanted to fight against the obvious humiliation of having to strip down for them. They already knew he was infected. The sore on his cheek was so deep now he could feel the coldness of the air on his gums and was certain that if he tried hard enough, he'd be able to force the tip of his tongue through. But he let his emotions go with a great sigh and peeled off his clothes, dropping them on the floor in a heap beside Madigan's. He tried not to look at his reflection, but there was no mistaking the bright red beacons on his upper chest and abdomen, the seething wounds on his thighs. It was only a matter of time now. The edges of the roughly circular ulcers were curling back, black with necrosis, the insides appearing to be little more than a slimy conglomeration of dead leukocytes and thickened blood unable to scab over the center of the wounds. They reminded him of the mouths of so many plecostomuses pressed to the glass in an aquarium, though rather than sucking algae, they were vomiting pus. At least he could be thankful that they didn't hurt nearly as badly as they looked.

He smiled at the thought.

"Proceed to the second stall on the right," the voice instructed him. "Use the soap in the dispenser and scrub until you've thoroughly cleaned every inch of your skin."

Avery walked away, shoulders slumped. He passed Madigan and stepped into the stall just beyond, the water firing from the nozzle as soon as he was inside. It was so hot it absolutely hurt his foot when he stuck it into the water. He held it there a moment before realizing that the temperature wasn't going to change, and inched into the stream little by little until every inch of his skin burned as though it was coated in a sheath of flaming gasoline. He waved his hand underneath the silver box mounted to his left, which issued a white and green powder that looked like the Comet scrub he used on his counters at home. It felt like boiling oil in his palm, but he managed to rub his hands together and scrub them across his chest.

Madigan let out a scream from the stall next door.

Avery's heart nearly stopped in his chest, his stomach sinking. It was barely a breath later that he learned why the soldier had screamed. The cleaning agent felt like it was eating through his skin, worse than the ulcers, worse than anything he'd ever felt in his entire life, like the barbed ends of so many fishhooks looping into his pores and tearing them open.

Before Avery knew it, his screams joined the chorus.

"Please," he called. "Please...It hurts!"

"Don't whine," Madigan growled from the other side of the thin wall. "It will only make it worse."

Avery looked at the gap beneath the stall wall and saw Madigan's feet, a peppermint twirl of blood spinning around the drain. His stare slowly followed the floor to his own drain, where it was nearly impossible to tell that it was water with all of the blood.

"Jesus," he whispered, inspecting his arms. The skin had opened up in dozens of different spots, swelling droplets of blood rising from what looked like so many crosses between abrasions and burns, the skin blistering beneath.

Avery doubled over with a sharp pain in his gut, dropping to his knees and vomiting all over the floor.

"Don't let them hear you," Madigan said. "Get back on your feet and kick it down the drain."

"I don't know...if I can," Avery said, a stream of blood-streaked fluid firing past his lips.

"Either do it or you're dead right now!"

"I'm dead...regardless."

Avery's shoulders bucked with the heaves, but only a long strand of blood appeared, hanging from his lower lip.

"Get up!"

Michael McBride

Avery pushed himself to his feet. The movement caused him to stagger back, but he regained his equilibrium and stood there in the fiery hot stream, swaying.

"You want a chance at living through this?" Madigan asked.

Avery nodded, knowing there was no way the other man could see the gesture.

"Turn around," Madigan said. "There's a towel hanging from the outside of the stall. Wrap it around yourself and meet me through the back door of the room."

Madigan blew past Avery's stall without casting even a sideways glance, the patter of his wet feet on the tile echoing in the large room.

Stepping out of the water, the stream ceasing behind his heels, Avery grabbed the towel and wrapped it around his chest beneath his arms. It was barely long enough to cover the weeping sores on his upper thighs, which bled right through the cotton. Blossoms of red opened like roses on his chest, blackening as he watched them grow. Whatever the cleaning agent had done, it had stripped away the burgeoning scabs trying to hold those wounds closed, which now bled freely.

There was nothing they could do now. He was going to die.

Shuffling his feet, barely able to raise them from the tile, he headed toward the doorway at the back of the room, the large rectangle teetering from side to side as though on a fulcrum. Madigan stood in the middle of the room beyond, climbing into a set of pale blue scrubs as quickly as he could. There was the flash of a sore opening on his right buttocks, another just beneath his shoulder blade.

"Get changed," Madigan said. He gasped when Avery dropped his towel.

289

"That bad, huh?" he said, managing a meek smile.

"Cover them up fast."

Avery slid on the white undershirt, the blood eating right through the moment it came in contact with the fabric. He pulled up the pants and slipped his feet into the slippers, donning the scrub top last.

"Do they hurt?" Madigan whispered, watching the widening amoebae of blood spreading on Avery's thighs.

"Do you really want to know?"

Madigan shook his head.

"What's next?" Avery asked. "Are we going to be quarantined or dissected?"

There was the hollow thud of footsteps approaching from the shower room behind them.

"Sit down," Madigan said, shoving Avery onto the bench. He stepped right into the center of the doorway and snapped to attention, saluting the Hazmat-clad soldier entering the room, who was flanked by two more men, both of whom stayed a respectful half-pace behind him at either hip.

The man in the center returned the salute.

Through the plastic shield, Avery could see that he was an older man, his face weathered by time, his eyes reflecting a sorrow only thinly masked by his grim determination.

"Colonel O'Conner," Madigan said, unable to hide the note of surprise in his voice.

The older man only acknowledged Madigan with a nod, entering the room and standing with his back to the doorway. The men behind him stood shoulder to shoulder in the threshold.

"I've heard that you might be able to shed some light on our current situation," the colonel said, regarding Madigan in what looked like pajamas through weary eyes.

"This guy's a doctor," Madigan said, the excitement causing the words to come too quickly. "We evacuated him from the roof of the hospital with another doctor—"

"That was a nurse," Avery interjected.

The colonel looked at him, and then quickly away, unable to hide the revulsion that pursed his lips.

"Anyway," Madigan continued, his lower lip slipping momentarily between his teeth. "He seems to think he has a pretty good grasp on what's going on."

The colonel turned to Avery expectantly.

"If my theory's correct, we're dealing with multiple strains of leishmaniasis, which is a disease carried by sand flies. We speculate it arrived from Cancun on that plane that crashed at the airport. The first strain is the flesh-eating variety that opens ulcers through the superficial strata of the skin, while the second filters through the bloodstream and causes massive toxicity in the liver." He doubled over to cough, gritting his teeth against the rise of acids from his stomach. Though the room started to spin around him, he managed to keep from vomiting. "From there, a third pathogen, which I speculate to be some sort of..." He winced at the pain in the upper right quadrant of his abdomen, pressing his hand to it to try to relieve some of the pressure and pulling it away bloody. "Some sort of toxoplasma. You've heard of feline aggression in cats? With the liver unable to filter out this normally benign microbe, it reaches the brain and causes violent rage and uncontrollable feeding instincts. In essence, the part of the brain responsible for higher thinking and rational thought dies, leaving only the hindbrain to control the body."

"You say you're a doctor?"

"Neurosurgical resident technically."

"That's quite impressive."

"Are you..." Avery started, interrupting himself with

a groan that forced blood through his bared teeth. It dripped from his chin onto his chest. "…patronizing me, Colonel?"

The colonel's face grew hard, his features rigid.

"Tell me something I don't already know."

Avery coughed, slapping a spray of blood onto the tile.

Everyone in the room backed away from him.

"So I was right," Avery said, smiling. The sheen of blood on his teeth shimmered even in the wan light.

"That will be of little consolation to us if we can't find a cure."

"I know the cure."

"That's right," Madigan said. "He told me he knew the cure."

All eyes in the room fixed intently on Avery, who managed to keep the smile on his face. The whole scene was surreal. The room spun and the floor tilted, and here he was in a locker room talking to three men who looked like they'd be right at home bouncing around in the zero gravity on the moon, with his blood covering the floor between them.

"You're wasting valuable time, doctor."

Avery rose to his feet, legs wobbling, swaying back and forth.

"It's the universal cure," he finally said.

"We've already tried penicillin," one of the men behind the colonel said. "So far it's merely retarded the phenomenal growth rate, but we haven't found anything to halt the progression."

Avery continued smiling.

Beyond the men in the doorway, he watched Lisa emerge from the steam billowing from one of the shower stalls and wrap herself in a towel, standing there shivering. Several angry red ulcers stood out on her legs like a

Dalmatian's spots.

Another woman shrieked in pain, her agonized wail echoing in the hollow room.

They hadn't been separated into showering rooms by sex.

"The colonel already knows the cure," Avery said. He didn't need to look down to know that his liver was so enlarged it distended his abdomen.

Colonel O'Conner locked eyes with Avery.

"We were hoping we might get lucky and you would actually know," he said, finally turning away when teardrops of blood rolled down Avery's cheeks. "I see now we've wasted our time."

"Time doesn't matter now," Avery said, closing his eyes against the enormous pressure welling behind them. It felt like they were trying to be shoved out through his eyelids from within. "It's the perfect disease."

The colonel turned away, the two men in the doorway parting to allow him through and then falling right back into place. He walked through the stark white room beyond and called out without looking back, "Quarantine them."

CHAPTER 20

Outside Cheyenne Mountain

There had to be a thousand of them on the other side of the fence by now. It was shoulder to shoulder as far as he could see, and he'd heard it rumored that there were ten times that many headed up the mountain toward them through the woods and along the roads. They could hold them out of the mountain indefinitely, but they wouldn't be able to keep them on the other side of the gate forever. Their instructions were to fall back into the mountain when it appeared as though their fortifications were about to crumble, distancing themselves as much as possible using one of the trucks that sat idling and ready in the mouth of the tunnel. There was no way that anyone would be able to keep up with the truck on foot for the length of the tunnel, but that was the point. They wanted them to try. Once they were safely inside the base, they could seal the entrance to the tunnel via remote and gas however many they trapped inside. There had been no mention of the plan following that point, but every soldier who worked inside NORAD knew good and well that they were stocked to withstand the half-life of a Cobalt 59 nuclear warhead detonated on their front porch.

"We should hose'em down again," King said, nervously eyeing the wall of humanity through the plastic shield of his space suit as they started to bow the fence inward.

"I'm with you, but we don't do anything without orders," Little said, grating his teeth. He wanted a cigarette but wasn't about to take his protective helmet off for anything in the world.

"What? You just want to wait until we're face to face with them?"

"Hell, no! I just don't want my ass court-martialed for torching a bunch of civies."

"You'd rather let them make a meal out of you?"

"Now you're just being stupid."

"I don't know, man," King said, leaning against the guard shack. "I don't like the way things are playing out. We've got a ranking colonel under our feet and there isn't a wall of artillery at our backs. My money says they expect this gate to fall."

"Either that or they're going to strafe it from the air."

"No way I'm going to be standing out here when either happens."

"I hear you." Little patted the square bulge on his suit beneath where he knew his pack of Marlboro's was. "God. I'd kill for a smoke."

"I say we cook'em."

"You're on crack."

"How many have we burned already? A hundred? Maybe more? We'd just be buying ourselves more time. It's not like we won't have to spray'em down soon anyway."

"True."

"So instead of sitting here with our thumbs up our

butts, let's actually do something productive."

"I'm not holding the hose," Little said, taking a step back.

"Shoot, man. I'll hold the damn hose. You just turn on the juice for me."

"If the boot comes down, it's stomping you."

"Oh, would you quit your whining and just turn the handle?"

"Then I'm having a smoke."

"Do what you need to do."

Little walked over to the side of the building and turned the lever to release the flammable flow, while King clicked the igniter. A twenty-foot spray of flame fired out of the end of the hose between the soldier's gloved hands. He strode forward, the arc of flame hitting the asphalt and growing closer to the fence with each advancing step. The people beyond appeared oblivious to the flaming death drawing near as they jostled for position, curling their fingers through the fence and smashing each other forward. Red eyes stared ravenously at King, showcasing an animalistic hunger that positively made his skin crawl. They were an abomination and he knew it. They both simultaneously scared the living hell out of him and stirred a primal desire to wipe them off the face of the earth. There was nothing even remotely human remaining within them. No love. No thought. No sentience. In the same sense that one finds himself staring into the eyes of a cobra before it strikes, he could see only evil within them. Not an evil quality one prescribes to those capable of making a choice, but an evil that exists simply to kill and feed.

He yelled at the top of his lungs as he raised the stream of fire. The molten flame poured down upon them, torching hair, blackening skin and eating straight down to the bone. Flesh melted like candle wax, sloughing free from exposed skulls that grinned demonically through the diamond-shaped holes in the fence before becoming little more than charcoal. Fingers still clung to the fence, curled around the metal, though now completely bereft of skin, poking through like twigs before cracking and dropping the skulls forward. Those closest to the blazing stream were cooked where they stood while those farther back in the churning maelstrom of bodies still flailed against the fire burning from their clothes and crackling from scalps fried like pork rinds, curling back from the exposed scalp. Boiling blood poured down their cheeks like lava from a volcano, carving channels through flesh before dropping in wads to the ground where they burned until there was nothing left to consume.

And not a single voice cried out.

It was like watching a silent reel to reel of the German atrocities in World War II. People dying in the most excruciating way possible, stumbling over each other, slamming headlong into one another without the slightest inclination as to what was going on. Without their tortured cries it didn't even seem real. Bodies fell where they stood, simply crumpling to the ground as the fire ate through them, fading slowly from red and gold flames to a meek amber glow that produced only a wretched black smoke. Corpses piled on top of corpses, one falling atop the next until it looked like an apocalyptic vision of hell. Blackened skeletons smoldered waist high, those still living climbing onto them to try to get through the fence in their stead. King turned the flamethrower on them as they rose, the smoke thickening around the remains until it was an impregnable wall of blackness, and still he continued firing the magma into the center of it, walking first to his left, and then to his right, testing the limits of the hose.

The Infected

The soldiers ringing the helipad cheered him on, pumping their fists to the heavens.

King didn't even realize how hot the nozzle had grown in his hands until he dropped it with a scream, the pain finally overcoming the adrenaline rush. It clattered to the ground at his feet and he brought his hands in front of his face, tendrils of smoke rising from the charred palms of his gloves.

"Damn that felt good!" he whooped, flinging his arms down and tossing off the gloves. His hands were so red they nearly glowed.

Little cranked the shut-off valve and walked back over to his partner.

"Nothing like the feeling of mass murder, huh?"

"Ah, forget you, chump. You're just jealous 'cause you didn't get a turn. I could always turn the juice back on and —"

Thump!

They both turned toward the sound, facing the fence.

A wall of smoke clung to the chain link, obscuring it from view. Small puddles of fuel still burned on the asphalt between.

Thump! Thump!

"What the hell?" King said, taking a tentative step forward.

The wind rose just enough to reveal an orange glow in the middle of the fence. As he watched, the light split into two and widened like diagonal yawning lips.

Thump!

"Breech!" Little screamed. "You melted through the fence you stupid —"

His words died as a dozen dark shadows materialized in the smoke.

A man sprinted from the churning smoke, the sides of his face carved with deep lacerations spilling blood from where he had forced himself through the fence like a newborn emerging from the womb. His hair was burnt back to his skull, flames lapping up his chest. Little's stare fixed on the man's face, blood red eyes and a tortured snarl framed by seething gashes, and then his flight reflex kicked in and he whirled to run in the opposite direction.

He'd barely made it five yards before he heard King scream behind him. He whirled in time to see the man slam down on King's back, smashing the soldier's plastic face shield on the asphalt. The man reached over the crown of the helmet and grabbed the upper portion of the fractured remains, yanking it backward with such strength that the back of King's head nearly touched between his shoulder blades. The helmet bounced off across the ground. The man raised his opposite hand and drove his fingers through King's eyes, jerking the head from side to side until the screams stopped and blood poured from the sockets. Opening his mouth so wide the jaw cracked, he bit down on King's head, his front teeth snapping off.

Little jerked his eyes away in terror and saw the fence clearly through the dissipating smoke. Bodies poured through the tear in the fence, pushing so hard from behind that they spurted through with momentum enough to rush on at full tilt. Others trampled corpses beneath their tread atop the cooked mess of bodies, clambering through the razor wire atop the fence, which cut so deeply through arms and legs and torsos that a waterfall of blood poured down to the ground. They fell from the top of the fence, splattering onto the ground only long enough to regain their strength and push themselves to their feet, stumbling forward, dragging useless bloody legs behind them, nearly severed arms flopping at their sides, spurting rich arterial blood.

The Infected

Little whirled and ran, wishing to God he weren't wearing that cumbersome isolation suit. It was like trying to run through knee-deep mud. He fixed his eyes on the transport vehicle idling at the mouth of the tunnel and watched it growing closer at a maddeningly slow pace.

The prattle of gunfire filled the air, bullets sparking from the asphalt as they ricocheted in all different directions. A shape appeared from the corner of his right eye, slamming into one of the gunmen who'd only barely turned to run, throwing him to the ground. The soldier's finger tightened on the trigger as he was pounded against the ground, a volley of bullets flying at Little. One tore through the pant leg of his suit and grazed the back of his calf. He felt the hot pain and screamed, running as fast as he could until he finally outran his legs and sprawled face-first onto the ground. Teeth slamming together with the impact, he nipped off a chunk of the inside of his lower lip. The impact knocked the wind out of him, dotting the plastic mask with a fine mist of blood.

He tried to push himself up, but they were already upon him, crashing over him like a tidal wave. Teeth tore through cloth while grappling hands wrenched bones from their sockets. Burnt hands weeping amber fluids and covered in blood slapped at his facemask, trying to pry it away from him. Through the smears he could vaguely see the driver of the truck as he made the decision to save himself, leaping up onto the seat and stomping on the clutch. The gears slid into place with a screech, but he didn't even have time to close the door before a herd of people swallowed the side of the cab. One grabbed the driver through the window and hauled him out, tossing him to the ground as the truck rolled toward the tunnel. He'd no more than hit the ground before he was swallowed by the crowd, the truck rolling away until it crashed into the side of the tunnel entrance, the hood crumpling and issuing a cloud of gray smoke.

A crack split across the plastic in front of Little's face and hands blocked his view.

His breath returned in a lurch and he screamed as his head was jerked from side to side, his neck snapping before he was forced to endure being torn apart.

*   *   *

Second Lieutenant Vincent stood in the middle of the tunnel, his right hand shielding his eyes from the overhead fluorescent glare, watching intently for the first sign of headlights rounding the bend. His legs were already tensed in anticipation of sprinting toward the door so he could trigger the thumb scan in time to let them all into the base. He already knew their outer fortifications had fallen. He'd heard the brief spurts of gunfire before they'd been overwhelmed by silence. The report that command had lost contact with the guards came through only moments later.

It took all of his strength and resolve to stay his ground while he wanted nothing more than to run to the doorway and ride the elevator down to safety.

What if he abandoned them? he thought. He could only imagine leaping out of the truck with a swarm of the infected preparing to overtake him only to find that there was no one there to let them inside, knowing that the thundering footsteps brought his death, but there was absolutely nothing he could do to prevent it. Raising his side arm and debating whether to waste twenty shots on a useless cause or one to prevent the suffering to come.

No. He couldn't do that to them. He wouldn't. He would stand his ground until he saw those headlights coming and they would reach Heaven together, one way or another.

There was a distant clapping sound coming from down the tunnel, faint at first, but growing louder with each passing second. It wasn't the grumble of an engine or the squeal of tires he'd been prepared for.

He wiped his sweating palms on his pants and drew his pistol, the barrel trembling in his grasp to the point it tapped his leg.

The sound grew louder until there was no mistaking it was the sound of footsteps. He turned, preparing to run for the door and then stopped. What if the outer guard had been cut off and unable to reach the vehicle and they were running for their lives mere steps ahead of the blood-lusting mob? He gauged the distance to the furthest extent of his vision, where the bend in the tunnel obscured everything beyond. Fifty yards maybe. If he didn't see uniforms, then they would probably be able to close another ten yards before he could start sprinting toward the door. Forty yards. The door was ten yards directly to his right, but they'd still have to round the corner before following. All he had to do then was press his thumb to the scan pad. In the time it took for clearance to be granted, they could easily close another ten to fifteen yards. Twenty-five yards. He could be through the door with it closing behind him in three seconds, ceding another ten yards. He'd still have fifteen yards, forty-five feet, between them and him when the door closed. He knew it sounded like a lot more than it actually was, but he was sure he could do it.

The thunder of footsteps grew louder until it sounded like a stampede, drowning out even the thudding of his heartbeat in his ears.

Vincent licked his dry lips, his right foot cheating away from him toward the door.

"No mistakes," he whispered, his dry voice cracking.

He couldn't even allow himself to blink.

It sounded as though he was in the middle of a construction zone with the sound of a million hammers echoing all around him.

A line of shadows stretched ahead of them around the corner like a stream of tar flooding across the floor.

He could barely think clearly over the roar of footsteps.

Several bodies flew around the bend with nothing but churning legs and arms and bobbing heads behind.

Vincent took a quick mental snapshot and turned, scrutinizing the image as he burst to motion. Muted yellow light reflecting from wet faces like the sun glinting from a trout's scales. Had it been blood on their faces or sweat? Their clothes were a blur in his mind. He couldn't determine whether or not he had seen uniforms, but there was no time to turn around and look.

The thunder grew into a deafening roar.

His eyes locked on the small black touch-screen beside the elevator, his legs working faster than they ever had in his life. He was too frightened to even breathe.

The people running at the front of the pack. One of them had been wearing shorts while fabric flagged behind the one beside like a dress or a shawl.

They weren't military.

The ground shuddered beneath him with the pounding advance, the silver door appearing to teeter in his vision.

Please God, five more yards.

He didn't dare take his focus from the scanner even to look down at his footing. There wasn't a second to spare.

Reaching out, he pressed his right thumb to the reader before he even stopped. It slid off the screen leaving a smudge of sweat.

All he could hear was pounding, his whole body

vibrating with it.

He brought his trembling hand back in front of the screen and pressed his thumb against it. His heart froze in his chest as he waited for the horizontal red laser to appear.

"Come on!" he screamed.

It felt like he was standing on a fault line in an earthquake.

"Come on!"

Jerking his thumb away, he swiped away the smear of sweat with his palm and tried again. This time the red light drew a horizontal line beneath his thumb, glowing through his thumbnail as it started its descent.

He glanced quickly back over his shoulder, his worst fears confirmed. They had already rounded the corner and were rapidly closing the ten-yard gap between them.

"Hurry!" he railed. The laser reached the bottom and began the return journey to the top.

Don't let me die, don't let me die, DON'T LET ME DIE!

The silver door slid away into the wall, revealing the open elevator chamber. He lunged forward, diving through the open doorway and landing on the floor. Pushing himself to all fours, he turned and all he could see was a wall of humanity bearing down on him. Red eyes flashed with hunger. Salivating mouths snapped in anticipation. Fingers curled to claws, slashing at the air. The stench of death on hot breath.

With a whoosh, the door emerged from the wall, sliding toward the opposite side.

A woman leapt for him, her hands falling only inches shy of his, her body sliding along the smooth concrete until the elevator closed on her midsection, biting into her with the sound of cracking ribs. Her head rocked back and she vomited a spray of blood on the floor between them.

Vincent scurried away, backing against the rear wall of the elevator, his legs still kicking the floor as though trying to propel him through the reinforced steel wall.

The motor in the door groaned and the whole cab shook as the door struggled to force its way closed, retracting and slamming back into her side, expelling gushes of blood through her gritted teeth. She raised her face and all he could see was the blood dripping from eyes that looked like gelatinous capsules of crimson fluid. Her jaws snapped like a rabid dog's.

"Get away!" Vincent screamed, his voice degenerating to a shrill wail.

A man stomped over the woman, squeezing between the closing door and the wall. Another man was right behind him, followed by a woman, and then Vincent couldn't even see them all as they swarmed upon him. The red warning light blossomed overhead, filling his vision with scarlet, a prelude to the freshets that washed over his face as his scalp was torn back.

The floor shivered and then finally started to descend, the flailing woman propping the door open rising as if levitating until she reached the roof of the elevator and was efficiently sliced in half. Somewhere above, her legs thrashed madly at the floor as the crowd funneled through the doorway to the left of the elevator, stampeding down the staircase as pipes mounted into the ceiling finally started gusting gas into the tunnel.

Vincent could only scream until his windpipe was ripped away with a crack of tearing cartilage, his final breath escaping through the hole in his neck in a burble of blood as the relentless hands continued to peel his flesh.

CHAPTER 21

The Gates of Heaven and Hell

Avery watched the colonel stride past the final shower stall on the left, and then he was gone. His eyes fell to the two remaining men in Hazmat gear. Both had their automatic rifles clutched in front of them, gloved fingers inside the trigger guards.

Avery could only nod.

Their features were emotionless, their fixed eyes unblinking.

"Come on, guys," Madigan said. "You don't have to do this."

"We're under orders to quarantine you."

"Don't think I don't know what that means."

There was no reply.

Avery started to laugh, blood trickling down his chin. The whole thing was so surreal.

"Through the doorway behind you," one of the soldiers finally said, gesturing with the barrel of his gun.

Avery turned and stumbled forward. Maybe once they were quarantined he'd be able to lie down and finally get some sleep.

"You too," the other guard said to Madigan behind him.

"No! Please...You can't do this!"

Avery stood in front of the door, swaying back and forth. There was no handle, only a flat metal surface that reflected his frightening visage back at him. The vessels in his eyes had ruptured, sending tears of blood down his cheeks. He could even see the lower portion of his zygomatic arch through the open sore beneath his eye. His scrubs were covered with large black puddles of blood, clinging to the wounds on his skin.

The soldier stepped to Avery's right and typed a series of numbers into the combination pad beside the door.

There was a thud of bolts disengaging within and then the whir of the door being drawn into the recessed wall. A gust of hot air flooded into his face, forcing him to close his eyes and raise his hand to shield them against it. He immediately smelled the scent of cooking meat.

"Go on," the soldier said, nudging him from behind.

Avery opened his eyes as he crossed the threshold and found himself looking at the floor beneath his hand, the back of which was starting to feel as though it was burning. There were spattered arcs of blood all over the floor, dried to a rust-colored crust. He managed to raise his eyes just enough to see the flames roaring in the mouth of the incinerator at the back of the room.

"God, no! Please!" Madigan screamed from behind him before being silenced by a loud thud, followed by the sound of a body crumpling to the floor.

Avery's legs gave out and dropped him to his knees, his limp neck dropping his chin to his chest as he wavered there.

His shoulders shook gently with the swell of understanding, a combination of frightened laughter and tears.

The Infected

He felt the cold tip of the barrel against the back of his head. The last thing he saw was a flash of his blood, riddled with the white bits of his skull, spattering the floor in front of him.

*   *   *

Angelica stepped through the doorway into Heaven, an enormous white room the size of a warehouse. The stark white ceiling glowed with the pale light from the rows of fluorescent tubes. On the far wall was a large screen like in a movie theater, the floor between was filled to capacity with single-sized white beds covered with white linens. With so many beds packed together and barely any room to walk between them, it reminded her of the old photos of wards in a sanitarium. Some of them were occupied with slumbering people while others milled about aimlessly. All in all, there couldn't have been more than fifty people in that monstrous room.

She slowly started to walk forward into the sterile chamber.

"Please register over here," a man called to her. He sat at a small table just to her left with a computer before him, his fingers poised over the keyboard. As he was wearing the same attire, she thought at first he must have been like her, but his name was embroidered above the pocket on his left breast, his blonde hair cropped closely to his skull. She didn't bother to read the name.

The world passed around her as though in a daze.

She sat in the chair facing him.

"Congratulations on surviving," the man said, his smile warm and genuine. "We've seen what it's like out there and finding your way here was definitely no small feat. You should be very proud."

"Thank you," was all she could think to say. "Can

you tell me where the man I came in with is?"

"What's his name?"

"Avery Martin."

The man typed in a few keys.

"He hasn't been processed yet, but that doesn't really mean much. Once he's been officially registered, we'll be able to tell you where he's quartered." He smiled. "Now what's your name?"

"Angelica Morgan."

"What's your social security number?"

"Five-two-two, one three—"

The door leading into the room slid back again, a child's cries piercing the stillness like a scalpel.

Angelica rose and walked toward the door. Dr. Roberts stepped inside with a young boy held against her chest, his face beet red from the screaming.

Angelica recognized him immediately.

"Where's his mother?" she asked.

"She apparently hasn't been processed yet. Do you know this boy?"

"We came in together," she said, leaning in so that her face was close to the boy's. "Hi, Nick. Remember me?"

His hair was still drenched from the shower, and she could only imagine how he must have screamed in the scalding water.

"I can take him," Angelica said, noting the relief in Dr. Roberts's eyes as she passed off the crying child. "How long before his mother's processed?"

"I don't know for sure," she said. "What's her name?"

"Lisa."

"Do you know her last name?"

"No...sorry."

"Well, I'll let you know first thing when I perform her physical. Okay?"

Angelica nodded and turned away, cradling Nick to

her chest. The door hissed shut behind her.

"Come on back," the soldier at the computer said. "Let's finish up your registration so we can find you two a bed and get you something to eat. I've heard it rumored that there's orange juice and bagels on the cart, and there's always a full stock of bottled —"

The overhead lights blinked off and then on again.

"Watch the screen. I'll finish when I return," the man said, rising from his seat, any residual effects of his smile erased from his face. He rushed to the door and pressed his thumb against the scanner. The moment it slid open, he hurried through.

"It's okay," Angelica whispered, stroking the back of the boy's head.

He buried his face into her shoulder, finally succumbing to the wiles of sleep. She could only imagine how exhausted he had to have been after what he'd lived through. No child should have to endure such horrors.

"This is Lieutenant McNeal with the updated news," a voice said, amplified through speakers all around the room. There was a pleasant looking redhead on the screen at the far side of the room. The lights dimmed to make the image more clearly visible. "The infection has reached global pandemic levels. All across the globe..."

Angelica allowed the voice to fade, no longer listening to what the woman had to say. She'd lived it. She didn't need someone else to give her a running commentary of her own life.

She looked at the computer and wondered if she could track down where they might have put Avery. Walking around the side of the desk, she was just about to sit down in the chair when she saw the monitor. It was divided into four quadrants, each containing a black and white image with a date and time stamp. In the upper left, she recognized the room with the ultraviolet chambers as the camera swiveled from one side of the room to the next. The screen beside it to the right showed the very room she was in now. Each of the bottom screens showed a shower room from a high vantage so that she could see down into the stalls. The man who had been sitting at this computer only moments prior ran down the tiled aisle between the rows of stalls on the bottom left screen.

Movement in the top left drew her eye as men and women poured through the main entrance at the front of the room at a sprint. The guards beside the purple chambers raised their weapons and started to fire, the tips of their barrels flashing. Dozens of the attackers were dropped, only to have even more swarm over their fallen bodies. Still firing, the guards backed toward the camera, but were overwhelmed in seconds and dragged down by the infected. There were no more flashes from their weapons, only tatters of cloth from their suits filling the air around them as they were shredded. Other bloody faces streamed past beneath the camera and emerged in both of the bottom screens.

She looked up into Heaven at the sound of footsteps. Five men in scrubs wove through the slalom of beds, machine guns clasped in their grasp. They ran straight toward the door leading back to the locker room, pausing only long enough for one of the men to scan his thumb and let the others pass, the door whirring closed behind them.

She lowered her stare to the monitor again. Naked men and women ran out of the stalls and toward the back of the steamy room while crowds of people poured into the room. Angelica could see the terror in their eyes, the silent screams on their lips. The soldiers who had just passed by her appeared on the screen, shoving their way through the wet bodies fighting them to get away. By the time they raised their weapons, it was already too late. They were buried beneath a flurry of slashing arms and snapping teeth, their blood washing over the ivory tile. Like scavengers they mobbed the bodies, painting themselves gray with blood while others raced past and under the camera.

There was a barrage of pounding against the door.

Angelica stumbled backward from the monitor, watching the steel door. Fists pounded furiously against it from the other side, but she knew there was absolutely nothing she could do. She could only imagine the naked and cold men and women beating their fists bloody trying to escape that death chamber before being butchered where they stood. The pounding grew louder and louder, until finally it ceased completely.

Other survivors gathered around the door, keeping their distance as they watched breathlessly.

Angelica distanced herself from the door as far as she could, her back pressing against the wall.

A gentle gust of air blew against the back of her neck from a duct, bringing with it the mortifying sound of their dying screams, pinging through the aluminum ductwork like so much dust. Their cries petered into nothingness marred only by a soft humming.

A woman screamed by the doorway when the pounding began again, louder and faster. Fevered.

The humming grew louder in Angelica's left ear, but she couldn't bring herself to tear her eyes away from the door. Nick awoke with a wail passing his lips. She held him tightly to her chest, praying for him to go back to sleep.

Everyone who had gathered by the door turned as one and ran for the far side of the room, tripping over beds and trampling each other in their hurry to get away.

Something small tickled Angelica's cheek. She unconsciously swatted the small red fly away, feeling a sharp prick as though the hairy creature had bitten her.

All she could hear now was the pounding at the door, the deafening metallic drum roll of their impending demise.

From the corner of her eye she saw movement.

Fuzzy red sand flies.

Dozens of them.

ABOUT THE AUTHOR

Michael McBride is the author of the *God's End* trilogy, *Spectral Crossings,* and the *Chronicles of the Apocalypse* series. He was born and raised near the locations fictionalized in this novel and now resides in suburban Denver, where he apparently spends the majority of his time fantasizing about the end of the world. He's always thrilled to hear from his fans at michael@mcbridehorror.com.

Printed in the United States
220482BV00003B/8/P

9 781934 546154